THE ELRIC UNDOING

cassandra celia

THE ELRIC UNDOING

CASSANDRA CELIA

The Elric Undoing

First Edition | Publication Date: October 31st, 2023

ISBN-13 (Paperback): 979-8-9858659-7-4

ASIN (EBook): B0CGTMDW2W

Cover Design © Quirky Circe Book Design @quirky.circe

Map Design and Interior Art © Alyssa Konkel @alypaca.doodles & Jacob Konkel

Edited by Alexis Aumagamanaia @threemuses_editorial

Proofread by Bear Lee @bearleebooks

Interior Formatting by Cassandra Celia @authorcassandracelia

CONTENTS

CAUTION!

By reading past this point, you are recognizing that THE ELRIC UNDOING is an adult book that features mature and at times triggering themes and material. For a complete list of relevant content warnings, please visit my landing page located at the end of this book.

We are all in control of our own content consumption.

Thank you, and I hope you enjoy!

For the creatives who pour from empty cups.
Your art matters.

Matilda's Apothecary
Coffee Shop
Café
B.U.S.
The Lantern's Church
Superette

Elric
Pyet's Manor
Library
Winona's House

PROLOGUE

Life was different here.

It was in the way darkness loomed overhead, and in the way time seemed too still. It was in the way the wind howled through twisted branches, mirroring the tortured screams of lost souls.

The town was nestled deep within a forest, its winding streets whispering secrets to those that traveled its roads. Every evening, as the sun set and cast long shadows across the cobblestone paths, the air thickened with an ominous weight. The town circle, once a lively gathering place, now resembled a desolate cemetery, with gravestones made of stone benches, its lampposts casting a dim glow like the flickering lanterns in the depths of a haunted house.

There was something different in the way the old mansions stood tall and imposing on the outskirts of town, their crumbling façades concealing history that could only be guessed at.

The nearby forest was a labyrinth where one could easily lose their way, forever wandering among the skeletal trees. The rustling leaves sang a ghostly song, a symphony of spirits long departed, but never freed. The church that stood tall and imposing was not abandoned, but is decaying exterior let it dissolve into the surrounding foliage, desperate to shield itself from too much scrutiny.

Life was different here.

It was in the way the townspeople huddled in their homes, chanting prayers in a desperate attempt to ward off the night. Their hushed conversations were laced with dread, tales of blood-curdling memories a constant reminder of the unspeakable terrors lurking just beyond their doorstep, and within themselves.

This town was a place where nightmares thrived, like sinister creatures under the bed. Every shadow seemed to have a life of its own, creeping along the walls, waiting to engulf unsuspecting victims in its cold embrace. The night was an accomplice, its inky blackness giving birth to grotesque monstrosities that danced in the moonlight, mocking the feeble attempts of mortals to defy them.

But despite the palpable fear that clung to the air, there was a morbid fascination that held the town in its grasp. It was the irresistible lure of the unknown, the intoxicating allure of confronting one's deepest fears. For it was in Elric, amidst the horror and the uncertainty, that one could truly experience life in its most raw and untouched form.

Yes, life was different here, where nightmares and reality became one, where every moment held the promise of heart-stopping dread. It was an unraveling story brought to life, a tale woven with ghostly threads where the lines between the living and the dead blurred together to create a haunting tapestry.

Life was different here, and once its smokey, invisible strings wrapped around your bones, it would be too late.

Elric would never let you leave.

October

FROM THE DESK OF

VIOLET CABELLO

My dearest granddaughter, Pyet Cabello,
I know you do not know me, and I'm so terribly sorry that this letter is going to reach you before you get the chance to. If you are reading this, it's because I have finally passed on, and left the world behind. I know you'll be wondering why you've been slated to receive this, and I wish I could tell you. Truly, I do. But it's something that cannot be written across a page or something that could be understood without being seen. And I want you to see, Pyet. I tried to make your mother see, but she refused.

She left.

It was probably for the best. It's why this

letter is addressed to you, and not her. Though I desperately wish that life was different.

I know your mother hasn't said the most flattering things about me. In fact, I don't know what, if anything, your mother has said about the place she used to live. Or what she's said about me. All I can hope is that she didn't scare you too much. I loved Elric with all my heart, and I would hate to see everything that I've worked for be left to someone that doesn't deserve the beauty of it.

I really do hope that you deserve it.

Once you receive this, I want you to call Winona Fairchild. She's the only one I trust to handle my estate. Elric recognizes her as a state of authority, and she will handle everything you need once you arrive. She will be reading my last will and testament. You can find the address and phone number below; she is expecting your call.

Please don't bring your mother. I don't think she could handle coming back here.

I hope you both are well.

Your grandmother,

Violet Cabello

DAY 1

5:30 PM

Even without catching the battered, run-down *"Welcome to Elric!"* sign out of the corner of her eye, Pyet would have known the second the Greyhound crossed the town line. The sun disappeared behind shadowed clouds, and the accompanying silence was so deafening that it made Pyet's ears ache with the absence of life. She turned her head to rest against the window and watched as chips of paint flaked off from the sign, falling to the ground as the bus drove into town, bouncing as smooth black pavement turned to cobbled roads and loose gravel.

Coming to Elric, she knew, would change her life. Pyet could feel it in the way the trees turned to watch them as they passed. She could feel it in the way all signs of life died the further they went. She could feel it in the way her bones stiffened, in the way her muscles strained, and in the way her body recognized the danger that awaited her. But it was too late to turn back now.

The energy in the air was palpable. Pyet could swear there was an electric current vibrating underground as they moved, pushing them further into Elric. It was as if the bus was no longer moving on its own, carried instead by the whispers of the wind and the pull of the electricity that filled their space.

Pyet shifted in her chair, wincing at the feeling of her skin separating from the itchy gray seats. She was afraid moving too much or too loudly would aggravate the currents around her. The underside of her legs felt raw and chafed from spending too much time sitting in one place, in one position, for far too long. The muscles in her back were cramped and her shoulders were so tense, she felt like she'd snap in half if the bus shook a little too hard in either direction.

Static buzzed through her fingertips and, if Pyet had known the feeling of rigor mortis, she would have complained that the feeling was too similar to appreciate. Three days was too long to be sitting so still. She felt like a sitting duck, vulnerable and exposed, too paralyzed to escape as she waited for some hunter to shoot her down.

Pyet shook her head and tapped her fingers against the top of her thigh, the sting from a torn hangnail making her wince on impact. Apart from being left alone with nothing but her thoughts, another benefit of sitting on a bus for an ungodly amount of time was the reigniting of bad habits. She'd pick at her nail beds until they were red and raw, and when it seemed like it was time to stop, she kept going.

Her hands were torn to shreds. It hurt, yes, but it gave her something to do, something to distract from her nerves and the growing need to vomit. She would take healing fingers over an anxious stomach any day.

The urge to dig at the already swollen nail bed was too much. She forced herself to look away. There was no winning—either the dead expanse of the town or the rawness of her hangnail was trapped within her line of sight. That, or the bland grayness of the seat in front of her. Pyet was stuck, wading through layers of panic that never seemed to leave her.

She forced herself to swallow the anxiety down, pushing it away until it was small enough to tuck into a little box and store it on a shelf. Despite the sense of unease that hung in the air, smothering her like a wet blanket, Pyet still couldn't see herself turning and running in the opposite direction. Not yet, anyway. Elric, as strange as it was, would be better than the place she'd left behind. It had to be; she was sure of it.

She was three days away from constant paranoia.

She was three days away from inevitable danger—a danger that seemed more apparent than the one she was quickly approaching.

She was three days away from her *mother.*

Ultimately, that was enough for her.

The gloomy exterior of Elric was lonely, but there was the possibility of *home* here. It was a thread of hope she clung onto desperately. As soon as Pyet had been lost to the temptation of Elric, her mother abandoned her; she was left to freefall from the nest, left behind like an orphaned baby bird. It was as if she no longer saw Pyet as an extension of her family, but as an enemy. She flipped faster than a coin, marking Pyet as a target to be eliminated.

Her mother would admit no fault, but it was there, woven into the seams of their relationship. It was in the secrecy and trepidation, the ability to paint vague horror stories of the place that called to Pyet like a siren song. It was as if she *wanted* Pyet to dig deeper, to find out more about the town she'd run from so long ago. All while threatening her demise if she so much as mentioned the dreaded name...*Elric.*

It was no wonder Pyet found herself here.

She had no intention of returning to her hometown, or her mother, anytime soon. She'd find solace here in Elric, whatever that looked like, even if it was…different. *She'd find home again.* Pyet had made peace with the fact that, now, she had nothing and no one but a mother who wanted her dead. While the thought was bleak, she found she could finally breathe.

Sometimes, she found, heartache was only relief in disguise.

The bus shook again and Pyet looked up from the window she'd settled on, casting a quick glance across the seats in front of her. She'd been too caught up in her own worries to keep track of how many people had come and gone from the bus over the last few days and now realized she was one of only four people left within the cavern of the Greyhound. It seemed Elric wasn't a place too many people traveled to on their own. No one seemed to know much about the town either. Their eyes started to drift and glaze over the minute the name escaped her lips. It was like a spell had been cast over them, only breaking once Elric's name had gone from the conversation completely.

The bus stayed quiet, no whispered words traveling back toward her seat. The overbearing silence was making her uncomfortable. Pyet feared closing her eyes, the images of her mother holding the blade of a sharpened kitchen knife to her throat overcoming her each time she did.

She could still feel the ghost of the steel pressing into her neck and she brought her hand up to rest against the column of her throat, where a thin scab now married the suntanned expanse of skin. It wasn't the first time her mother had threatened her, but it was the first time Pyet had thought her capable of following through with the threat.

Pyet's upbringing had been nothing but a revolving door of paranoia, never knowing who she could trust or confide in. Her mother had always been a volatile presence, content to make her own daughter a victim of her warpath, her own childhood in Elric the catalyst for a lifetime of fear. She never said a word, never explained what it was about this place that made her so intent on being prepared, or *ready*.

Pyet was keen to believe her mother was crazy. It was easier to deal with than it was to accept that there was no rhyme or reason for her to act the way she did. There was no reason for the secret, for the paranoia. And if there *was* a reason, Juliette would never tell her, not directly. Pyet hung on to every word she could squeeze out of her mother, crazy or not. Elric was a puzzle that could be solved if she just tried hard enough.

The problem was that she had just tried *too* hard this time, pushing against the steel trap of her mother's mind until it snapped, too focused on the *what-ifs* to remember her mother wasn't *normal*. Nothing about their life, their *world*, would ever be normal.

Now, Pyet had nothing but a backpack full of junk, a bus taking her to the place her mother hated most, and a letter from a woman she'd never met. She had no money, no home, and she certainly didn't have a family. She was unmoored, drifting, and looking for a place to land. The letter was both her ticket out and her ticket in—out of her mother's house and into the puzzle she'd spent so long trying to solve.

Pyet rubbed the tingle out of her hands again, shifting her gaze from the passengers at the front of the bus to her new home, separated only by a single-paned window. She could see the trees, with their gray and naked branches piercing the sky, bending against the wind as the sun disappeared into the cloud cover. Pyet imagined this was how cave explorers felt, that the farther they went into the darkness, the more frayed their nerves became at the thought of what could be lurking in the vast unknown that stretched out in front of them. She could feel the frigid arms of isolation welcoming her home, begging her to find warmth in the cold.

Beyond the trees were homes different from anything Pyet had ever seen. Each house was more grand than the last—tall marbled columns framed the doors and sizable stone structures guarded entrances. Elric's history reeked of dark, dirty, old money, but there was magic here too. Pyet couldn't quite place her finger on it, but she could feel it in the air as they passed through town. It was unmistakable, and not so different from the electricity vibrating underneath her.

There were no people walking the streets, no stray dogs or feral cats weaving through the underbrush. Pyet sighed, running her hands through her hair. If there was anything her mother taught her about this place, it was that Elric didn't welcome visitors kindly. The empty streets were proof of that. It was a ghost town compared to the hustle and bustle of the city she'd left behind.

The panic started in her chest again, her heart pounding harder and harder against her ribs until her entire body quaked. Pyet was used to being alone. Life with her mother secluded within their home had taught her not to rely on the company of others. But seeing the barren streets of Elric dampened her hope. Pyet was convinced she was running to a place to call home; she wanted a place where she could speak to people, a place where she could put down new roots. Pyet wanted, and was expecting, a place opposite of what her mother had taught her about. Because surely, no place was as cruel or as isolating as she painted it out to be.

Pyet wasn't expecting a welcome wagon, but she expected *something*.

She was going to drown; air filled her lungs, but breathing wasn't coming easy. The panic attack was coming down the barrel and if she didn't sort herself out, she was going to go under. The overwhelming feeling of what she had done and where she had gone was settling in her gut and Pyet felt overcome, submerged in uncertainty.

Fuck, she hated feeling so unprepared, and so out of control of her own body.

The feelings in her chest were only getting more intense, questions filling her mind faster than she could find answers. Pyet grabbed the seat in front of her, grateful there wasn't someone occupying it. Her head dropped between her arms and she forced herself to take deep breaths, holding the air in her lungs for a few seconds before she released it and repeated the process her mother taught her a lifetime ago.

This panic was unwarranted, she knew. Normal, functioning adults moved away from their cities and their families all the time. It wasn't anything new. Pyet needed to get a handle on herself quickly, or she wouldn't be settled enough even to wade through the water.

Drowning, she thought, seemed inevitable.

"Shit," she murmured to herself, feeling tendrils of frustration crawl up her spine. Pyet sat up, shaking her hands, trying to rid herself of the excess energy caged in her bones. She was cursing herself for her own anxiety, and her mother, though she couldn't pinpoint what for—for *everything*, maybe.

Now that she was here, her feet about to touch the soil of the place she'd been chasing for so long, slivers of doubt wove their way into the fibers of her being. Was her mother right? Was the world just a monster waiting to sink its sharp teeth into her and rip her limb from limb?

Pyet was nothing but a beast for slaughter in the grand scheme of it all. The realization that nothing her mother put her through—the paranoia, the abuse, or the dystopian overpreparedness—ever really prepared her for anything.

She wasn't sure she was ready for the freedom that would come from escaping her mother—there would be no restrictions, no need to ask for permission. She would be free to wander as she pleased. Pyet was fresh and new, and absolutely unsure of who she was or her place in this world. She was an outsider to Elric, warned away by someone who escaped too long ago to remember exactly why she'd run.

As the bus bumped along, bringing her closer to the town center, Pyet wondered if her grandmother had planned for it to happen this way, or if it was just her luck.

BEFORE

Pyet and her mother's two-bedroom home was not large by any stretch of the imagination. It was a little cottage tucked away in the city center, shrouded by an unruly expanse of bushes and wired fencing—no one but the postman would know that there was a house buried deep within the greenery. It was exactly what her mother wanted: heavily guarded, protected from all the things her imagination could conjure up.

A smaller space makes for sharper instincts. That's what her mother always said.

Pyet never understood what she meant, but she wasn't in the habit of questioning Juliette, knowing that doing so would only make her life that much more difficult.

Her mother was insistent on keeping them away from the outside world at whatever cost, so much so that she had become agoraphobic in her pursuits of safety. Pyet was usually subjected to those same fears, no matter if they were genuinely reciprocated or not.

Life was less intense when she was young. At first, her

mother would only beg her to stay safe, and her efforts seemed nothing more than reasonable parenting. Pyet couldn't remember when it morphed into something *more*. One day things seemed normal, and then the next…

Now, it was Pyet's duty to pay the bills. To get the groceries. It was Pyet's job to do the things her mother could no longer physically do, the things that made her human. She did nothing but hide in their home, content on feeling discontented, and it left Pyet to pick up the pieces of their life on her own. She was meant to sew together the lost remnants of someone who should have cared for her, lost in the lacing of another world. It was a life she *knew* wasn't normal, but it was the only normal she knew.

Their reality was nothing but a bleak routine. Several hours of homeschooling with nothing but her own wits and determination to get her through. Specially delivered groceries that Pyet had to carefully inspect before her mother rationed and stored them away every month, and the daily chores around the house that she would do alone.

Pyet only looked forward to checking their mail once a week, if her mother allowed it.

Their mailbox was secured just outside of the fence lining their property, and each week Pyet would count the days until she could coerce her mother into letting her leave the safety of their urban cottage. She once coined it as their most dangerous necessity, and at once her mother abandoned the torturous thought. She was far more inclined to put her daughter in the line of fire if it meant she was safe from the risk herself. It didn't surprise Pyet in the slightest that she could just as easily send her daughter to slaughter.

At the familiar sounds of the tin van crawling along their secluded street, Pyet's mother disappeared into the depths of their home, behind traps and doors as if the man in the van had any other motive than to just deliver his goods, and go home to his own family.

Not that she minded being the keeper of this particular errand. It had become her favorite part of surviving in this world her mother created. They never received mail that wasn't a bill or a letter from a debt collector, and she hadn't died yet. Instead, Pyet's weekly trips across their front yard were met with copious amounts of appreciation for just being outside. The crisp breeze was far more welcoming than the stagnant musk she'd find inside their home. She loved how it felt when the sun beat across her forehead, or when the rain puddled beneath her feet. It was the closest feeling to the magic that seemed to be missing from her life. Magic was not real, she knew that. But, submerging herself within the elements seemed to be the best place to start.

That morning, as she grabbed for the familiar weight of the sealed envelopes, knowing that several of them were from collectors, she was also struck by the weight of something unexpected. Pyet didn't dare take longer than necessary, lest her mother send a search party for her, and she quickly returned to the stale air of their home, her heart thudding rapidly in her chest.

The paper was thick, like cardstock, and her name was embossed on the envelope. Although she would have sworn that it wasn't meant for her at all, the proof was right in front of her. The card was heavy in her hands, eggshell white and just as smooth, the gold letters of her name catching the light and flashing as she shook. Pyet forced a nail under the thick lip of the wax seal, covered it with her fingers, and tried to muffle the sound of it separating from the paper. She knew if her mother heard her, she'd have hell to pay for it.

The letterhead listed a name Pyet had only heard mentions of before, and when she'd read through it—exactly five times—she doubled down on her belief that it wasn't real at all.

I really do hope that you deserve it.

If Juliette found out, she would tear the letter from her grip and rip it to shreds, as she had just last week with an ad from the local grocers—the same place they ordered from weekly. If she knew it was from *Violet,* her own mother, there was no telling what Juliette would do. Even so, Pyet couldn't tear her gaze away, couldn't force herself to tuck the letter away in the back of a drawer or tear it to shreds. It felt important, valuable. She couldn't let this piece of her history be destroyed, no matter the cost, even if it meant defying the person who had protected her for all these years.

Pyet's mother rarely talked about Violet, and when she did, she shared nothing but horrific stories. Once, she told a story of being locked away in a closet with no food for forty-eight hours because she disobeyed an order. Another time, she spoke of the way her mother only ever sided with the residents of her peculiar town, putting her faith in them rather than her own child. Juliette wasn't just angry with her mother, but terrified. Violet was as much of an enigma as Elric, but there was always an edge of skittishness whenever her mother mentioned her name.

This letter was the only real connection to the family Pyet's mother kept her from. It felt like a double-edged sword of betrayal—one to her mother if she kept it, the other to herself if she destroyed it. This was uncharted territory.

Torn between two supposed evils, Pyet could do nothing but stare at it. She knew she needed to move, to hide and find some place safe, but she couldn't—she was frozen to the spot, locked in a cycle of fear and possibility. Her mother could come down the hall at any second, and there was no telling what she would do if, and when, she saw the letter. There was no place to bury a treasure like this, even if Pyet wanted to. Her mother, vexed with childhood trauma she could never understand, would *know*.

In some ways, Juliette was so in tune with Elric and its mysteries that she saw everything. And in other—most— ways, Pyet's mother was a ghost of her former self. There were days when she wouldn't come out of her room, nightmares plaguing her waking hours so much that Pyet worried her mother wasn't fully there at all. Other days were worse, the ones where she screamed and thrashed, tearing carpet from the ground and pounding holes into the drywall. It scared Pyet, having to live in this home with her. She wouldn't admit it to anyone, not that they would listen anyway, but apprehension rolled through her body just as often as the blood that pulsed through her veins.

A secret like this wouldn't last long in this house. At every point where Pyet thought she could navigate the cold waters of her mother's motives and emotions, she found herself mistaken. It seemed a futile pursuit, to wonder after the place that haunted this home.

A place she had never even gone to.

Pyet blinked several times, and each time, the letter still stayed glued in her grip; not a dream, but a reality she wasn't sure she could handle. The corners of it frayed now at the edges from her constant fidgeting. Her anxiety wouldn't let her fingers rest, bending the corners between her nails and scratching at it to the beat of her erratic heart. Tear stains soaked through the parchment, blurring the ink; Pyet scrubbed the sleeve of her sweater over her eyes, desperately trying to absorb the wetness before it could ruin the letter further.

Why would this woman, who never so much as called her,

send her…this? Her grandmother had done so much harm to her family, and this attack seemed malicious. There would be no other reason for this letter but revenge on the daughter that left her behind.

And, it *was* her. Her name was written in delicate script, centered at the top of the page–

Violet Cabello

A threat from a feathered pen. Her handwriting was equally entrancing and beautifully curved, with big loops and daring strokes painting the page. It was written with the confidence of a person who didn't know fear. Pyet rubbed her thumb over the family crest above it, caressing it, wondering what life she might have lived if her mother hadn't abandoned her home all those years ago.

The crest was beautiful, strings of ornate teardrops dripping from a triangular tapestry, a gothic "C" stamped across the center. Pyet gazed at it longingly, details from the filigree and black lace surrounding the emblem her family had used longer than she'd been alive creating more questions than answers.

"What the hell is that?"

Pyet's blood ran cold, a terrible fear consuming her as her mother screeched at her from the kitchen entryway. The voice didn't startle her as much as her sudden appearance. Juliette was dressed in nothing but a short nightgown that hit her at mid-thigh, her hair in tangled knots as if she'd just gotten out of bed, though it was late in the afternoon. Pyet could smell the alcohol on her breath even from this distance.

It was a bad day. The liquor always left the cabinet on bad days.

Fuck.

She took several violent strides toward Pyet, stopping just a few feet from her, not close enough to touch, but close enough for Pyet to see the lines that wrinkled her mother's face. Pyet swallowed hard, hyper-aware of how the saliva hit the back of her throat, scorching her insides as it traveled down her esophagus.

She hated drinking, and she especially hated when her mother did it.

Pyet hated drinking *because* her mother did it.

Her posture was rigid, and she was poised to run if the moment struck. Pyet tried to crack the knuckles of her empty hand to relieve some of her anxiety, but found that it helped none. It was always best for her to be on her toes whenever her mother was near. Juliette wasn't the peaceful type, resorting to violence more often than not—the odds higher whenever the liquor cabinet had been opened.

Claiming ignorance would be her savior.

Her mother's body swayed from side to side—from drunkenness or disbelief, Pyet was unsure—as if her mother could *feel* the letter nearby. Its presence roused her from sleep, her body unsure of itself as it tumbled forward. It was as if she knew exactly where it was and *what* it was without looking at it. Not that it would be hard to recognize. Pyet's fingers still grazed over the family crest like it was something delicate that needed to be protected, and she watched as her mother's eyes widened as she caught a glimpse of it in Pyet's hands again. Her mouth fell slack, and for a moment Pyet wasn't sure if she was going to say anything at all.

The letter, the emblem, it was all too much; it overwhelmed her mother. The letter caused a circuit in her brain to malfunction. Pyet could see it in her eyes, millions of nightmares dressed as memories flooding the deepest pits of her mind. Though she was incoherent before, she was no longer.

They both stared down at the parchment in Pyet's hands, a temporary truce suspending them in time. The damage Violet could inflict with just a few written words was alarming, and though she was subjected to horror stories, it was different to see them manifested in real-time. It was either her grandmother had too much of a deadly touch, even this far away, or they were all entirely broken to begin with. Just fractured pieces of a whole, held together by wishful thinking.

She wondered when the last time her mother had seen their family crest was.

It must have been decades. Pyet didn't know when exactly her mother found her way out of Elric; the timeline was full of holes, and she didn't know enough to piece together more than small fragments of the life her mother refused to let slip.

Juliette's eyes glazed over as they slid from the crest to the body of the letter. Pyet shook as Juliette descended into her own darkness. She wasn't close enough to read it, but Pyet's fear heightened as she watched her try. She wanted to pull it away, but she couldn't find the strength to. Any movement would be considered threatening, and Pyet knew better than to test the woman in front of her.

Even without the clear letterhead, her grandmother's handwriting would be distinct enough to remember. Juliette hadn't needed to know what was written to be afraid, all she had to distinguish was that it was truly from Violet to begin with.

"I don't know!" Pyet panicked, her grip tightening on the letter. The shrill sound of her voice was enough to snap her mother from her trance. It was the first thing that slipped through her lips, and it was *a lie*. That mistake would not be her last, but Pyet knew the minute it escaped that it would be her undoing. She worried her bottom lip between chattering teeth, sucking hard enough that her eye twitched at the echoing pain. The woman in front of her didn't respond to her hurt. She cared not for the girl she birthed or the child she raised, but only the nightmares that plagued her waking thoughts.

Instead, Juliette Cabello, her mother, the person with whom Pyet spent all of her life, broke.

Juliette screamed as loud as she could, the sound sharp enough to shatter the windows. It ricocheted off the walls, bouncing from floor to ceiling with no way to escape. Pyet covered her eardrums, shielding herself from the worst of the noise.

That was her next mistake.

Her mother used that moment to reach for the letter, crazed desire and longing in her eyes. Her face contorted, eyebrows rising too high for her face to catch up, mouth baring her teeth in a sadistic rage. Juliette curled her long, bony fingers around Pyet's wrist, and fastened her eyes onto Violet's letter. Pyet wasn't ready to abandon the one thing she'd ever been able to call hers; she stood firm, her hands raising higher and her grip tightening.

Another mistake.

Juliette tugged hard on her daughter's wrist and grasped desperately with her free hand until her fingers met with the edges of the parchment and the sound of a tear filled the room.

"Let go of it," Juliette growled in warning. Pyet shook her head fiercely, the soft brown curls that rested on her shoulders whipping through the air with each shake.

"No," she whispered, more to herself than to her mother, whose face all but lost any residual signs of empathy. The face that stared at her now was cold and unfeeling; her skin was cool to the touch, her eyes burning coals of distrust.

Instead of responding, Juliette pulled once more, testing her daughter's resolve. On another day, Pyet might have relented, but this letter was too precious to her now. It was a gateway to another world, a lifeline to the past she was so desperate to uncover. She couldn't let this treasure go, not even to silence her mother's demons.

"Why have you been talking with Violet?" Juliette accused, suspicious eyes grazing hungrily over Pyet's short frame.

"I haven't!" she said with equal force, making a point to lower their hands, the letter poised between them, "I promise. I don't know why she wrote to me!"

"Don't lie to me," her mother seethed, "I can see your name written by *her* hand! It's right there, Pyet. I'm not an idiot. Do you think I'm an idiot?"

Pyet recognized the tension simmering just below the surface. It swirled inside of Juliette, bouncing from rib to rib as it waited to manifest outside of her. She crouched over as if in pain, never daring to unlink their hands. Uncertainty filled the room, leaving them no room to breathe as it suffocated them. Pyet and her mother were drowning.

She wouldn't win, not like this. Not here.

Pyet's grip loosened, her fortitude weakening. She winced as her mother finally tore the letter away from her, but it wasn't victory that filled Juliette's eyes. It was relief. Sadness. Overwhelming defeat.

Juliette clutched Violet's letter between her hands and crumpled it until the paper was unrecognizable. She tore the letter once, twice, three times. Pieces of it fell to the floor in a sorry heap.

Pyet's lifeline disintegrated before her eyes.

"I just opened it! It said my name and—" She didn't know what to say because it didn't matter anymore. Pyet looked at the torn shreds of parchment, the family emblem now indistinguishable. Her mother wouldn't care about the reason she was so attached to it. Juliette saw a threat, and she eliminated it. Pyet's head dipped to her chest in defeat, tears threatening to fall from the corner of her eyes.

"And what?" Her mother challenged again, "You know our rules. You know why we have to stay safe, Pyet. This letter isn't safe. We're not safe!"

Her mother started to shake again, her entire body looking as though it was ready to collapse. She rocked back on her heels, her teeth rattling so hard she could have chipped one. Pyet reached to wrap her arms around her slender shoulders. Even through her frustrations and fear, Pyet felt *empathy*. The hollowness that echoed throughout Juliette was trauma-born, something Pyet could at least understand. She hated how soft she was.

"I'm sorry, I'm so sorry," Pyet murmured, gently caressing her mother's shoulder. She rubbed idle circles across her shoulder blade, and old routines resurfaced.

How was it that they always found themselves here?

"Why is she back?" Juliette whined. "Why does she continue to haunt us?"

Pyet couldn't tell if she was supposed to answer, and so she didn't. Instead, her eyes stayed focused on the crumpled up parchment littered on the ground.

Her mother turned away suddenly, causing Pyet's heart to skip a beat as she escaped to her bedroom, leaving the torn letter and her daughter behind her. Whether embarrassed or distraught, Pyet couldn't tell. She knew her mother had disappeared completely when the smell of liquor finally faded. The sounds of her bare feet scurrying across the tile quieted until there was nothing left but the soft sounds of Pyet's quickened breath.

It was nothing but a fever dream.

Pyet waited until the door clicked shut and looked again at the scraps that scattered the floor before her. She knelt to grab the small pieces of paper, brushing them each into her hand before dropping them onto the table and arranging them like puzzle pieces.

It was like looking at physical pieces of her torn soul.

The address was there, hidden in the tears. Pyet pieced it together as night loomed, desperate to reclaim the piece of her that was hiding within those pages while her mother snored in her drunken slumber. She wanted to know what exactly made Juliette this way, because despite the horror and pain she'd inflicted in this house, she could only think of one person and one place to blame. There were reasons why Juliette kept those secrets so close to her chest.

Pyet could save her, if only she knew where to go to find those answers. And maybe then, once her mother was healed, she could have the family she was robbed of.

The family crest formed amongst the remnants of her mother's violent destruction as she worked, Violet's cursive stringing the pieces together until Pyet could at least find the address she'd been searching for.

She treated it like Pandora's box, waiting to be opened, but when Pyet looked at the torn letter, all she saw was potential.

She hadn't moved for hours. The letter was still sitting in front of her, though the strips of paper were thrown together like jigsaw pieces—every time she breathed, she could see a few of them threatening to flutter to the ground. She couldn't find it in herself to fully repair it, at least not permanently.

A door in the hallway creaked open, causing Pyet's breath

to hitch in her throat. Juliette stepped out in the same clothes she'd been wearing earlier, but she looked like a different person. The distinct stench of alcohol had left her, and it looked as though she'd run a comb through her hair. The only evidence of her breakdown was the swollen skin around her eyes. She looked like Pyet's mother again, not the stranger that had assaulted her before.

"Mom," Pyet said softly. She knew her mother was listening. She could see the twitch of her head as she acknowledged the words that hung in the air, but she didn't respond. "Mom, Violet is dead." It was dangerous to mention the letter again at all, fearing Juliette's relapse. But Pyet was still so young, and so afraid. She needed her mother, not this shell of a person in front of her.

The word *dead* seemed so concrete. Pyet wondered why the finality of it wasn't something they were celebrating. The mere memory of her own mother plagued Juliette, and the letter—though oddly addressed—should have been a victory. But she should see the ghosts still lingering in her mother's eyes. It haunted her, a leech that couldn't be removed, sucking the life from her blood. Not even the death of her tormentor could rid her of her nightmares.

Juliette's head cocked to the side. When she opened her mouth to respond, her voice was raspy from wailing, though it came out sharper than Pyet expected it to.

"She lies. That *witch* will never be dead."

"It's notarized by—" Pyet caught herself before she said the name Elric, lest she had to survive another meltdown. "It's notarized. Official. She's gone, and the fact that they sent this is confirmation. She can't hurt us ever again." Juliette needn't worry about a dead woman, after all.

And Violet Cabello was certainly dead.

She wasn't sure she entirely believed herself, but the words rolled off her tongue easily. There were too many lies

Pyet had become used to telling. Her mother's face snapped up to glare at her. Her eyebrows were drawn together in an exaggerated frown, her eyes swirling with new bouts of suspicion. Pyet curled away from the intensity of her gaze.

"Mom, it's me," she said again. "We're safe here. She's gone."

Pyet clutched her bag close to her chest and breathed in deeply, feeling the fullness of each inhale as it settled in her lungs. Memories circled inside her mind like sharks in the water and she felt a familiar tug at the back of her eyelids, begging her to close them just for a second. The eternal exhaustion of being alive encased her, sticking to her like the center of a spider's web. Pyet leaned her head against the window pane to rest as the heaviness weighed on her, sitting dead in the water like chum. No wonder the sharks closed in on her so quickly.

They always did know when to overwhelm her—just when she felt safe enough to sleep.

The squealing of the brakes stopped her from fully falling into her own thoughts. Instead, Pyet's forehead crashed into the seat in front of her. The collision shocked her out of her daze, making her frown as she rubbed the soreness from her temples. She hadn't realized they'd been so close, but she was grateful for the sudden, physical halting of her spiral. Three days felt like so long, but in fact, it wasn't long enough at all. She really couldn't win, it seemed.

"Last stop, Town Circle!" The driver's harsh voice echoed through the cabin. "Everyone off, everyone off!"

The three shadows she'd been keeping track of moved towards the front of the bus, leaving Pyet to be the last to step off the Greyhound. She rubbed her head again, wincing from the sting and slung her backpack over one shoulder. Pyet pushed off the seat and felt all of the blood rush back into her legs, uncomfortable prickles sliding through her bones with each step. It was slower than she intended, and Pyet tried to ignore the incessant tapping of the driver's foot and huff of frustration as she made her way forward. She didn't know how often the bus passed through Elric, but they seemed just as eager to leave it behind as her mother had.

As *she* should be.

Pyet took slow, deliberate steps down the stairs until her feet settled onto the cobblestones. The driver wasted no time before shutting his doors and leaving her there, a cloud of dust and smoke left in his wake.

She had made it to Elric, finally, and at least no one here was trying to kill her. Already it was exceeding the expectations her mother had imprinted on her brain.

Being a Cabello signed you up for a lifetime of tests, of having to prove yourself worthy of surviving. Juliette survived Violet, and now Pyet was proving that she could survive Juliette. Two decades of her own hell surely was enough to get her through...whatever this was. Despite her family's cursed paranoia running through her veins, Pyet would prove them all wrong and get the answers she so desperately craved. Maybe it would help her save her mother in the process.

When the air settled, Pyet dug into the pocket of her jeans. What she retrieved was a small, seemingly insignificant scrap of folded paper. She gently pulled the pieces apart, flattening the paper across her palm. Though the details were smudged, Pyet could still make out the faded address scribbled onto it in her chicken scratch. She'd quickly transcribed it from memory before she left home.

The timing of the letter was a catalyst for violence, and Pyet noticed the exact moment her mother turned on her. It was subtle, only noticeable in the way she averted her gaze and how she kept tapping her fingers across the countertops the day after its arrival. The belief that Pyet had intentionally called upon Violet was, ultimately, her mother's undoing. It was almost Pyet's end.

Her life had changed so much in just a few short days.

Elric had been a source of apprehension for so long, and here Pyet was, running to it. Some place she knew her mother would never come to find her.

The letter was long gone now, ripped and torn, burnt up into ashes and sent into the air, but not before the truth stuck a dagger in the heart of her family—Violet's final wound. Pyet was requested at the reading of the will, the only member of their family. Not that her mother would ever go back anyway.

Violet knew exactly who Pyet was, even though they'd never met, and it tore her mother to shreds.

Pyet needed to leave out of necessity; when it came to Violet, her mother would stop at nothing to erase her, even if it meant erasing her own child in the process. She didn't have time to look at a map before she fled, so Pyet had no idea how close this stop was to the home Violet and Winona wanted her to go to. From what little she could see from the bus window, Elric didn't seem like a large town, but here within the Town Circle, it felt massive.

What worried her were the nooks and crannies, the alleyways and shadowed corners. She felt like it was easier to get lost here than it was back home.

Pyet wasn't even sure if this place she was summoned to

was a home, and there wasn't anything in her letter indicating that the place she was going to was meant to be a place for her to stay overnight.

Did her grandmother believe she was more self-reliant than she actually was, or was she even aware of the leash her mother kept wound so tightly around her throat?

Pyet shivered as a breeze tickled the nape of her neck, the frigid February air cutting down to the bone. The sun was hiding behind ugly-looking clouds that showed no signs of parting, and it cast an eerie blue-gray tint over the Town Circle. This place was a hyperbole in itself, the shadows and darkness exaggerated so much it seemed like it was something out of a horror novel.

Elric's Town Circle looked like it had been carved out of an old stop motion gothic masterpiece, oversaturated with blacks and deep grays, leafless trees whipping around in the wind. It was large and overwhelming, with overgrown dead things and neglected foliage filling all of its empty spaces, inhabiting within the cracks of the cement walkways. Pyet stood at the bottom of the arch facing the center, focused on finding a friendly face or an open storefront.

Neither of those seemed likely in this gray arena.

Dead grass and four paths came down to meet at the center. Pyet sized up the large statue in the middle, perched atop a fountain with no water. Standing from a distance, the weathered stallion was an impressive sight. The years had taken their toll and changed its color to a dull seafoam green, the intricate details that once made up its mane and tail were now faded and eroded like it had been left out to weather the storm for centuries. The once polished metal now a quiet shadow of its former self, but it still stood proud.

There was something unsettling about it that Pyet couldn't quite put her finger on. Its eyes, once fierce and powerful, now held a dull, lifeless gaze. She couldn't help but feel like it was watching her every move, like a predator stalking its prey. Its once mighty muscles were now deflated, giving the impression that it was ready to pounce at any moment. Pyet couldn't shake the feeling that this statue was more than just a lifeless sculpture. The stallion was an oddity within the Circle, the only thing that felt alive amongst all of the dead.

Despite its rough exterior, the Town Circle was well loved. Though it wasn't properly groomed, it was obvious that it was traveled across often. The walkways looked worn from years of use, and the stallion's base was littered with dried floral arrangements, tokens, and other things one might have found intentionally placed at a shrine or altar. It was beautiful, a diamond surrounded by the roughness of the Town Circle. The surrounding trees seemed almost intentional in their placement, as if the sharpness of the branches were meant to guard the treasured stallion and the gifts left at the fountain. They were sparse and dying from the crisp chill in the air, and Pyet could see through the wispy maze of saplings that separated Elric's sacred space from the world beyond.

As an outsider, the scene painted before her was ethereal; Pyet knew that this place was something special, something unusual.

She tore her gaze away from the statue, and squinted her eyes to see through the grove. Just beyond the stallion, Pyet noticed a small light flickering, illuminating the front of what seemed to be a first-floor superette. She took off in that direction, hoping the light meant signs of life inside. It was her only shot at finding the address on the crumpled piece of paper she still held in her hand. Pyet shoved it in her back pocket as she walked, its safety within the confines of her jeans a small comfort.

A heaviness lifted from her chest as she passed the last

tree and stepped onto the gravel road opposite of where she started. The Town Circle, though empty of occupants, felt charged. It was as if all of the electric currents that vibrated underneath her stemmed from the same source.

The stallion centered at the heart of Elric.

Pyet found she could breathe again as she traversed the unpaved surface of the road, and it was that surge of confidence and comfort that allowed her to continue her journey towards the storefront with the lit lantern.

Movement from behind the glass doors caught her attention, the lantern above the entrance dancing with flame. After the last three days, it was nice to have small tendrils of hope for a change. Pyet charged forward, needing the comfort of conversation. Without her mother, she didn't know how to talk to anyone. She missed connecting with someone that didn't know about the haunting nightmares that ran rampant inside her mind.

It was exhausting living through those on her own.

The sign out front was old, swinging back and forth and squeaking against its rusted hinges. This building, much like everything else in Elric, was ancient, a little unknown pocket of the universe. Pyet made her way over and attempted to push through the door with no luck. It was locked. Her heart sped, her body falling easily into the beginnings of another panic-driven spiral, but she took several deep breaths to settle herself.

It was hard to remind herself that she no longer needed to worry about the dangers her mother put her through. Locked doors no longer meant the same things they did when she was within her mother's compound.

She didn't have to be alone anymore.

Refusing to be thwarted by the simplicity of a locked door, she tapped on the glass with two knuckles. Pyet couldn't hear any sounds of footsteps or rustling, and after a few seconds with no answer, Pyet knocked again. She didn't want to relent, not when this might be her best shot at finding Violet's home before dark. Pyet could have *sworn* she'd seen someone inside.

She almost knocked a third time, but the distinct sound of something falling to the ground behind the door made her pause.

At long last, a small figure pushed against the door, a frown settled neatly on the face of a petite gentleman. He had that bookish look about him, glasses that sat atop a small button nose, freckles dotting across his cheeks like shooting stars. He wasn't friendly looking now, but he seemed to be the type that smiled frequently, specifically when his nose was stuck in a book and not behind a cash register.

She could tell that he was unimpressed by her appearance. He made no move to open the wooden door further, even as Pyet tried to peer into the convenience store behind him.

"It's half past six. We're closed," he said sternly, shaking his head.

There was something haunting, almost ghostly, in the way he looked at her. She watched as his eyes trailed down her body, widening in surprise at her dusty jeans and blue cardigan. He was looking at her as he would an outsider, like it was obvious Pyet didn't belong here. It made her curl in on herself, feeling suddenly self-conscious.

"I'm so sorry," she said warily, pulling the scrap of paper from her pocket again and reaching toward him. He created a barrier out of the door, closing it so that only one eye was now in view. "I was hoping you'd be able to help me. I'm looking for this address," she said with a nod towards the slip in her hand.

The man looked at it, scrunched his button nose, and narrowed his eyes in her direction.

"We're closed," he said again.

"Please!" Pyet begged. "I just need to know the direction I'm going in. I just need you to point."

Reluctantly, and with a loud sigh, the gentleman took the paper from her hands. At once, his skin paled, the corners of his mouth drawing into an even more pronounced frown. His hands started to shake until shivers traveled up his arms and throughout his body. He shook his head immediately.

"We're closed, and you're breaking curfew." The man dropped the slip of paper onto the ground and shut the door completely. Pyet heard a distinct click of several locks being set into place.

What if her mother was right?

Even if the letter had told her to, even if it would save Juliette, Pyet shouldn't have listened to it. She shouldn't have come here.

She bent to pick up her lifeline, tempted to leave it there in the dust, just as the bus driver had left her. Pyet kicked the ground and turned to walk alongside the sidewalk. The shops that encased the Circle were cozied up next to each other, the alleys between them no larger than a few feet on either side. Each building was consistent in the blues, blacks, and grays she'd come to accept out of Elric, deepening as the sun continued its descent.

In less than a few hours, she'd already failed. And worse still, she didn't have a home to go to any longer.

With one foot in front of the other, Pyet kept the sea green stallion in her sight as she hobbled across each uneven cobblestone, now on her fifth lap around the Circle. She couldn't tell how long it had been since she encountered the shopkeeper, but she knew that soon, she would be needing to set up a makeshift bed on one of the benches around her. Pyet had given up on meeting whoever Violet intended for her to meet tonight. She was hopeless here in Elric. No map, no sense of direction. She might as well have submitted to her fate at the hands of her mother.

Pyet would walk until her legs fell off, that was what she decided. Lost in thought, she wandered, unaware of the sounds of small footsteps that followed each step she took.

The footsteps stopped when she did, faltered when she stumbled, and followed her effortlessly, not that Pyet was paying close enough attention. Her thoughts were still too focused on her impossible task, and of the future she was still so unsure of. This town kept playing a game that Pyet wasn't used to playing.

The footsteps needed to be quiet too, of course. Much like Pyet, they were used to having a stern hand. They were used to having rules. Pyet was breaking all of those rules, and it intrigued them. The figure attached to the footsteps was small and lithe, too small to harm or fight. It was curious, that was all. Even if it was also out past curfew, Pyet was too interesting a risk to avoid.

"What are you doing out so late?"

The quiet voice made Pyet jump. Goosebumps broke out along her arms, and she snapped her head around to reveal a young girl looking at her curiously. There was a hint of concern in her expression at Pyet's quick movement, but the girl let her curiosity win out.

Pyet, in comparison, had her eyes drawn up, her eyebrows arched so that she perfected the 'deer in the head-lights' look. It took a moment for her heart rate to calm down, her hand pressed against the place where her heart nestled behind her ribs. The silence that stretched between them made her instinctively take a step back as she caught her breath.

Pyet wasn't entirely helpless. She knew she could outrun this girl if needed, but if life had taught her anything so far, it was that she should always be on her toes. Elric was already proving to be nothing like she'd ever experienced. It pained her to say it, but Pyet was starting to believe that her mother was more sane than she knew—a realization that shook the very core of her beliefs.

The girl continued to stare at her. She hadn't done anything wrong, other than be curious. Curiosity wasn't a crime. Even still, Pyet rubbed at her arms with closed fists, frowning. It had been so quiet, the Town Circle seeming so *empty*. She was caught off guard, and it put her on edge. Years of being pressured to *stay alert* by her mother went to waste at the first moment she had been tested. Juliette would have been so disappointed in her.

"I, uh—" Pyet started, trying to get her words back. She swallowed, her throat suddenly sore and dry. "I was looking for this address." She unclenched her hand to reveal the same crumpled paper with the address she had just tried to show the store clerk across the street. It was getting increasingly worn and torn, the smudged handwriting fading each time she handled it. She wasn't sure why she was answering the girl's question so nonchalantly, or why she hadn't already run off. The girl was a bit off-putting, but she didn't seem like a threat. Maybe Pyet was craving the company of someone so badly that just the mere sight of the girl tugged at her heartstrings.

"Why are you out so late?" the girl repeated.

"Why do you all keep repeating yourselves? No one here can give me a straight answer," Pyet grumbled. Her hand shook the paper in front of her, finally catching the small girl's attention.

"I'm just looking for directions," she repeated, "and then I'll be on my way. I'll be on the next bus out of here once I handle some business." *And figure out why my mother can't even speak Elric's name without crumbling to the floor in panic.* The girl nodded in disbelief, chuckling as she grabbed for the address and looked at it very closely.

"I don't think you'll leave," she replied casually, like it was impossible for Pyet to believe that she would want to, or *could*. Pyet didn't know how to respond, and so she didn't.

The mystery of Elric would never cease to confuse her.

After a few seconds, like the shopkeeper, the girl's face dropped as she read on. She shook her head fiercely.

"You don't want to go there," she said seriously.

"What do you mean I don't want to go there? I've just spent days trying to get here on *purpose*."

The girl looked at it again curiously, frowning and pursing her lips. It took a long, drawn-out moment before she deigned to respond.

"You're out really late tonight," she said, looking up from the paper and right into Pyet's eyes.

"It's not too late," she counter-argued, "I have a standing appointment there." Pyet punctuated her statement by pointing directly at the paper again. She tapped on it a few times for emphasis. "And," she continued, letting the full force of her frustrations out with each breath, "why are *you* out so late?"

The girl waved her off, refusing to answer. She did draw inwards a little, not ready to defend herself to the stranger that stepped an unwelcome foot in her town. Pyet felt vindicated, at the very least.

"I don't see why it's such a big deal. The bus just dropped me off, and no one seems particularly helpful. I'd love to be in a warm bed soon if you could just. Give. Me. Directions."

Pyet was not usually this direct, but sitting in an uncomfortable seat with very little food for so long had made her delirious with frustration. The girl either didn't catch on or ignored her spiteful comments, instead continuing to look at her with that curious expression, like she was a puzzle. It was infuriating.

"It looked like you were walking to sit at a bench, not looking for an address."

"Have I mentioned that this town continues to be unhelpful?" *No wonder her mother wanted to leave so badly.*

The girl shrugged her shoulders. "You're out past curfew."

"I'd love to not be outside at all, if it's any consolation."

"Why do you need to go here?" the girl asked, shaking her hand with the torn slip of paper in it before handing it back to Pyet. Pyet tapped her foot impatiently. She was starting to get sick of this game of twenty questions.

"I have an appointment there," she reiterated, "and to be completely transparent, I don't even know if the person I'm meeting is still there. They said they'd wait, but at this rate, I'd be surprised if they did."

"I can take you there," the girl said softly. Her voice was neither sure nor confident, and Pyet narrowed her eyes suspiciously.

"No, really," she said again. Without saying anything more, she turned on her heel and started walking away. Pyet took off right behind her.

"I don't under—" Pyet started, but the girl turned on her quickly, startling her.

"I can take you there, but you must be careful," she insisted. It was as if Pyet had given her no other choice, that she was being forced into showing her this place that no one else had wanted to take her to.

"Careful of what?" Pyet cracked the knuckles on her left hand, crumpling the slip of paper in her right. She was close to tossing it, getting rid of the thing that made her come to this place to begin with.

The girl turned back around to stare at the statue in the middle of the Circle. She breathed in deeply, and Pyet could see the steam escape her lips, dancing out into the crisp cold that surrounded them. Stars were starting to litter the sky as the sun finally sank down below the horizon. Darkness was a welcomed friend.

"That place is cursed," the girl said, shaking slightly. "I'm afraid if you go in, Pyet, you'll never leave it."

The girl continued walking again, but Pyet wasn't sure she wanted to keep up. As night began to creep around them, it felt like there were eyes everywhere. She felt shivers down her spine, and Pyet couldn't shake the feeling that they were being watched. She couldn't trust her instincts anymore. Elric after dark was a far scarier place than it was when the bus dropped her off.

To never leave? It felt daunting. The girl's joking was now long gone. Where she laughed at Pyet's initial assumption that she'd want to leave, now her face was nothing but fearful of the possibility.

Pyet still followed her strange companion. They said very little to each other, keeping close to the walls and carefully watching their surroundings as they walked. The girl stayed several feet in front of Pyet, not letting her catch up even as she tried to match her pace. Soon, Pyet had to be content with wrapping her arms around her shoulders and trailing her reluctantly.

The girl had long hair that cascaded down past her shoulders, far longer than Pyet's had ever been. Her body was wrapped in deep smokey-colored clothing—a short-sleeved top and long, comfortable-looking pants. She looked as if she was wearing scrubs, coming home from a long shift at a hospital. Pyet couldn't help but stare at her from behind to analyze, longing to discover her origin as they trekked through the winding roads of shops and ancient homes.

Pyet didn't realize until they left the circle in the distance that she never did tell the girl her name.

They didn't walk much farther than just past the edge of the Town Circle and the collection of shops that were housed there. Pyet could see the statue from where they stood in the distance, up the hill of cobblestone they climbed. Each home they passed was drearier than the last, as if the Circle and its rusted stallion were the heart of this tiny town. The further they moved outside of it, the quieter it became.

Each building was a deep gray or purple, clouded even further by the darkness of the night. Curtains were drawn and lights were dimmed; it was a miracle the girl was able to find her way around. There would have been no way Pyet would have found where she was going on her own. There were very few lampposts, and the ones that were situated every hundred meters or so only gave off the faintest orange glow, not quite reaching further than a foot.

Pyet hadn't yet learned the girl's name but it was not from lack of trying. After a few fruitless attempts at getting the girl's attention, however, she gathered that she was being ignored purposefully. Pyet quit trying to engage in conversation after that. She never did ask how the girl knew her name, either, fearing the answer that might escape her lips.

She was pretending that she had to go looking for reasons to leave Elric already. She wouldn't, *couldn't* leave, and so Pyet blissfully ignored the oddity of it all. She was insistent on figuring out what her grandmother wanted from her and her mother first. It was becoming increasingly difficult, but she was too afraid of failure. Her life back home was no longer suited for her, and where would she go if she couldn't find a home here?

Pyet followed dutifully, her mouth sewn shut as her feet clacked against the cobblestone in the road. Sooner or later, when only a sliver of the stallion was still in view, the girl stopped walking and Pyet almost ran right into her backside.

"This is as far as I can take you," the girl said solemnly. Her voice had a new creakiness to it. Pyet turned her head and looked around. The small gloomy homes that were so close they touched one another had turned into large estates with yards and wrought iron fencing without her realizing. The homes this far out from the Town Circle were meant for the old money that she smelled from the town line. These were the homes her bus drove past on her way into Elric.

It felt like a different world out here. Even the air was irregular, staler. No one walked these streets on their own; it was as if there was a large pair of pearly gates stationed at and guarding Elric, granting entrance only to those worthy of staying. The imagery that accompanied the afterthought frightened Pyet more than she cared to admit. The gates she envisioned were not what you'd expect them to be; the white had worn from years of abandonment and disrepair, its purity tarnished by darkness. All of its virtue was uncovered for the sinister turpitude that it was, a mask of nobility. It had been there all along, Pyet thought. The overbearing threat of damnation scared people out of thinking for themselves. It left them as blind as herded sheep.

It certainly was enough to destroy her mother beyond repair.

Pyet could tell in the jittery mannerisms and frantic glances the girl kept giving her that something was amiss. She was not welcomed here, and if *she* wasn't, how on earth would Pyet be? Surely no outsider could be worthy of a home like this, in a place this full of history.

"Where is it?" Pyet asked finally. The girl stretched out a long, pale arm and pointed her boney fingers towards a house on their right. Across the street sat the most beautiful house Pyet had ever seen. Even amidst these large, wealthy mansions, this manor was a standout. It was a gorgeous marbled white, the contrast against the darks in the sky striking in the dead of night. The grounds were clean, sporting the same shades of oranges and yellows that she'd seen in the Circle, though much more polished and well taken care of. There were glorious columns that hugged the front doors and steps. Everything about this mansion signaled an ugly amount of wealth. The décor was gaudy and over the top. Pyet was at a loss for words.

She collected herself and swallowed, turning to face the girl.

"Why can't you go any further?" she asked, watching as the girl shook her head before Pyet had even finished the sentence, her features fear-stricken.

"Blessed land," she said between shakes of her head. "I can't go any closer. I am not allowed."

"If you are not allowed, how can I be?" Pyet insisted.

As if the mansion recognized her presence, a light in one of the first-floor windows flicked on, illuminating the left wing of the manor. The girl's eyes looked toward it, and immediately she shook her head again.

"You must go," she said.

Pyet nodded, even if she was worried and full of questions. The girl was shaking so hard that Pyet could hear her teeth chattering. She didn't want to say any farewell or thank you, opting instead to nod in the girl's direction and started walking toward the manor. There were no sounds of cars from either side of the dead street, and she didn't even bother to look both ways before crossing.

"Pyet!" the girl called after her. Pyet stopped in the middle of the cobbled street and turned around. She looked like she wanted to say something specific, instead sending Pyet a disappointed, disdainful look. The girl frowned weakly at her.

"Don't fall prey to the talking walls or the walking moths. They're all dangerous."

Pyet was about to ask her what that meant before she heard the creaking of the manor doors open. Her full attention was now on the gaping entrance to the manor, the shadows dancing off the marble steps from the light inside. When Pyet turned back to look at the girl for an ounce of reassurance, she was nowhere to be seen.

She had disappeared into thin air.

Startled, Pyet moved quickly towards the massive door. As she crossed the street and neared the gate that surrounded the home, a figure finally came into view from where the light originated. She took up the entirety of the entryway, shadows darkening her features so much that she couldn't make out any details. Pyet didn't know who it was she was walking toward, but maybe that was a good thing.

Maybe she would have run in the other direction if she knew. From what little experience of Elric she'd had so far, Pyet wasn't sure she'd have gone through with it if she saw the face of the person she was about to meet. It was the mystery and curiosity of it all that pulled her closer. Pyet was always one for intrigue, it came from a lifetime of being starved of it.

"I was beginning to wonder if you would show!"

She was close enough now that she could make out the features on the figure's face. It was the kindest she's seen since stepping foot in Elric, creases lining her soft skin that pulled up as she smiled. Her eyes were sincere too, a Coca-Cola brown that warmed her from the inside. Pyet's muscles instantly relaxed. She shared a shy smile and shrugged.

"People weren't the helpful type," she explained, nodding in thanks as the woman turned into the doorway to give her space to enter. If she was captivated by the outside, the inside of the estate was far more impressive. Pyet couldn't stop from gaping the further into the manor she went, her eyes continuing to find one grand thing after another. A wide set of stairs sat in the middle of the foyer, long hallways situated on either side. The room she was standing in was so large that it made her feel insignificant. Pyet didn't belong here.

She felt rooted to the ground, not unwilling but *unable* to take one step more.

"Ah," the woman said in understanding. Pyet could hear the soft clicks of her shoes against the tiled floor and turned to face her, tearing her eyes away from all of the things housed in the manor. "They don't like this place. They worried you."

It was an assumption, but the woman was correct in her observations. The odd girl made an impact on Pyet, as did the shaky store clerk, and she cracked her knuckles and tugged at each finger to calm her anxiety.

"Why?" Pyet asked quietly. It was puzzling that a place as beautiful as this wasn't admired by the people of Elric. It seemed like such a waste.

"They believe this place is cursed."

"Who is they?"

"The people. Elric." She spoke as if the town itself was a living, breathing entity. She spoke just like her mother did—with admiration and a hint of fear.

"Do you?" Pyet pressed.

"Do I what?" The woman smiled. It seemed an innocent enough question, but Pyet didn't miss the tightening of her lips or the length of silence that stretched between them.

"Do you believe this place is cursed?"

"I think it's something you need to discover on your own," she replied honestly. "This place has history, and history scares people. I implore you to learn about this place on your own. Elric is...*different* from most. History doesn't really leave it, and I suppose the history of *this* place in particular isn't something the people here want to remember. But that is on them, not on you, Pyet."

Pyet didn't know how to respond, and she stood there dumbfounded instead. The woman laughed lightly and gestured towards one of the hallways beyond the stairs. She was starting to hate their familiarity with her, and her lack thereof with them.

"Come. It's getting late, and I'd like to leave you to explore the manor after we're done. Or get some sleep." the woman smiled, knowing, "At least inside you won't be breaking the town curfew."

As if on command, the tension in her legs loosened. Pyet no longer felt rooted to the ground, and she shook out the muscles in her thighs before following dutifully.

When they emerged from the hallway and into another too-big room full of luxurious sofas, the woman invited her to sit on one. There was an array of folders on the coffee table before it. She sat across from Pyet, crossing her legs and sitting up straight. She seemed so at ease here, far more comfortable than the girl had, or the storekeeper that refused to bring her here. This woman was something else, entirely.

Pyet shivered as a cool breeze fluttered about her. She could have sworn she smelled roses as she sat, scrunching her nose from the odd, unwelcome aroma. The woman across from her was unfazed.

"My name is Winona," she said, ruffling through the folders on the table. "I am the executor of your grandmother's will."

Pyet nodded, happy to finally put a name to a face in Elric, and a familiar one at that. Winona was who she'd spoken with on the phone at the bus station, the one that promised she'd stay, no matter how late it was when she got into town.

"Do you live here?" she asked suddenly, not realizing that she had interrupted Winona's long winded sentence she barely listened to. Winona looked shocked, but not frustrated.

"I live in Elric, yes," she replied, not missing a beat. "Not too far from here. Just over a few streets."

"Did you know my grandmother?"

"Violet was a lovely woman," she nodded. "She was kind to me. I think by the end of her time she would consider me a friend to her, and a friend to the manor."

"Did she know about me her entire life? Forgive me for my intrusiveness, I know you want to go home. I just...I'm finding it hard to understand why I was named in the will as her successor when I never met her, and why my mother wasn't invited back." *And why she was so petrified of her, and this place.*

"I'm sorry you didn't know her," Winona frowned. There was something more beyond those words, but she didn't expand on them. "I knew Violet for a long time. She sought me out years ago to get her will in order. It was the only time I'd known her to do so. She trusted so few people; I find it unlikely that she went to anyone else to change it. So, for several years or so, your name has been on these papers. She has at least known of you for that long."

Pyet sat silent for a moment, her body filling to the brim with more questions than the woman in front of her could surely answer.

"Can I proceed?" Winona asked patiently.

Pyet nodded, albeit reluctantly. She had a feeling she would be haunted by this letter, by the spontaneity of her grandmother's decision-making for the rest of her life.

What other secrets did Violet Cabello have?

She left her a fucking *fortune*.

A new home, money, and assets. Pyet was glad her mother wasn't invited, if she had, there would be nothing left of it. She would burn it all to the ground. And surely, after all was said and done, Pyet would be dead. She couldn't find it in her to say much of anything in response, her mouth hanging open with each new inheritance mentioned. It got grander and more obscene with each passing reward.

Winona seemed pleased when they neared the end of their appointment; she kept throwing Pyet uncertain glances throughout her reading. It felt like an eternity, but other than naming things off, there wasn't much else to go over. Violet truly left everything to her. In all, it was over in a matter of half an hour. This morning, Pyet wasn't sure where she would be sleeping tonight, and now she had more money than she could count. And a mansion. *A fucking mansion.*

"Do you have any questions before I go?" Winona asked gently, interrupting Pyet's private, internal monologue. She couldn't help but laugh in response.

"I have about a million," she replied honestly. Winona nodded in understanding, a shy smile creeping up the corners of her mouth.

"Yeah, I'm so sorry. I know it's a lot to take in. I didn't realize you would be so…in the dark." Her face flushed in embarrassment.

"It's not your fault. It's just so overwhelming. I can't believe…" She looked around and waved her hands in the air. "All of this is mine."

Winona smiled again, though Pyet was sure she saw a hidden bitterness cross her face as she replied.

"It *will* be. It'll take a few weeks before everything is finalized, but I'll be in constant contact with you to keep you updated on the progress. As I said, I live close by. There isn't anyone in this town that knew Violet—and the mansion—as I did. Here's my card." She dug in her pocket and reached to hand her business card to Pyet. The card was a deep plum with raised gold lettering. Pyet noticed it outlined a number and her name, Winona Fairchild.

"Please call me if you need anything, okay?"

"I appreciate it," Pyet took the card and flicked it back and forth between her fingers. Winona took that as dismissal, getting up from her spot on the couch. There was a moment of panic that shot through Pyet. Was she just supposed to stay here? All alone?

Winona seemed to recognize the fear, touching her shoulder lightly as she walked by.

"While the paperwork finalizes, I expect you'll stay here. Get yourself accustomed to the manor. I don't know what your plans are, but I hope you don't tear down this place. There's history here, remember? I would hate to see that history taken away from Elric. Don't listen to what people tell you, Elric needs this place."

Pyet didn't even think that was a decision she *could* make.

"I'd like to think that I can form my own opinion," she said cautiously. She didn't know what else she could say. "I… I do have one question though, if you don't mind?"

Winona kept walking through the living space and into the foyer again, Pyet following. When she reached the door, she turned around. Her brown eyes shimmered with curiosity.

"What's that, Pyet?"

"Do you know where I'm supposed to sleep?"

Winona used that moment to throw her head back and let out a yowl of laughter. Pyet could feel her cheeks flushing red; it seemed like such a silly, stupid question to ask—like she was ten years old again and not the fully-fledged adult she was pretending to be.

"Pyet," she said, so much like her mother might have before she left, "You're the Lady of the Manor now; you get to decide where you sleep. But, if you're looking for something a bit more…formal, Violet's room was upstairs and to the left."

With that, Winona smirked and opened the door to walk down the marbled steps. The evening had blackened even further, the street lamps still emitting that faded orange glow. She reached the bottom of the steps and turned around to wave goodbye.

"Oh, I forgot to mention, Pyet," she said quickly, "Violet also had a cat. I'm sure she's walking the estate, somewhere. Don't worry, once she gets to know you, you won't be able to shake her. Her name is Kit, and her stuff should be in the kitchen. Violet never hired anyone to clean or watch the manor. I, uh…don't recommend it. Not many people would come near this place even if you tried. I'm sure you can figure out where the rest of her things are as you explore. Have a good night, Pyet."

Pyet waved half-heartedly, suspending her disbelief, and,

as she watched Winona walk through the iron gate, she shook her head.

She was seeing a woman out of her new mansion.

A fucking *mansion*.

She wondered what her mother was doing back home, and if she had worried about where her daughter had gone. Pyet gazed longingly towards the darkened street again, as if Juliette would manifest out of thin air. It was wishful thinking; Pyet knew her mother wouldn't set foot in Elric again. She disappeared long ago, ran away, and never looked back.

Elric would haunt her mother until her last, dying breath. It was her hope that maybe one day soon, Pyet could understand why. It wouldn't make any of her later actions excusable, but maybe knowing would help Pyet find some peace. She hoped it could let her finally put the past behind her, and build a new family she chose for herself.

As she retreated into her new home, she turned and locked the door—in case her mother *did* decide to make an unexpected appearance in the dead of night. For as much as she wanted to see her again, the dread that built in her stomach at her prospective return churned.

Pyet had no idea where to start, so she rubbed her hands along her thighs to release some of the built-up tension. Her bag was sitting close to the door, and she grabbed it and headed toward the stairs with the intention of finding Violet's old room. It was getting too late to do any looking around in the dark, and Pyet was sure it would take a lot of exploring to really get an idea of what this new home had in store for her.

She wasn't sure how many rooms a place this large could hold—another question she'd forgotten to ask—but finding a place to sleep was priority number one.

As it turns out, a place this large can hold at least five rooms upstairs. Pyet hadn't been in a space so lavishly decorated in her entire life. She was taken aback by its opulence—gold-framed paintings, floor to ceiling velvet curtains, plush furniture upholstered in the most luxurious fabrics. Every surface was dripping with gold accents and intricate carvings. Expensive vases of freshly cut lilies filled the air with a sweet aroma, and a grand marble fireplace was carved into the center wall.

In the end, she did choose the largest room in the bunch, which just so happened to be Violet's. Some might have thought it was odd to sleep in the same room as a dead relative, and an estranged member of her family, but Pyet was exhausted. She didn't even know the dead woman well enough to care.

The room was covered in patterns, some carpeted, others painted on the walls. Silk tapestries hung from the ceiling and draped from the columns, creating a riot of color before her eyes. Gold-framed mirrors covered every wall, ornate to the point that they were eclipsed by their own decorations, embellished in mosaics depicting scenes from mythology. While she had never seen anything so beautiful or decadent before, Pyet understood it as a reflection of who lived within this house.

The room's large platform bed had posts in each corner. She had never felt more comfortable in her life than when she tossed her bag to the side and flopped onto the room's large platform bed. Pyet crawled all over it, sliding underneath the duvet and curling up into herself. She was like a fish in the ocean, there was so much bed around her.

It didn't take long before Pyet succumbed to sleep.

She wasn't used to dreaming. In fact, Pyet could count on one hand the number of dreams she could bring to the forefront of her memory. But, as her eyes fluttered underneath the curtain-draped four-poster bed in her new home, it was the most vivid dream she'd ever had.

From the moment she stepped foot in the manor, Pyet was never alone. At first, it felt like a looming presence over the entire town, but the longer she stayed in the manor, the more she realized the energy was coming from the house itself. It wasn't the Elric Town Circle or the stallion statue that was the heart of this town, it was this place.

And Pyet was right in the middle of it.

DAY 2

3:33 AM

The dream she had was so potent that it felt real. Her body twitched and spasmed, as though Pyet was being physically touched and prodded all night. The goosebumps that peppered along her skin broke out over her body constantly, the hair on her arms following the feather-like touch wherever it went. It wasn't so much a dream, but a heavy awareness. Pyet could sense herself sleeping, a sort of cognizant REM sleep that had her hovering over her own body. She couldn't move, paralyzed on the bed. Feeling. Sensing. Knowing. Though she couldn't see much of anything other than the rise and fall of her chest, she *felt* it.

Sometime well past midnight, she heard the soft tapping of feet out in the hallway. It could have been Kit, her new cat, but she couldn't be too sure. Pyet wasn't convinced that she even had a cat—she hadn't yet seen or heard her anywhere within the manor.

It wasn't like she could go looking anyway. She was still chained to her bed, her sleep paralysis gluing her body under the duvet.

The manor is old, she couldn't help but rationalize. *It was settling, that's all it could have been.*

It was mid-morning when Pyet finally woke up in a cold sweat. Full consciousness washed over her and she sat up immediately, feeling the tingles trail through her toes. Her hand went immediately to her throat, touching the place where her mother had gently slid the kitchen knife against it. There was no knife there, no indication that anyone was in the room with her at all. But even just the relief of regaining control over her body calmed her some.

The sun dripped from the window to the right of the bed and illuminated the entire room. She could have sworn she was hearing things, though it was nothing like the creaking of a settling mansion, but something *more*—voices and laughter from the other side of her bedroom door. Petrified, Pyet slowly crawled out of bed, careful to tiptoe towards her shut door. She pressed her ear to the wood. The noises she thought she might have made up overnight were still present, even in the sunshine.

The manor was her *home* now, but it felt the furthest away from it. Pyet gathered her nerves, creaking the door open and listening out for voices. There was nothing but footsteps nearby, although the source of the noise was further down the hall toward the stairway, still much too loud for an otherwise empty house.

It was possible that Winona stopped by this morning, Pyet thought. Maybe she'd been doing it every day since Violet died. If they were as close as Pyet gathered, she couldn't blame her for wanting the comfort of the manor to help her grieve.

It still felt weird to think about people knowing Violet better than she did.

Pyet, feeling more confident from her vividly spun story, pulled the door open and stepped outside of her suite.

Something brushed up against her leg and Pyet almost lost her balance, covering her mouth to stifle the scream. When she jumped, she couldn't help but stumble a few feet forward and stub her toe into the stair railing. It made her curse fiercely under her breath, hobbling on one foot and grabbing her leg. Pyet collected herself, squinting her eyes against the pain and looked for the source of the soft caress against her calf. The pain had masked her initial fear, but she was oddly grateful for it.

A small black cat meowed, purring so loud it sounded like a motorboat beneath her. It looked at Pyet happily before sitting on its hind legs, lifting its paw to lick at it with a sandpaper tongue.

"Is that you, Kit? What are you doing?" Pyet hissed incredulously. The cat didn't seem to mind her frustration, blinking large green eyes and licking its chops. She thanked whatever God was out there that Winona had warned her about the resident feline, or else she might have toppled down the stairs in fright.

Pyet bent at her knees, rubbing her fingers together until Kit sat up delightfully and stepped closer to her. The cat was velvet soft, her onyx fur gleaming from a fresh washing. Winona hadn't been lying. She was incredibly friendly.

"You're lucky I'm a cat person," Pyet whispered. She hovered there for a moment, hoping she hadn't caused enough commotion to disrupt the happenings downstairs. After she regained her composure, she patted Kit once more on the head, making sure to tug lightly on her whisker before slowly descending the glorious staircase, her nerves no longer peaked.

There were women everywhere. Literally.

Pyet couldn't stop to think about what it was and who it was she was looking at. Instead, her jaw dropped, gaping at her kitchen full to the brim with absolutely breathtaking women. They all wore seemingly timeless garments, long dresses cinched at the waist lavishing in all sorts of colors. They all looked like they belonged in a different time period.

She felt as she had in bed and in the foyer the night before, paralyzed and unable to walk away.

A small squeak left Pyet, and her sudden outburst caused the talking to cease at once. Several faces turned to her in shock, and before long, one by one each woman disappeared.

Pyet rubbed at her eyes, trying to burn the image into her brain. She wasn't crazy, she didn't imagine this. Kit seemed disinterested, but not oblivious, staring at where the women once stood and her tail flicking silently.

It was when she was in complete silence that Pyet finally

screamed. Her fear now overtook her curiosity, and her voice finally found its volume again. She could hear herself echoing through the not-so-empty halls.

And then she ran.

She ran out into the foyer, practically tearing the door from its hinges trying to escape this ghost house. This haunted house. This cursed house.

The sun was high in the sky in Elric—though still hidden behind another batch of heavy rain clouds—but Pyet didn't care about the town, or how it looked quite the same as it had when the sun was gone. Instead, she looked around desperately for a pay phone. When Pyet breached the iron gates of the manor's property, she spotted something resembling one down the street and sprinted to it until she was out of breath.

She was only about four to five houses down the way, but just being out of the house was enough to settle the rapid-fire pounding that was Pyet's heart.

The phone was old and rusted with paint flaking from its handle, but she grabbed for it anyway. Pyet dug deep into the pockets of her jeans from the night before and pulled out the business card Winona had given her.

It was still simple, plain gold lettering in a pretty font, with nothing but her name, title, and phone number. Pyet dialed the number quickly, relieved when she heard ringing.

"Hello?" A groggy voice answered. At first, Pyet didn't say anything. Instead, breathing heavily into the other line, she scrambled for the words. "Hello?" The voice grew more aggravated. She didn't even check what time it was.

"H-h-hi. Winona?" she said breathlessly.

"Who's calling?" It felt good to hear her familiar voice.

"Winona, it's… It's Pyet. From yesterday? You helped get me settled at the manor."

She could hear scuffling on the other end as if she was just getting out of bed herself.

"Pyet, yes of course! I'm so sorry, I don't get many phone calls."

"That's no worry," Pyet said. She gazed back towards the manor and the open door, swinging on its hinges. Kit had walked out and down the steps and was sitting lazily at the entrance gate, grooming herself. After a few seconds of silence, she heard Winona clear her throat expectantly.

"Did you have a question for me?"

"I, uh, I do. But I have a feeling it's going to make me sound crazy." She was met with more silence, and she could only imagine the regret Winona was feeling at this moment.

"I'm listening, Pyet."

"Did Violet—did my grandmother ever mention seeing ghosts?"

Silence.

"I don't think I understand the question."

"Did Violet ever tell you that she saw ghosts in the manor?"

"I don't really think this is what I meant when I told you to call me if you had any questions." Pyet shuffled her feet, taking curious glances back towards the manor in hopes of catching a glimpse of the women she could have sworn filled her kitchen. Nothing but the swinging door met her eyes. The harshness of Winona's tone made her uneasy, she thought she found the one friendly person in this God-forsaken town, and now she was scaring her away.

"I know, I'm sorry," she said earnestly.

"You do realize it's just after eight in the morning, right?" Winona prompted. Pyet shook her head, knowing full well she couldn't be seen on the other side of the line.

"I do, I'm sorry. I just had a dream—"

"I find it difficult to believe that you would be calling me over a silly dream you had last night." Pyet tapped her toes and felt her hand curl around the receiver. Now *she* was getting frustrated.

"This house has something in it. I'm not crazy. This is the first time anything like that has ever happened to me!"

"What exactly happened to you, Pyet?"

She hated being talked to as if she was a child.

"I saw ghosts, Winona!" she exclaimed, exasperated, "I walked into the kitchen this morning and they were everywhere! And then they just...just, they disappeared!"

Winona let out a long-winded breath, as if she was gearing up to talk Pyet off the ledge.

"Do you have a history of sleepwalking? I know it's possible for people to hallucinate while they sleepwalk."

"I wasn't hallucinating!" She'd never been one to sleepwalk. If she had her mother would never let her forget it. It would be a weakness.

"Pyet, I know you knew it would sound crazy. I'm sorry to tell you that you were right. You sound absolutely bonkers right now." Pyet could feel the tears start welling in her eyes. She wiped them away vigorously with the palm of her hand.

"Can you just answer my question, Winona, please?" There was a pause as she gathered herself.

"No," she said solemnly, confidently. "Your grandmother has never explicitly talked about seeing ghosts in the kitchen of the manor."

And that was that.

"Was there anything else you needed from me, Pyet?" Her voice had lost the edge, returning to the soft, nurturing one she remembered from last night. Pyet sniffled, wiping the snot from her nose and the tears trailing down her face. She didn't feel like she was adult enough to handle all of this on her own. She didn't want her mother, but she wished she had *someone*. Pyet hated being so alone.

"N-no, I'll be okay. I'm sorry to bother you, Winona."

Winona sighed again, and Pyet was sure she was going to hang up the phone.

"Listen, Pyet," she said softly, "There is no other living thing in that house with you, other than the cat of course. No one will harm you at the manor. I have been there more often than anyone, so please trust me on this. Let's meet up for lunch today. I can show you around Elric a bit, get you acquainted with some of the friendlier residents. It would be healthier than continuing to think about those women you thought you saw."

Pyet felt herself nodding, "I'd like that."

"Okay, I can be at the coffee shop in just a few hours if you'd like. It's not that far from the manor."

"Okay."

"I'll see you soon, Pyet."

"See you."

She hung up the pay phone with a satisfying click and slid down its post to wrap her arms around her knees. Pyet looked back at Kit, who licked her lips and wrapped her tail around one of the iron posts.

Pyet felt her heart race, knowing that she had kept a heavy secret from Winona. These weren't just any ghosts that she had seen. These were the souls of lost women, their wraiths forever trapped within the walls of the decaying manor. They were women that Pyet didn't know, even if she felt them in her soul and her mind long after she ran through the marbled columns.

The ghosts were women, but Pyet never told Winona that they were.

As she stood in silence, a detailed vision of a moth fluttered in front of her eyes. Pyet could see the intricate details of its wings, its feathery antennae twitching in the breeze.

It was a sign, she knew. The moth was a messenger of the spirits, warning her of impending danger. Pyet took a deep breath, her hand instinctively reaching into her pocket for something, but coming up short.

She always came up short.

They never specified a time for their meeting, and Pyet, who hated being late, found herself wandering the streets until the Town Circle was in sight, trying hard not to think about the ghostly women she'd stumbled upon at the manor.

The sun was hovering behind gray clouds, the dark buildings still somber, even in the daylight. She paced back and forth along the sidewalk, keeping her head down and rubbing her arms so fiercely that the friction could have caused sparks. Thankfully, the café was not difficult to find; it sat catty corner to the corner store—which Pyet skittered past after her unfriendly encounter with the clerk yesterday. She hoped this cafe was the only one in town because Winona wasn't exactly *descriptive* when making their plans. Pyet knew she looked insane pacing outside the coffee shop, but the place looked closed, and she was feeling restless.

Pyet took a peek through the windows and nodded once to herself—confirming that she was, in fact, near a place that served coffee—before stepping around the corner to fully assess Elric's Town Circle again. It was just as dead and dreary as she had experienced last night, even with the sunshine ricocheting off of the stallion sitting in the center. The town was oddly still, even at this early hour; Elric was as quiet during the day as it was at night. Back home, the city was bustling even before the sun came up, but everything in Elric was different, and the empty streets were no exception.

What she hadn't noticed last night was that the Circle was littered with more than just shops. It was not just the corner store she'd tried to enter yesterday, or the café she would be visiting today, but loads of small signs lining the streets. There was a post office, a library, a laundromat, anything anyone could ever need. Pyet imagined people weaving in and out of the doors, wondering, not for the first time since arriving, where all of the Elric residents *were*.

Making sure to keep the café in sight, Pyet walked down the sidewalk. Every single shop she passed was closed, and her brows furrowed deeper with each darkened window.

Catching movement from the corner of her eye, Pyet raised her eyes to find an older woman, wearing the same gray canvas scrubs as the others she'd seen, propping open a door with a large rock. It was the only shopfront with some semblance of movement, and Pyet was inclined to investigate.

The small, rotted sign out front simply read Matilda's, and had no discernible objects in the front windows. She wasn't sure it was even a shop at all until she stepped through the doors and heard the tinkling of a bell signaling her arrival.

The shop was nothing like she had ever seen before.

The distinct smell of cedar wood and herbs assaulted her senses, so much that she could taste it on the tip of her tongue. Pyet noticed a small stream of smoke coming from a lit incense stick in the corner, and a small, plump woman with a head full of curly gray hair pulled back into a bun atop her head. Her face wasn't exactly friendly, but it wasn't *unfriendly* either. She looked Pyet's way, nodded once in greeting—but not before giving her a terribly disgruntled once over—and returned her attention to the pendulum swinging in her hands.

Pyet walked slowly through the menagerie that was Matilda's. Tiny bowls of gemstones and rocks littered the countertops, and bottles of various liquids were sprinkled across bookshelves. She found herself reaching towards a book that was laying on its side, running her finger along the cover, and coming up with a thick coat of dust.

"Can I help you with something?" The woman's voice was low and toad-like, croaking with each syllable. Pyet shook her head quickly, pulling her fingers back to her chest in embarrassment.

"No ma'am," she said quietly. "I'm just passing through."

"People don't just *pass through* my shop," she—Matilda, presumedly—said, uncertainty coating the words as her gaze narrowed in suspicion. Pyet physically shrunk back from her. *Unfriendly, then.*

"I just moved to town," she said desperately, trying to explain. "I'm meeting someone at the café for coffee and I wanted to see what was around here,"

"You're...meeting someone?" Matilda scoffed, unbelieving. "People don't just *move here*, either."

The verbal abuse made Pyet visibly recoil, and she backed into one of the shelves in her retreat, causing a bunch of the bottles to rattle as they threatened to fall. She wasn't used to such animosity in such a small space. The people here were terribly unwelcoming, despite Elric seeming like a close-knit town. This was where her mother got it, she decided. Her wickedness was a product of the people Elric birthed.

"Where did you move from?" Matilda pressed, slapping her wrinkled hands down on the cash counter firmly.

Pyet took a small few steps around vases that covered the floor, moving away from any other breakable objects. It also acted as a barrier between her and the shop owner. Matilda tapped her fingers impatiently on the counter, rubbing the pendulum in her other hand as she waited. Pyet didn't feel as if she owed her any explanation, but she also felt scrutinized. Would Matilda let her leave if she didn't answer? She wasn't entirely certain.

"My grandmother died. She lived in an old manor up along the road that way," she pointed for emphasis. Matilda's lips pursed as she listened.

"You are Violet Cabello's granddaughter?"

"I didn't know much about her," Pyet answered truthfully. "She knew me, though, apparently. She let me have the home. Gave it to me. It's the largest gift I've ever received." She looked down towards the floor and shuffled her feet awkwardly.

To her surprise, the woman guffawed.

"That's not a gift, girl. She must not have liked you too much. That home is cursed."

Pyet cringed. It seemed everyone knew more about the manor than she did, and it was infuriating. She rolled her eyes and took a few steps closer to the old shop owner.

"Do you know why it's haunted?" she asked. The woman looked at her and frowned, shaking her head.

"Ain't nothing you need to be looking for, girl. That there's trouble if I ever saw it."

"No one will tell me *anything.*"

"Get used to it. I doubt they ever will. They're afraid they'll catch the ick just looking by looking at it. Being associated with that house is bad. Don't be surprised if they come at you with pitchforks soon. Wouldn't surprise me."

"But why?" Pyet begged, "I don't understand why no one

will tell me what the hell is going on in the manor. I can't leave if I don't know what's going on."

Matilda looked at her and shook her head slightly. "Do you really want to know?"

"More than I want air to breathe, at this point."

Matilda laughed at her candor. Pyet didn't want to like her —she was rude and odd and didn't seem to like her so much either, but it was hard not to relax the longer she stood in the shop. Fear still shot through her bones, but Matilda's bluntness made her feel a little less crazy than she had this morning.

"I can't do it here. You're ruining business just by standing. Cursed, remember? There's no way people are going to want to be anywhere near where you've been or what you've touched, I should have pushed you out the minute I recognized you. Come by after we close, I don't mind telling you the stories. It might scare you off though, so be prepared."

It's too late for that, she thought to herself. Pyet found herself nodding anyway.

"What time do you want me here?"

The old woman looked at her and cocked an eyebrow, her eyes directed toward the door and the small sign hanging on it.

"Are you blind?" she asked, sounding serious. Pyet rolled her eyes again and shook her head.

"Fine," she said sharply, "I'll come around after you close."

Matilda scoffed in annoyance and turned away from her.

"And one more thing," she added, both of their heads turning as a small ding echoed from the entrance. The patron kept their head down, not looking either of them in the eye, and slid along the wall in an attempt to avoid them as best as they could. Matilda narrowed her eyes and whispered, "Come 'round the back."

Pyet took that as her dismissal and maneuvered around

the various apothecary items scattered across the floor, scurrying out and away from the strange woman and her shop. She should have run, and between the manor and Elric's odd company, she almost wanted to. However, her curiosity got the better of her and, while a part of her wanted to catch the first bus out of there, Pyet felt rooted to this small town.

Curiosity killed the cat—that was how the saying went, right?

Pyet chose the furthest table from any other patron in the now-crowded café and sat with her thumbs rubbing circles on the tabletop. She grabbed her iced coffee and took a long sip. It turns out this *was* the only coffee shop in the entirety of Elric. They didn't offer any milk substitutes, either—strictly black coffees and pastries. She grimaced at the bitterness of her bagged sugar coffee, sucking in air through her tight lips and clenched teeth. It would have to do.

It felt as if a switch had been flipped after her conversation with Matilda. Where the streets were empty before, now they were crowded with Elric residents. The clang of a bell rang from somewhere unseen, as if it were a siren giving its people permission to finally be awake and functioning. People of all shapes and sizes moved about town, all wearing the same gray canvas scrubs. They blended into the muted colors of the town, melting into the shadows of buildings.

It felt as if her clothes were a beacon. Everyone who noticed her gave her weird looks and, even if she wasn't sitting at the furthest table in the café, she doubted anyone would approach her. They all avoided her like the plague. She felt as if people knew she'd come from the manor, just with a single look.

Her dry, flaky croissant sat untouched in front of her on a napkin. The barista behind the counter kept glancing her way and the unwanted attention made Pyet's face burn berry red. She shrunk into her chair, waiting.

Winona was later than Pyet wanted her to be. Though the day was still young, she'd sat in the god-forsaken coffee shop for two hours, her foot tapping incessantly with anxiety.

"Oh, Winnie!" she heard the girl behind the counter exclaim suddenly.

Pyet lifted her head—had she dozed off?—and found her lips rising in a small tilted smirk. She raised her hand in a small wave, and when Winona caught her attention, she seemed to smile right back. Winona ignored the barista completely, walking straight to the table Pyet was slouched over. She straightened her posture and crossed her legs.

Winona was breathtaking. Pyet didn't notice it last night but as she moved closer, her long sable-colored mane cascaded down her back in loose waves that practically imitated Pyet's shoulder length curls, framing her plump, rounded face. Pyet could feel her heart pounding through her chest; it hurt so bad that she wanted to clutch at her ribcage. Something about her looked and felt familiar, but Pyet couldn't place it. Winnie was the closest feeling to home she had here.

"Pyet," she said warmly, sitting across from her and mirroring her crossed legs. Pyet's fingers shook as she took another sip of bitter coffee. She decided not to comment on her obvious tardiness, watching as Winona got comfortable in her seat without so much as an apology.

"I appreciate you taking my half-crazed phone call this

morning," Pyet said sheepishly, lowering her face to hide the red that bloomed across her cheeks.

Winona didn't say anything for a long moment, taking the time to stare at Pyet until the silence was too uncomfortable to bear.

"It's okay," she said at last, "I told you to call me for anything, and this fell under the umbrella of everything. I've had worse, truthfully."

Pyet couldn't help but smile. There was something that was so easy about this, about being around her. She was… comfortable. Winona was soft and kind, an anomaly in Elric.

"I feel like you're too nice to live here," Pyet said offhandedly. "Sorry, I know that's probably not the nicest thing to say. But, I haven't had the best luck with the people here so far."

"I noticed."

"So, uh," Pyet continued uncomfortably. It was hard to focus when there were eyes staring daggers into her back from all angles.

"It's not you," Winona fumbled. She rubbed her hands awkwardly. "I'd be acting similarly if I was in a situation as strange as yours. I really thought you'd at least have known who Violet *was*."

"Well, I knew she was my grandmother, but that was the extent of it. She and my mother had a falling out when she was young, so I never got the chance to meet her. She really didn't tell you a single thing about me?"

"Not much more than a name and where you were living. You know, so I could send the letter—"

The barista that had been eyeballing them both walked towards them, steps falling heavily against the waxed floor. Pyet's eyebrows raised as she dropped a nice hot cup of coffee in front of Winona.

"Caramel macchiato with an extra shot of espresso. Just how you like it."

Pyet hadn't seen her order anything, and a caramel macchiato was different from the "just coffee" she was told was the only option. Her eyes narrowed in frustration. Winona must be a regular here—but who wouldn't be? The barista stood there for half a second too long, and Winona offered a quiet thanks so that the girl would leave them be. She didn't touch the coffee, pushing it away from her instead.

"My ex," she supplied easily, as if answering Pyet's unasked question before continuing. "I thought you'd be more informed is all." She raised her index finger to her mouth to chew lightly on the nail. "Honestly, I thought you'd be able to answer more questions for me than I'd have to answer for you."

"Answer questions for *you*?"

"Yeah. Violet was a very private woman. I always felt like she thought of me as a daughter, in the end. I was the only one that ever came by, and you know by now that most people in Elric try to avoid the manor. We were close, but she had her secrets." She sounded bitter, and the harshness of her tone cut like glass.

All that said, the people here didn't avoid *her* like the plague. They all seemed to be pleasant, waving at Winona and whispering their greetings, all while ignoring Pyet. She noticed that Winnie recognized each one individually, making them feel important, special.

"Didn't you know her for several years?" Pyet asked. Winona grimaced.

"I knew her for far longer," she said with a nod, "but she had no reason to pay attention to me until I was in early adulthood. My career had me in a chokehold when I was twenty years old. This town…encourages work to benefit its people, and I wanted to help Elric in the best way I knew how. I was groomed for it, as most children here were. Helping your grandmother was a debt I took on for the town. And I grew to love her, eventually."

She was around the same age as her mother was when she left Elric, Pyet decided, and Winona had a career while she was having panic attacks over leaving her mother's prison. The thought made Pyet shrink further into her seat. How incredibly humiliating. She felt like such a child.

"I should have known that Violet had her own agenda, but I always felt like it was odd that you were the one she was giving everything to."

There was a hint of accusation in her tone, but Pyet ignored it.

"Try not having a relationship with her at all."

"I know that now," Winona said defensively, "I actually thought that *you* were her daughter, which I now understand was your mother—she was a piece of work I hear."

Pyet couldn't help but start laughing. The barista glared at her from behind the espresso machine, but Winona only looked at Pyet curiously. Between bouts of laughter, Pyet actually had to grasp at her chest.

"You don't know the half of it," she said, catching her breath, a tear sliding down the right side of her face. "My mother burnt my letter and ripped it to shreds. I'm lucky I was able to write down your number and the address to the manor."

"Oh Lantern, I'm so sorry. I had no idea."

"Of course not." Pyet waved her hand dismissively. "It's not the worst thing she's done. I swear she was going to kill me." Winona's eyes widened in surprise. She didn't expect her to say anything—it was a heavy confession and the first time Pyet thought to admit her mother's suspected crimes out loud. She didn't care as much as she should have; the person who birthed her had forgone being her mother long before this incident.

"She tried to kill you?"

Pyet nodded, "A story for another time." She didn't expect the light touch of Winona's hand to cover her own trembling ones. Her fingertips grazed the roughness of her knuckles and it made Pyet suck in another breath. Such light touches hadn't been felt in too long and she was so starved for them.

"I feel like it's awkward to bring this up now." Winona finally retracted her hand from Pyet's and reached instead for the coffee in front of her. Pyet half wondered if it had gone cold. She took a long drink, almost draining the cup before setting it back down again. "But I think you should tell me about what you saw."

Pyet was dreading it. The sooner they touched the elephant in the room, the sooner they'd be done, the sooner Winona would realize that she was out of her mind.

"I feel like I overreacted," Pyet stuttered, retreating inward and grasping her hands against her rounded thighs. Her fingers dug in, marking her. Her eyes twitched from the pain.

"No," Winona said sternly, "Don't do that. You sounded... freaked out. I want to help."

"You're just going to think I'm crazy."

"No, I just thought you were lying." Her head dipped sheepishly.

Pyet's nose scrunched up and her heart raced. "About the ghosts? See I told you—!"

"Not about the ghosts, Pyet. Could you let me finish?" Winona reached towards her, their hands colliding again. It did little to stop the rapid pace of Pyet's heart. Her tone carried through the small coffee shop, causing several heads to turn their way. Pyet's cheeks raged with rose coloring. Winona straightened out her shirt and ran her hands along her pant legs. She looked as uncomfortable as Pyet felt.

"I thought you were lying about your grandmother when we met."

"I don't understand."

"Of course you don't." Winona smiled slightly. "I was the closest living person Violet had considered...family. I was a friend to the house, and I promised her I would never let anything bad happen to it."

"That's a big commitment you gave...to a house."

Her face broke into another grimace. "I know, but there are things you need to know about the manor, and I don't think you're ready to know those things yet."

"But it's *mine*. Shouldn't I know everything there is to know about it?"

Winona's palms grabbed the edges of the tabletop suddenly, startling Pyet. She looked up to find her face contorting into anger, her brows arching menacingly, and the beginnings of a snarl crawling over her thin lips.

"You did not earn the respect of that manor. You do not *deserve* to know."

"You speak as if it's a living, breathing entity." The fire in Pyet's eyes matched Winona's, and for a second she felt electricity swirl around them. Winona's eyes flicked in recognition before she settled. The rage behind her features was gone, disappearing as quickly as it appeared.

"It's..." she wavered, uneasiness coating the words. "It's hard to explain,"

Pyet raised her hands in frustration, their confrontation seemingly forgotten, "You don't seem like you're trying to explain anything!" She tapped her fingers against her thighs anxiously.

"I didn't trust you. I thought you knew Violet, I thought you knew that she was giving you everything. I thought she told you things and when I found out that you really didn't…"

"You were jealous?" Pyet could see it coming. It was in the guilty shift of Winona's eyes and the way she turned her face towards the window overlooking the Town Circle.

"Violet was *my* family, and she didn't tell me half the secrets she carried around with her. Which is her right. But then she leaves all of her secrets to you? You, who had no relationship with her. You didn't care for her when she needed it, you didn't protect the manor with your life. You weren't there the day she was…the day she died. I just don't understand."

Pyet didn't know what to say. She couldn't apologize for something she had no control over. And what could she give Winona anyway? This conversation was starting to feel like emotional whiplash, and she was still no closer to getting the answers she was desperate for.

"Now you must think that *I'm* crazy, right?"

"No, not really," Pyet answered. She understood how Winona saw things, at least more clearly than she had before. It couldn't have been easy to have a stranger walk into your life, so soon after someone you cared for died—Pyet would have been wary too.

"I understand, I think. And I'm sorry for your loss. I didn't know her, but I wish I did," The words sounded weird coming from her lips, and she knew if her mother were here she would have been dead on the spot. But they were true. Despite growing up with nothing but disdain for Violet, she couldn't help but be curious too. "She sounded like she meant a lot to you."

"She did, and I'd love to come to the manor and talk to you about her. I know where she kept her photo albums. I think she wrote in journals too. I'm sure she'd have wanted me to share them with you since she's gone. That is, if the house hasn't scared you away yet."

Pyet took her time to respond. She noted the hint of bitterness that laced Winona's tone, whether intentional or not. She wasn't too clear on the ins and outs of the estate settling, but she knew this much: Violet didn't leave Winona anything. For someone who was so close to her grandmother, why was it that she was excluded from the will? There was a sadness about her whenever she talked about Violet, and if they had the relationship Winona was convinced they did, none of it made sense to Pyet. But Winona knew more about that house and its belongings than Pyet did, and she was offering to help her understand.

"You should take them. The albums, anyway, or the journals," she insisted. Winona quickly shook her head.

"They're yours, I could never-"

"They're not mine," Pyet countered, "Like you said, I didn't earn the respect of the manor yet, and I hardly knew her. While I appreciate and accept your invitation to teach me, it feels wrong to keep something that seems to mean so much to you." There were a few beats of silence, and Winona looked too stunned to say anything. After a while, she nodded.

"Thank you," she whispered. Pyet could feel a pull at her heartstrings for the broken woman in front of her.

"She should have left you something. Anything."

"Violet always had her reasons, Pyet," she said, shaking her head. "No one but her could ever know the true intention. She was full of secrets; you'll learn that soon enough."

Pyet took a glance at a clock on the wall, her eyes widening in surprise. The day had flown by, and though she wasn't entirely convinced that they had been here for over three hours, the clock wouldn't lie to her. It had been so distracting that Pyet had almost forgotten about the apparitions she'd seen in her home earlier. Winona didn't answer her questions, so to speak, but Pyet had another source she could go to. That she *needed* to go to. Pyet continued to stare at the clock for a moment longer before cutting Winona off with some long-winded sentence.

"I'm so sorry, I have to go!" she said hurriedly. Winona's eyebrows arched in confusion, before settling into a narrowed expression, her train of thought forgotten. She looked so much like all of the other people in Elric at that moment—anxious, angry, suspicious. She looked, Pyet thought in disbelief, a lot like her mother.

"I'm sorry?" Winona asked, catching Pyet's hand as she scooted her metal chair back with an ear-shattering screech. Pyet couldn't resist the urge to swipe her hand away, bringing it close to her chest. It was hard not to miss

Winona's stunned, hurt reaction. She recovered quickly, uncrossing her legs and leaning forward. "Where on earth do you think you're going? Everything in Elric is closed, or closing, by now."

"That's sort of the point," Pyet said vaguely, pointing her face in the direction of the barista wiping tables on the other side of the café.

"Oh, are you going back to the manor? I can join you, I'm welcome there,"

"No, it's okay," she said quickly. Winona kept saying things like that, like she was welcome there—like there were people that weren't.

Winona's face fell, her mouth turning over into a frown.

"I don't mean to give you the wrong impression," she muttered quietly. Winona played with the rings on her finger with one hand. She was delicate, her skin stretching over fragile bones that were unsure of themselves. Pyet couldn't explain, not really. She couldn't tell her how truly frightened she was, how she had nowhere else to go but Matilda's. She couldn't tell Winona that her presence wasn't enough to ease her worries.

Yet, the look in her eyes was too much to bear. Distant, forlorn. Not once in their time spent did she talk about anyone but Violet and the manor; Pyet was her last connection to it. The old woman and her haunted home were the only things Winona seemed to have ever cared about, and Pyet felt like she owed her something. Maybe not everything, but enough to let her know that she wasn't leaving. Not yet.

"Matilda asked me to stop by the shop after they closed. It seems rude to keep her waiting," she tried to explain quickly. Even saying it out loud sounded bizarre. Winona looked like her jaw was about to drop to the floor.

"What do you mean, Matilda? Like *the* Matilda? The old crone that tells everyone she's a witch? The same one that parents sing about in their nursery rhymes to keep their children in line? God dammit Pyet, you've been in Elric for only twenty-four hours, and you've already made friends with the second most alienated person in this town!"

The first being her, that is. Winona didn't have to say it for Pyet to know that's exactly what she was implying. The reminder made her frown more prominently.

"She's the only one that's even remotely interested in letting me know what's going on." If she wanted an honest answer, Pyet was going to give her one.

Winona clamped her mouth shut, disapproval written across every twitch and flattened scowl that crossed her face. She looked as if she wanted to argue with her, and Pyet *wanted* her to. She didn't want to go to Matilda—she wanted Winona to tell her. But, judging by the way she kept her lips pressed together, Pyet knew she wouldn't get her answers here in this coffee shop. Winona's trust will be much harder earned.

"I'm going to go now, Winona," Pyet said. Every moment was an opportunity, and despite her promise to herself to not have any expectations in coming to Elric, she continued to find herself disappointed.

"You will know in time, Pyet, but not yet."

"Matilda promised me answers *now*, Win. I can't wait until you believe it's the right time for me to learn about my family, my mother, my *grandmother*. Why my mother was terrified of all of you. Why she abandoned my grandmother and fled. Why there are *ghosts* in my manor."

"She can't be trusted, Pyet. Please, listen to me!" Winona sounded desperate, and she grabbed Pyet's hand. "You cannot trust these people, least of all Matilda. Promise me you won't go there. Promise me you'll let me explain what is happening here to you in my own time."

Pyet frowned, her eyes glancing down at their entangled

hands. She shivered at the warm touch, but refused to meet Winona's eyes. After a few long, steady beats, she finally nodded. It was so much easier this way, and Pyet wasn't yet ready to let Winona go. She knew too much, and her information was invaluable. And, Winona continued to feel like home. She gave Pyet the comfort her mother might have, if she had been normal, if she cared.

The longing in her chest outweighed her desire to find the truth.

She had time to wait.

"Fine," Pyet said through clenched lips, "I won't go."

Pyet stared at her small closet, pulling the sliding door open to its full width to get a better view, but she wasn't surprised at what she saw inside of it anymore. She was coming to expect the gray slacks and shawl wrap tops that she'd seen Elric's residents dress in. They weren't medical scrubs like she originally thought, but the required uniform for all of town. Winona mentioned the dress code in passing a few days after their coffee date, and at first, Pyet simply laughed it off.

She didn't realize that Winona was *serious*.

The gray was jarring, at first, but after weeks of staring at it, the monotony had lost its sharpness. It was just…normal now.

Pyet noted how easy it was to fall into the customs of Elric, even after just a short while. She was so starved for a community, a place to call her own, that the town's idiosyncrasies didn't startle her as they once did. She wondered if, at some point, *all* of her surprise would be gone. Pyet wondered if her blade would start to dull, or if the edges of her vision would start to blur. She wondered if, sooner or later, rose tinted glasses would replace the blanket of dark blacks and grays and purples before her.

Elric had, without even trying, become familiar. It could have been the lingering memories of her mother's stories, or the home that had nothing but haunting souvenirs left from Violet, but she felt a kinship here that made her lower the walls that had stood tall for so long. It scared her, how effortlessly she was falling into this lonely town's clutches. The teachings of her distrustful mother, the paranoia and the unhealthy levels of preparedness, were lost on Pyet as she navigated this new life without her.

Though the grays were not her first choice, Pyet grabbed for the fabric, shaking her body of the goosebumps that started to freckle along her arms. She was a beacon everywhere she went anyway, no matter what she wore, so it was better to at least attempt to blend in, to conform. Though she was fastly accepting this odd, unusual town, Elric didn't seem to reciprocate or acquiesce. Its people were still wary of her, skirting out of her way even as she stayed close to the walls, taking up as little space as possible. Winona promised it wouldn't last long, but Pyet couldn't see their suspicion waning anytime soon.

She still couldn't find her backpack with the change of clothes she'd brought with her that first day. It had gotten lost or misplaced, even though Pyet could have sworn that she had just thrown it near the bed. There were so many questions Pyet collected in the last week in Elric, her missing belongings only a small fraction of what she came up with, but the ones involving Violet *had* to take precedence.

She couldn't let her familiarity or her relief cloud her from her initial objective—Pyet needed to know why her mother left, and seek out the reason for her grandmother bringing her here. She really didn't have a choice, it seemed. It was gray or gray, with little to no variation of the shade.

So, they became her regular garments, too. The clothing called to her, and maybe that was why she never brought it up to Winona again. It was probably for the best that Elric's residents were still wary of her. She couldn't stomach the idea of letting go of her own convictions just to be part of theirs.

God, Pyet missed having a family.Winnie seemed to think that they would come around eventually, but she wasn't convinced.

She hoped she would have her answers long before that time came.

Thoughts about Elric's odd wardrobe—and who had written it into law—fell to the wayside as she pulled a tightly folded pair of pants from the closet she had been staring at for too long now. She pulled up each leg intentionally, reveling in how perfectly made for her body they were. The pants were loose-fitting but comfortable. They slipped up her legs and settled along her waistline with little give. The canvas texture was rough against her soft skin, and she couldn't help but scratch at the outsides of her thighs to eliminate the itch.

Pyet's focus tried to return to her closet of gray, but it seemed her attempt to do the simple chore of getting ready would be wasted. A panic shot through her before she could stop it, the habitual gasping for breath assaulting her throat and lungs. She never learned how to calm the panic attacks when they came, instead grasping at her chest, trying to tear her rapidly beating heart from her body.

Pyet melted to the floor, wrapping her arms around her legs, needing to feel the solid ground beneath her to stabilize herself. Only when her cheek was pressed firmly to the wooden floor did she relax again, the coolness seeping into her pores. Although she had been facing the opposite direction of her closet of gray, just the feeling of knowing it was right behind her threatened to make her jump over the edge again. Her body tightened, her muscles tensed, and Pyet clenched and unclenched her fingers.

The overwhelming feeling of this place not really being *hers*, but *Violet's*, continued to haunt her. The manor sensed it too; she was an outsider here, no matter what she wore. Pyet was just a girl playing dress up in her grandmother's clothes, playing adult in her grandmother's house.

Nothing here would ever really be hers.

After a few moments, she breathed deeply, catching the scent of mildew from the dirty floors. Pyet pushed herself up off the ground, sitting up in nothing but a sports bra and the same itchy, canvas pants. Looking back at the closet again, she blinked slowly.

Nothing here was hers.

Nothing *here* was hers.

Nothing here was *hers*.

But maybe, that was okay.

That string of hope was enough to help her get off the ground. It was enough to make her face the closet again and grab for the shirt that hung ominously on the hanger. It was enough to get her through that moment, but she knew it wouldn't hold for long. If Pyet couldn't find her place here, or the answers she came for, she would break. Her string would snap in half, leaving the ends torn and frayed.

She pulled the shirt over her head. It was much the same as the pants were, tight enough to hug her curves without being skintight. The canvas itched the same, too.

But, at least now, she felt like someone that could belong in Elric.

Pyet walked over to the full-length mirror that hung from the back of Violet's bedroom door once she felt strong enough to move again. What she saw in the reflection was not the person she remembered being before she arrived here. The person that stood before her was…different.

She had put on some weight while she was here. Her body was fuller, she had color in her face—though maybe the swelling of her cheeks from her panic attack would leave its mark on her for hours to come. Pyet looked so much like the person she could have been if her mother hadn't left her to fend for herself.

Pyet could tell her attitude had changed too over the course of the last month. She was finally starting to dig through the layers of who she was, not realizing until now how much her mother smothered who she wanted to be, and who she should be.

If only the panic attacks would leave her be.

There was no place to hide here before the mirror. Pyet hated looking into it, scrutinizing every detail of her face, agonizing over how similar it was to her mother's, and wondering how much of Violet made it into her DNA.

There was a prominent frown that inevitably crept into her features as she pulled at her skin and tugged on her curls. Pyet looked at her face for so long that the figure before her morphed into someone unrecognizable.

Her hair elongated, darkening and transforming into loose waves that fell far past her shoulders as opposed to her shorter, tighter curls. The skin on her face melted into deep wrinkles, aging her well over forty years. Pyet patted her face with slender fingertips, noting how the skin felt the same— tight and flushed—despite the mask the mirror deceived her with. The reflecting light darkened, making the background of her mirror look eerily like shadows dancing behind her. She couldn't look away.

It wasn't real, she knew that, but it *felt* real. She lifted her hand to the mirror to touch it, feeling momentary relief when her reflection followed suit. It was her only tether to reality, knowing that the illusions before her were a figment of her bizarre, tortured imagination.

Her reflection moved again, opening its mouth into a shriek as long pointed teeth emerged from swollen, ruby red gums. Blood dripped from her mouth, and Pyet could have sworn that she tasted the metallic tang as she watched. The figure tilted her head, eyes wide with hunger and want.

Florals and foliage started to sprout from her hair, peppering her scalp with dozens of flowers, leaves, and thorns. They wrapped themselves around her ears and neck, making a home along the curves of her body. Pyet could feel red, sticky blood trail down her forehead, noticing, finally, that the vines had not manifested out of her hair, but her head. Clots formed at the roots, painting her face with red streaks that burned bright against her ivory skin.

Pyet was fascinated, leaning closer and closer to the mirror until she felt as if she could fall into it. When her eyes peeled away from the beautiful flowers in her hair, they caught on the bulging blue veins threatening to burst from her neck. The vines had entangled themselves around her, pressing into her skin and crushing her like it were an anaconda strangling its meal.

They wrapped around her neck like a noose, strangling her until she felt the burning sensation of her skin ripping apart. Strings of flesh and severed muscle groaned from the unrelenting pull. Blood sprayed out in every direction as her head tore free from her neck, ripped off by the unforgiving grasp of the twisted, thorny vines that coiled around her throat like a deadly serpent. Pyet's body convulsed and shuddered, thrashing against the ever-tightening noose until it was all too much to bear. Finally, with a sickening ripping sound, her head came free and remained suspended in the air, enveloped by an eerie stillness as its eyes stared out into the abyssal darkness below. Her lifeless eyes stared back at her own reflection in the mirror, the vines still clutching her body in their merciless grip as her severed head hung there in defiance.

Pyet's breath hitched, the space in her gut twisting in fear.

When she looked back up, the eyes of her doppelganger cocked its head again in a motion so slow that it seemed like time had stopped. Its wry, knowing smile filled her with an icy dread as she felt all the hairs on her body stand on end. Its dark eyes glinted like an animal's in the night as its piercing gaze drilled into her soul.

Pyet felt for her face, her fingers traveling across her lips. The monstrous teeth had gone, replaced by the smooth, straight teeth she'd known her whole life. Her thin lips were still the same, and she sucked in a breath, noting the downward tilt of her mouth.

Pyet was not smiling.

Her heart pounded in her chest, the sound echoing through the small room. Without even thinking, she stumbled backwards in a desperate attempt to escape the ghostly image that was manifesting before her very eyes. As she frantically shuffled back, her foot caught on something soft and furry, causing her to stumble even more. Pyet looked down in horror, realizing it was only just the boney apparition of her cat's thin tail that she had tripped over.

Kit screeched and hissed violently, sprinting out of the room.

"I'm sorry!" Pyet screamed after the tiny thing. Her arms shook aggressively, and she stepped out of sight of the mirror to avoid the face that wasn't hers. She couldn't bear to look at it, turning around to grab the comforter from her bed and throwing it over the reflection that stared back at her.

She was going to go crazy here.

Pyet paced back and forth, rubbing at the worn canvas

that trapped her body as it enveloped her. Her bed was the only safe place, the white sheets inviting her in, offering a space away from the panic building in her chest again. She succumbed to it, falling onto the edge and laying spread eagle against the crisp fabric. It did little to relieve her, but feeling tethered to something helped pace the beat of her heart and slow the blood racing through her veins.

Kit's howls echoed through the empty house, and Pyet used the awful sounds to ground herself as she closed her eyes.

It was only her imagination.

It had to be.

The house was quiet.

It had been two weeks since the apparition in the mirror. Two weeks since her mind began playing tricks on her; she allowed herself to believe that she imagined it all.

Pyet wondered if a life with her paranoid mother made her this way, wary of everything that might step into her path.

After several sessions of reassurance from Winona, and the lack of *activity* around the house, she was starting to believe that she didn't really see ghosts after all. It was her mother, it was Elric, it was the shadows in alleys and the stallion in the center of town. She was letting the horror stories from her childhood influence her interpretation of this house, and of the person who had most recently inhabited it.

Weird things happened in that house—strange whispers echoed through the halls in the middle of the night, doors slammed shut on their own accord, and the temperature in the manor would fluctuate from one extreme to another without any logical explanation—but it was nothing like what she had seen that first day. It made her wonder if she had truly seen those women after all.

Kit was still upset with her from the other day, howling from another corner in the manor while Pyet walked through the hallways, the creaking of the wood loud and ominous beneath her bare feet. She would never get comfortable with the sounds that came from within the manor.

Winona did let slip simple bits of information every now and then, just enough to keep Pyet on the line. She mentioned things like Stone Tape Theory and frequency illusion, all things that were more complicated than Pyet cared to look into. Ultimately, what she said made sense, and so it was easier to believe her than to question it. She knew it was to put her at ease, but it was working.

"I'm sorry!" she called out to Kit again for the fourth time that week, knowing full well that the cat could not hear her, but saying it for the guilt-ridden heart she was carrying.

Pyet felt immediate relief when she stepped outside the manor. No matter what assurances Winona was giving her, there was something off about that place that unsettled her, and the tension melted from her shoulders the minute she was away from it. Pyet was not used to feeling so uneasy about herself and what she was seeing. She liked to think that she had at least an ounce of self-preservation—the one good thing her mother ever did for her was teach her how to survive.

Uncertainty in anything she did was not like her, but Elric seemed to bring out a lot of that.

She crossed the threshold of the iron gates and turned to look at the manor, as she had every day since leaving it. There were no figures in the window, no unusual things to see, but she needed to make sure. Pyet wrapped her hand around the metal, feeling its grooves under her fingertips.

They twisted around and around, coming to a pointed fleur-de-lis. Pyet let her hands bounce against the iron as she walked to the end of her property. The instant she let go of the manor's entrance, it seemed as if everything around her lit up.

Pyet covered herself with her arms and exhaled slowly, letting the wind caress her face and chill her bones. Out here in the open, she found that she was able to breathe fully again. The walk into the heart of town was not long, but it *was exactly* what she needed to calm herself before submitting to Elric's less than welcoming residents.

As she made her way across the final street before the large, imposing mustang came into view, she looked around expectantly. In the last month, she'd been caught up in the whirlwind that was Elric. It was a busy, populated town. People usually lined the streets, going in and out of the storefronts. They weren't all friendly, but at least she could see them, hear them, touch them.

Most days, Elric was bustling with activity, but there were others when it felt like a ghost town. There were days that felt so much like her first, where the streets were empty and the people gone, like they had simply disappeared from sight. Pyet was never sure which version of Elric she was going to get. It seemed like there was no rhyme or reason to it. It was as though everyone had a means of communication that she was not privy to.

And, though she wished she was wrong, Pyet knew they *were* communicating.

When the large bell, visible from the Town Circle, tolled out its resounding call, people gathered in excitement. It was the same as the day she first met Winnie, and even though it had been several weeks since then, they still flooded the streets each time they heard that sound. Pyet hadn't been able to mark down the days properly, or see if there was any pattern that she was missing, but it happened without fail. The bell was loud and powerful, a presence not to be missed in a place as small as this. Wherever they were hiding, the people would reemerge at its beck and call.

And, every time, Pyet went uninvited. She never did know where the people of Elric went before the bell sounded. Days and weeks had come and gone, and she was no closer to figuring out the mysterious bell tower, and the reason for her town's bizarre relationship with it.

The streets today were empty, despite how high the sun sat. Pyet shuffled along the silent sidewalks, her feet dragging in frustration with each step. She kept her head down, quietly navigating the empty Town Circle, sticking so close to the wall that she could have scaled it. Pyet loved letting her fingers fall against the brick, each groove and divot of the stone matched her breathing as she walked.

She didn't want the plaza to be so full of people that she couldn't move about as she pleased, but Pyet missed the feeling of people. She found she enjoyed sharing the same space as someone else, even if they avoided her. She was kept prisoner in her home with her mother for so long, she craved the attention of passersby.

She craved conversation. Connection.

A sense of belonging.

There was nothing to do in Elric when its people were gone. The shops were closed and the electricity underneath her didn't vibrate with the same kind of intensity.

Elric was, in the truest definition of the phrase, a ghost town.

As she approached the curb that separated her from the stallion fountain sitting at the center, Pyet looked up, stepping off the ledge and onto the uneven road before her. The cobblestone was littered with tree roots and protruding weeds that broke through the bricks. Just seeing it made her skin pimple with fear. The vines reminded her so much of those in her illusion, and Pyet's hands went immediately to her throat to tear the serpentine greenery from her neck at the memory.

No longer dragging her feet, Pyet sprinted across the cobblestone until she was safely on the other side. She clutched at her chest as panic started to rise like bile. Pyet took two deep, long breaths before leaning her head back and closing her eyes.

It was only in her mind, it was not real.

It was not real.

Biting back another bout of fear stricken paranoia, she kept walking. That was the only thing she *could* do—keep moving forward.

She couldn't allow her panic to cloud her judgment. She couldn't allow her weakness to cause her failure. Elric felt more right than any other place had before. There were secrets here that she wanted—*needed*—to figure out. Not for Winona, her mother, or Violet. She wanted to figure them out for herself. Pyet needed, more than anything, assurance that she could be on her own after all.

She stretched out her hand to feel the dead bushes as she glided across the Circle. They started to change, she noticed. The branches were less dry, and she could have sworn that she could see some yellowing that looked almost like new growth. Pyet was always paying too much attention to the metal horse in the middle of town. More than she should, anyway.

The stallion was so much scarier this close up, its beady black eyes staring into the pits of her soul. Pyet was not put off by its size or menacing exterior, instead walking straight up to it and placing her palm on its hind leg. She spread her hand wide across the rusted surface. The metal was cool to the touch and ice shot up through her veins as she rubbed her fingertips across the beast's rippling, rusted muscle.

"Pyet?"

She jumped back in shock, feeling a jolt of electricity shoot through her fingers as she turned to see Winona looking at her curiously. Her brows were pulled up, the dimple on her chin prominent as she smirked in apology. Elric's residents had a tendency to sneak up on her, and she hated it.

"I'm so sorry, I didn't mean to spook you. What are you doing here?"

"I was coming out for a walk. I wanted to hit some of the shops for groceries, but…" Pyet gestured around them to the darkened storefronts. "I'm out of luck today. I'm sure I can find something in the cupboards somewhere." She grimaced. Despite her exceptional reliance on herself, she had neglected to tend to some of the more important things that came with living on her own. Making sure food was in the house, of course, was one of them. Her stomach growled in frustration.

Winona's expression changed, but it was too quick to narrow down. It flashed briefly across her face before she nodded.

"I'm *so* sorry, Pyet. The Lantern called a town meeting. It's required. We drop everything we're doing to attend."

"How does everyone know? I didn't hear anything." As if anyone would come close enough to talk to her, anyway.

Winona scrunched her nose apologetically. "I'm afraid you wouldn't. They don't usually invite newcomers. The Lantern has to deem you worthy enough for an invite."

It seemed she was the only one in town that didn't receive one, then. Newcomers to Elric were few and far between —*she* was uncommon. If there was anyone worthy of attending their secret meetings, it couldn't be Pyet, either.

She wasn't even important enough for them to give her the time of day in a conversation.

Trying not to let that ruffle her feathers, Pyet huffed silently and tilted her head toward Winona. "And you? Did you not get an invite?"

"Oh I did, I had to—" She stopped mid-sentence, showcasing a small embarrassed smile. More secrets, more things Winona refused to tell her. Pyet wanted to scream at her, to demand that she finish the words that stuck in the back of her throat. Winona refused to look at her, her arms were drawn in, her fingers rubbing together in an anxious rhythm.

Pyet would get nothing from her.

Pyet's eyes narrowed and her otherwise content expression darkened. "That's okay, I know I'm keeping you."

"It won't be too long, Pyet. We could meet up afterward if you wanted?" Winona's hopeful tone was lost beneath Pyet's grunted reply. It didn't seem genuine, but she was no longer surprised by vague, unusual nonanswers. Especially from Winona.

Her frustration was not lost on her friend, who's anxious ticks manifested more prominently with each passing second. The color in her face mirrored a ripe tomato, her eyes forecasting past Pyet, still not wanting to make eye contact. She looked so familiar from this angle; it was in the sharpness of her jaw, and in the pointed cheekbones that starkly outlined her face.

If only Pyet could place it.

Winona continued to shuffle uncomfortably before digging a hand into her front pocket. Pyet couldn't see what she retrieved, but before long there was a balled hand shoved into her chest.

"Here, at least take my house key. I told you, I live only a few streets from *the* manor." She couldn't help but hear the weird inflection as Winona mentioned the manor, but took note of it to ponder at a later date.

Winona turned over her fist and opened her fingers delicately. The key that sat inside of it was old and made of brass, looking more like a key from a movie than one that served any real purpose. It looked entirely make believe, like everything else in this town.

"You can't miss it, I promise," Winona continued, forcing herself to finally look at Pyet. Pyet couldn't help but notice the flash of suspicion cross her features. Before she could articulate it fully, however, it was gone—replaced by the feigned friendliness that she was so used to seeing.

"And there's *food* there. Eat whatever you want."

Winona smiled again before shaking the key in her hand. When Pyet finally took it, Winnie took off in the opposite direction without another word, past the stallion and into the menagerie of Elric's buildings, cutting a path towards the bell in the distance.

A part of Pyet couldn't help but feel punished for coming here. She didn't want the key to Winona's own old, gaudy mansion. She wanted nothing but the home she went looking for when she crossed into Elric, the one her mother robbed her of. Pyet wanted to find a way to make them accept her, to find her *worthy* of being a part of their odd, twisted pack. She couldn't go on as she had the last month—without answers, without friends or a family any longer.

She was sitting on the Circle benches, thinking about her mother again, and about going home to the place she knew so well—risking being killed. Would that be better than where Pyet was now? Effectively a pariah, and no closer to understanding what Violet was up to. Still, even with familiarity came uncertainty, and the thought of her mother still made her skin crawl.

She had no desire to see her again.

Pyet hadn't even been sure if Juliette was looking for *her*, or what she would do if she found her. The more time spent without her, the easier it was to see the cruelty nestled behind her mother's eyes. Her fear of the consequences of seeing Juliette again after all they had been through made Pyet weary. There was a darkness in those memories, a monster that she was convinced Elric created.

Pyet looked up toward the sun and kicked the ground with her feet. Life had dealt her a shit hand of cards. She wasn't a bad person, or at least she didn't think she was.She was just born at the wrong place, at the wrong time. To the wrong person.

She begrudgingly slouched forward, her feet taking her into a now familiar direction away from town. As she moved further and further away from the statue, Pyet felt magic take root in her bones again. She relied on that feeling the last few weeks. The energy was addicting, and even if it was dangerous and unusual, it helped her feel grounded. The stallion acted as a deterrent; while she was near it, no hint of Elric's devilry touched her. Now, as she crossed the dead street again in the direction of Winona's home, she couldn't help but feel the wind pushing her along. At once, Pyet felt herself settle into the arms of the shadowed magic.

Spiritual or not, she was becoming quite the believer. This little town was making its mark on her, and Pyet didn't think she could leave. Physically, she'd be able to climb the stairs of another Greyhound, but mentally? Pyet could never leave Elric without understanding its purpose. Maybe that was why people stayed here.

Elric trapped people, and then never let them leave.

This walk was familiar, but it was never boring. Pyet would never tire of the winding streets full of homes in Elric. Though the buildings were decades old and musty, with a distinct rotting smell about them, it was peaceful. The stiff silence here was different from the tendrils of smokey shadows that coaxed their way along the shops within the Town Circle. It was as if the grays in the sky were less a menace out here. Color had started to seep in from the seams, bleeding greens and blues. The more days that passed, the easier it was to see muted remnants of color the town had been missing

Elric was not perfect, it was not pleasant, but as Pyet succumbed to its people, the easier it was to find life in the darkness. Elric's people seemed content, never bored or tired of their lives– they saw the color she was fighting to find.

It was taking so much effort for just an ounce of muted colors.

As each step lengthed, the sun dipped toward the horizon. Pyet's frown grew deeper with each passing minute as she felt her sense of loneliness and isolation grow. Her body tensed at the thought of being completely and utterly alone in another home, on yet another world. Her neck was sore, her body broken from exertion. It took so much effort to wake up, to survive. Loneliness was far more exhausting than a room full of company.

The sun wasn't so far past the Elric skyline before it shone directly on Pyet's face. Her eyes crinkled in the corners and she squinted one eye open, holding a hand out to shield herself from the sun.

Pyet didn't know where Winona lived, but it wasn't hard to guess. There were exactly two neighborhoods surrounding Elric's town, just several streets separating the two. She knew the house when she saw it, just like she was promised.

It just *felt* like Winona. The magenta panels that lined the house were old and falling off the structure, but still held a certain charm; it felt poised and quirky all at once. Pyet walked up the wooden steps—so unlike her own marbled ones—and fingered the key that she had been given. It slid into its slot comfortably, and when she turned the handle, a cloud of dust exploded in her face as she pushed the door open. The hinges creaked from disuse, and Pyet almost felt like she didn't have the right home at all. Did Winona even live here?

It felt weird being in a home that wasn't hers. She wasn't allowed to go to friends' houses when she lived with her mother; they weren't safe or approved. Pyet had only known what was hers, and hers alone, manor now included.

If she *had* actually inhabited this home, Winona lived a very different life than what she did. Her clothes were strung about, and Pyet could see half-empty plates of food lying on the couch, uneaten. She shifted inside, letting the door fall shut behind her.

What was the most surprising was the air; there was no

electricity here, no current shocking her bones. She was still not used to feeling *nothing* in Elric. It was as if the magic that flowed through town avoided this house and the stallion completely.

There would be time for questions later. With her stomach screaming bloody murder at her, Pyet beelined for the fridge, mouth watering over fruits and other snacks that lined the shelves. She could have sworn it had been years since she'd had them, though it had only been a few weeks. She grabbed a bag of grapes and went in search of a bowl to rinse them off in before finding a comfortable spot on the couch. Legs crossed, she popped each purple grape into her mouth, savoring the sweetness as she rolled it along her tongue.

Pyet looked around, desperate to cling onto everything she could, but her eyes were not moving fast enough. She wasn't sure how long this secretive town meeting would run for—the bitterness over her lack of invitation still soured in her mouth—and she wanted to drink in anything she could discover about Winona. She wanted to trust her, but something was holding her back; it nagged at a deep part of her brain, but Pyet was unable to pull it forward.

Shaking her head, she let her eyes continue to roam over the room before her.

Pyet sprawled along the couch, stretching her arms above her head and almost knocking over her bowl in the process. She sunk into the couch, turning her head so that the coffee table was now at eye level. Pyet didn't realize how much she needed to lay down. The leather was soft and plush, and Pyet could drown in this couch if she could. Her eyes started to glaze over, the lull of sleep trying to call her, but she willed the desire away.

She squinted as movement caught in the corners of her vision. A ribbon cascaded from the underside of the coffee table in front of her. It hung there idly, swaying back and forth as if it had fallen from some hidden nook. There was something so familiar about it, almost as if it was an old friend calling her home.

She reached her hand underneath, curiosity spiking when slender fingers traced the length of the silky ribbon, and her hand paused at the base of the shelf. She pried away a corner of the wood and discovered a small, rough leather journal tucked securely underneath.

Don't mess with it, it's not yours, she breathed to herself. Winona had trusted her enough to go to her home, not to go through her private things.

If the angel on her shoulder kept her away from the hidden book, then the devil on the other side was twice as loud. Curiosity, as it always had with Pyet, won, and she picked at the edges of the tape, pulling at it until the journal dropped to the ground with a satisfying thud.

It felt wrong to be intruding on the privacy of the woman who welcomed her into her home, but Pyet recognized the journal the minute it came fully into view. The maroon leather was worn from use, the ribbon leaking from the bottom pages. It belonged to her grandmother, pulled from the collections she gave to Winona before she even understood their worth, a treasure gifted out of guilt. As if to prove it to herself, Pyet delicately opened the front cover. They were originally part of *her* inheritance, after all.

Scribbled atop the first page of the journal was her grandmother's name in deep black ink.

Violet Cabello, 15 of 30.

Her face fell slack, the corners of her mouth dragging into a frown. She hadn't ever read the journals, never knew they existed before her conversations with Winona. She had given them all away, naive to the wealth of information a book like that could have within its contents. And then they were forgotten, never spoken of again before now.

Pyet didn't expect to see them again, assuming Winona had kept them only for nostalgia's sake. She thought they weren't worth going through, that they were nothing more than just the ramblings of a woman she'd never known.

So why keep this one hidden?

Pyet didn't want to risk Winona coming home to see her rifling through her belongings, but she wanted to find the other journals. The compulsion to uncover them was digging its way into her brain, carving a permanent home. Pyet couldn't help but wonder if they were all hidden this way, as if Winona was leaving her a treasure map, begging her to find her way.

But she couldn't.

Instead, she flipped through the book in her hand quickly, her hands tracing over the grooves of Violet's beautiful calligraphy. She could recognize that handwriting anywhere now. A few pages caused Pyet to hesitate, unfamiliar script littering the margins, an intruder in between the lines. It had to have been Winona's handwriting because it was neither beautifully curved nor elegantly placed like her grandmother's. Instead, it was hurried, rushed, and chaotic. It was less like the treasure map Pyet wanted it to be. Winona did not want anyone to find this journal. She wanted to figure it out herself. It seemed Pyet's grandmother really did keep secrets from them all.

She didn't read much of Winnie's scrawl, instead sitting upright and closing the book shut. Pyet stood uneasily from the couch and turned to leave, the journal tucked safely underneath her arm and the bowl of grapes discarded on the coffee table, rotting in Elric just like the rest of them.

FROM THE JOURNALS OF
VIOLET CABELLO

I hate this fucking house.

No, I don't. That's a lie.

I love this house, and the destination will be worth it in the end. The house, these women, is not the destination. They are all just vessels on the journey. I have to remember that.

I must.

My mother did this. And my mother before her. And now it's my turn. I will prove to them that I am not weak. I will be the strongest of my line, I will continue this legacy.

So no, Lantern no, I love this house.

Sometimes I wonder who even reads these things. Mother told me that our entire family had journals. I don't know where they put them, or why. I don't think mine have ever been moved.

I don't even think Mom has read them. But they keep making me write them. Even if I have nothing to say. Like now.

Oh well.

The house has been reckless lately, I think that's why my head has been all over the place. That's why none of this makes any sense. I'm sure my last few journal entries are about the same. Nonsensical.

I should have prepared myself, Vernal is coming and I know they hate it. They hate everything this town does. I can't say I blame them. But I'm not going to stop, no matter what they say. Lantern, they are the worst. Mom tells me to ignore them. But the more I ignore them, the more they bother me. Maybe it's just the women I hate after all. Not the house. Not the journey.

Just these terrible, murderous women.

I. Hate. Them.

November

DAY 40

8:42 AM

She hadn't seen Winona since stealing the journal. Pyet wasn't a terrible liar, but she wasn't keen on looking into her eyes and risking alienating the only friend she had here.

Instead, Pyet spent her days deeply involved with her grandmother, not leaving the safety of her manor. If she couldn't handle confronting her consequences, the most she could do was avoid them.

She learned hardly anything about Elric as she journeyed through her grandmother's journal, much to her dismay, but she learned a great deal about Violet. The journal acted as a portal to another time, one just as grim, but nowhere near as quiet as the one she was currently in. She was fascinated by the world in which she was transported, feeling like she was amidst an anti-tale of dark whimsy. Her grandmother was telling her a work of fiction, not the story of her life.

The house was eerily quiet the last few days, not even a creak in the foundation pulled Pyet's thoughts astray. It was as if the manor approved of her snooping through the journal, meddling in the lives of its past keepers. There were no apparitions, no things out of place. It almost made her feel like she had a home again.

Pyet could see the beauty of living in a place like this. It was like a fog was starting to clear. The walls were less dull, the flaking of the yellowed floral wallpaper now full, crisp, and bright. The wooden floors were not scratched from wear and tear, but shiny and new. Every time Pyet looked up from her grandmother's journal, she saw the world as if she was looking through Violet's eyes. It was as if Pyet had become Violet herself.

So much reading made her desperate to learn more about the manor. The journal mentioned rooms she hadn't explored, and memories described in places she couldn't tell still existed in the manor, making her realize that she hadn't quite surveyed it as much as she should have. The manor was still entirely new to Pyet, even after living here for an entire month. She was more concerned about the oddity of this portal world and less about the bed she slept in.

Pyet was foolish.

She wasn't going to find the answers out there, from people who ignored her, who skirted away whenever she was near. She was going to find answers in the place her grandmother sent her to begin with.

All it took was the journal to realize this, and there were more of them just waiting to be found, to be read. Pyet had just given them all away.

The silence in her self-imposed containment allowed her to focus. Pyet read the journal from front to back over ten times in just a week, but while she drank in every written word, she didn't understand half of it. Violet spoke in a language that sounded like her own, but so much of what she wrote felt out of context. Pyet was only an outsider looking in. It was as if she was in a car, desperate to see the road, and no matter how fast or how efficient her windshield wipers were, the rain kept pounding against the hard glass, everything around her a blur.

It was infuriating, trying to decipher it.

She did try to traverse the house as she was reading. Sometimes, if her grandmother had written about a room, Pyet would follow. It was weird, mimicking Violet's movements. She often closed her eyes and dreamt she was right there in the room with her, moving as each word dripped off the page.

She didn't have any photos of her grandmother, and Pyet made a mental note to continue looking for some as she raided the closets. Her mother refused to have anything in their home that resembled Violet. In her dreams, her face was nothing but a blurred visage, one that often turned to her, desperate for Pyet to see.

Without photos to place her face, she remained a ghostlike mystery.

Sometimes, if the mood struck, Pyet would walk to her nearest vanity mirror and pull at her own features. She wondered how similar she looked to Violet, or how similar her mother looked to her. She must have had Pyet's chocolate colored eyes, or her mess of wild, dark curls. Pyet kept forgetting that Violet was, in fact, family, and not just a random stranger that died and left her this inheritance. There must have been some sort of resemblance.

She wished she had Winnie to ask.

Though her friend was convinced that she had a deep relationship with Violet, there was no indication that her grandmother felt the same, at least, according to the journal. Not to mention, Winona's notes between the lines of Violet's entries felt more cryptic than her grandmother's. They were unusual and made no sense that Pyet could see. Words were circled, and short notes that were meant as markers were unreadable to an unknowing eye. It made Pyet want the other journals just as badly.

Did Winnie mark in those, as well? Could Pyet find the secrets that hid underneath the words if she just had more of them?

It was no longer a desire, but an absolute need. A necessity to the task she'd assigned herself. It gave her purpose, to seek information about Violet, about Elric. About Winnie.

Pyet found her perspectives shifting with each passing day. Her previous assumptions were abandoned, with new curiosities sprouting with each pass over Violet's scribbled words.

A level of her consciousness was lifted, her rose-colored shades slowly disappearing. Elric hadn't yet lost its gloomy exterior, but Pyet had torn back subtle layers of this manor, *her* manor. There was a color to it that was fascinating to look at.

It was impressive from the outside. The grandeur, the history, and the mystery of it were intoxicating. As she continued to experience the manor through Violet's eyes, Pyet could see herself starting to appreciate it far more than she had when she arrived. It was no longer intimidating, but *familiar.* It was starting to feel like a terribly unorthodox version of home. And the more she appreciated it, the further enraged she was with the people of this town.

How dare they look at this place with reproach? How dare they not worship it the way it was intended to be worshiped?

Because Violet *did* worship that manor. She often referred to it in her journal and spoke about it as if it was a delicate, fragile being. It was revered, loved in a way she couldn't articulate clearly. What started as hatred developed into a tender appreciation of the secrets that were kept inside. Of the *women* she often referred to. The Violet of this written world was their safe keeper. She was their protector, and that obsessive dedication was clear.

But, Pyet couldn't figure out *why*. Why would her grandmother care so much about a manor her peers despised? A home her town wanted to burn to the ground?

The manor seemed to vibrate at the thought. It was so small that Pyet thought she had imagined it, but it was there. The house hummed and purred in contemplation, and she wanted to believe that it was happy to finally have someone who was starting to understand it like her grandmother had. There was a moment of peace between the two of them. There was no haunting and no intruder; there was only family and belonging, mutual understanding. Someone who appreciated it when Elric, and even her own mother, did not.

Pyet felt like she could empathize with the manor, and she never did think of how bizarre it was that she had identified with a house. The insanity of it was not lost on her.

And did she find the same type of love for it Violet had? Pyet couldn't tell. She'd only been within its walls for a short time, but she started to coddle it. She walked through the halls with a hand against the wallpaper, tracing and caressing the home as she wandered its depths. Pyet found that the more time she spent here, the deeper involved she became. It was just *this* manor, it had a hold on her. It gripped her by the shoulders and wouldn't let go.

The way Violet talked to herself in her writings made it seem like she was constantly talking to *someone else*, and not just putting pen to paper. Pyet realized that her grandmother thought of this place as if it was living. She was not just talking to the women that she mentioned often, but to the house itself. And, to her dismay, Pyet was falling into the same pattern.

The parallels were glaring. She, too, was starting to see

the manor as a living, breathing entity. She was falling for it, just like her grandmother had, and the thought paralyzed her.

The sense of an oncoming spiral that could have rivaled her mother's crept into her periphery. She could see this path so clearly, and Pyet knew that if she allowed herself to go any deeper, she wouldn't ever escape Elric's clutches—she wouldn't even be able to escape her own mind. Goosebumps freckled along her arms and the familiar prickles of her hair rising ghosted across the back of her neck. Short, shallow breaths escaped her thin lips, and she tried to swallow past her dry, swollen tongue.

Violet felt so tangible in this space. It was as if she was standing mere feet before Pyet, though each time she looked up from her reading she was met with nothing but empty air.

The Violet of the pages before her was an outsider. She lived and breathed between the lines of ink and the leather that bound it. It was the closest Pyet could say she'd ever felt with a family member—though her only experience was that of her mother. She understood her grandmother's melancholy, her loneliness evident with each entry. Though she lived most of her life in Elric, it didn't seem to matter. This town sucked all of the good from her. It was not only sadness she read in each line, but an overwhelming delusion about what was happening around her that made Pyet worry. Violet couldn't tell what day it was half the time, and as she neared the end of her journal, her careful script turned to a messy scrawl. Like she was running out of time.

They did it again, she mentioned often.

Another moth gone.

One for the witch and two for her people.

Each line felt more unhinged than the last, and it was becoming more and more difficult to decipher her gibberish with each read-through. It was Pyet's obsession; hours passed before she tore her eyes away from it again. She forgot that Violet was dead half the time, the overwhelming presence of her grandmother surrounded her. It filled the manor. It burst through the seams. It leaked onto the marble staircase.

She was *everywhere*, and it was in that illusion where Pyet found the skeletons of the woman she desperately wanted to know. She craved more, wanted to devour each new piece of Violet that she was allowed, but past the pages of her worn leather journal, there was hardly anything else worthwhile to find. Pyet would have to live with what she had, for now.

And she read it over and over and over again.

Pyet had, in fact, read through the thing so much that the spine had broken. Some pages were torn, stained, and bent. She dog-eared seemingly important pages and bookmarked ones to come back to with anything she had on hand—used napkins, dirtied receipts that littered the house from shops downtown, torn bits off the house plant that had begun to die from her lack of care. She was as bad as Winnie was, destroying the journal in ways that felt wrong. But she couldn't help it. She'd read through it twice today, even. Secluded up in her room with the door tightly shut and the covers pulled up past her waist, Pyet escaped from this world and into the mind of Violet Cabello.

At one point, the silence had become too much for her. The lack of sound was almost deafening, as if the house's magic kept all notes of any whispers and creaks out of her ears just for her benefit. Just so she could focus, and learn. Pyet had missed something, and only by overindulging would she find what she was seeking.

The manor would make sure of it.

She clenched her fingers into fists, leaving raw streaks across sensitive skin and dropped the faded journal onto her lap, her head snapping to attention at a piercing noise that shook her bones. She wiped at her eyes as the familiar fog slithered away, noting that the sound echoing throughout the halls was not in her mind after all. The shriek of the doorbell scraped against her ears yet again and she flinched, ducking her head beneath the covers. The sound was loud and obnoxious, like a giant gong that rumbled beneath the floorboards.

She had no interest in confronting Winona yet. She hadn't had enough time. Pyet refused to answer the door—as she had many times over in the last few days—instead taking a big breath and letting the ring of the gong fade into the distance. Winnie only ever rang once or twice before giving up and leaving.

Pyet had been efficiently avoiding her calls, and every knock at the door. It was cruel, what she was doing, but she was embarrassed. She knew Winnie didn't have anywhere else to go, and by ignoring her, she was effectively keeping her from the one place she loved. A place Pyet took advantage of every day before now.

In a way, Pyet felt like she was becoming as bad as her mother was. Her wariness was warranted...but Juliette thought hers was too. Maybe she was more like her mother than she though. Maybe this fucked up way of thinking was just part of being in the family.

Another of Pyet's newfound obsessions had manifested in the form of the mysterious *Lantern*. Pyet had observed their name being used in casual, hushed conversations as she walked the busy streets, and even from Winona, but before reading the journal she had no idea *what they* were. People spoke of them with the same sense of reverence as one who speaks of their god.

Violet's own obsession with the Lantern was even more intense. She talked about them like she loved them. Wholly and truly loved them.

Most of the time.

Other times, she cursed their name as if it was no better than the dirt on the bottom of her shoe. Pyet guessed that they were a religious figure here, or an entire religion. She wasn't sure if they were real, but people talked about them as if they were. She had yet to see them in person, but she also believed that it had to do with the secret meetings Elric hadn't yet invited her to.

This world lured her in with lush secrets and promised memories, and she was finding it natural to slip into the same routines her grandmother often spoke of. Pyet had started bowing to residents and muttering their greetings as she passed them. Every day she sank further into Elric's odd customs; it was easy, now that she felt connected to someone.

She had to get out of her room. Not just because it also once belonged to Violet, whose looming presence was becoming overbearing and stifling in this small space, but because it had been *days* since Pyet had left it. Time kept escaping her, and Pyet slipped deeper and deeper into bed rot.

The journal was like a quicksand she couldn't walk out of. It kept her glued to her spot, sitting near the window, flipping each page over and over again until her eyes fell and she collapsed onto the floor in exhaustion. From her place on her bed, comforter brought up right under her chin, Pyet snuck in two long blinks of her eyelids and glanced towards the window that led to the front of her estate. There on the sill sat the red journal, untouched, taunting her.

She ignored the pull and turned over instead, back now facing the memories that lay dormant behind the cover. Pyet pulled herself out from underneath the comforter and planted her feet firmly on the wooden floor. Every move was intentional. She feared she would be easy prey if she was not strong enough in her convictions. Though the house had not spoken to her in a long while, there was still darkness here. There was no place to go to rid herself of its stickiness, Elric in its entirety felt the same sort of heaviness as the manor.

There was no escape from it.

If she didn't look at the journal, she could at least ignore the temptation, Pyet thought. The journal felt like a lifeline, like there was a physical string connecting her to it. It was agony just facing the other direction; all Pyet wanted to do was return to the world of her grandmother and the family she was robbed of.

She stood and practically ran past the mirror in the room, which was now covered by a sheet, and escaped past the door frame before she could talk herself out of it. Pyet could not get the memory of the mirror out of her head. Thoughts of teeth, vines, and rage circled her like a shark. It was never too far off from her memory, striking just when she was too weak to keep it at bay. It returned to her now as she shut the door behind her, and Pyet took two large gulps of air as her back pressed against the door, her hand settling against her sternum. Her eyes squeezed shut, the creaking of the manor no help in her plight. Every sound made her jump, and it took several seconds until she was able to breathe normally again.

She had done it, at least.

The journal lay left behind, and in an attempt to put more space between it and her, Pyet slipped into the darkness of the hallways. Even in the middle of the day, the manor still felt like a maze. The reality of how little time she had spent there, and how little she explored it, hit her in the gut. A small flame of guilt started in the pit of her stomach, crawling through her body and igniting each piece of flesh and bone it could. How could she truly understand her grandmother when she hadn't even the slightest clue what the rest of her estate held? The rooms and halls before her held so many possibilities.

The manor seemed to rumble in pleasure, reveling in her internal torment. Pyet swallowed hard, exhaling through her nose with each step she took, further and further into the manor's mouth.

It haunted her how little she knew about the place she slept in, lived in. As she reached a hand to touch a handle of a door, she couldn't even envision her mother or grandmother being in the same place, doing the same thing. The manor, regardless of the number months she lived there, was foreign to her. Despite its familiarity, she still wished she had her family here to show her.

Pyet twisted the brass handle, expecting it to give way. When the door didn't budge, she pushed harder, convinced lack of use was its cause.

It still didn't budge.

Frustrated, Pyet let go of the knob, reaching toward a similar door on the other side of the hallway. This too did not budge. Her brow furrowed, her fingers lingering on the metal. She pushed again, to no avail.

The corridor felt longer the more she walked it, almost magically so. Pyet let her hands trace against the wallpaper on the wall. It seemed as if she was walking forever, each step drawing out an extension in the manor. She didn't know why she kept going, or why with each door she passed, there was no temptation to open it. Maybe because as Pyet was drawn further and further into the shadows, something else called to her. Something darker.

She couldn't ignore it.

Pyet's slow wander broke out into a trot, and when she felt the soft whispers of a breath against the back of her neck, her trot morphed into a sprint. Tears streamed down her face, the hair rose along her arms, and the hallway continued to get longer, with no end in sight.

She regretted leaving the safety of her room. She regretted not leaving this manor and abandoning this city.

And when she couldn't run any longer, when her bones were aching and her muscles screamed for her to stop before she exhausted herself, Pyet came upon one final door. The hallway seemed to catch up to her, and the room—once cavernous before—now shrunk until she felt claustrophobic. The manor seemed to push her towards the door, the lights turning off one by one. She watched as each one flickered before it extinguished, until there was nothing left, leaving her alone in the darkness.

There were no windows to aid her, no journal to protect her from whatever dark magic this was. She looked around in horror, expecting blood and vines, expecting the woman in the mirror to find her again. What the manor wanted, it would get. Panic flooded in her chest again as Pyet's hand reached to the brass knob to turn it.

This door, unlike the others, gave way easily. It swung on its hinges, the light inside pouring into the dead and dreary hallway. Pyet's heart continued to race as she cautiously entered the room, the door creaking behind her before it shut with a loud bang. The sound made her hop forward, scampering toward the center of the room. A putrid stench assaulted her nostrils, as if the very walls of the room exhaled decay. There was a heavy air that seemed to weigh upon her like a thousand forgotten secrets.

The room was like a relic of the past, its decaying walls and broken furniture whispering tales of neglect and despair. Pyet couldn't understand how such a place could exist within her grandmother's manor. It was inconceivable that Violet's cherished journal had never hinted at the existence of this sinister room. It was as if this room had been intentionally kept hidden, its secrets lurking in the shadows, waiting to be discovered.

The sight before her eyes sent waves of horror coursing through her veins. Cobwebs hung from the corners of the room like menacing cobras, while dust-covered dolls with cracked porcelain faces stared back at her, their hollow eyes penetrating her very soul. The bed was a twisted mess of torn blankets and faded toys, as if it had been hastily abandoned.

Pyet felt an overwhelming sense of unease settle within her, causing her to fidget nervously with her fingers. She had found solace within the pages of her grandmother's leather journal, and now, she deeply regretted leaving it behind. Its comforting words could have provided guidance and reassurance in this nightmarish place.

A chilling breeze rustled the papers strewn across the floor, making her jump again. There was no logical explanation for how a draft could exist in this forgotten room, but Pyet knew that logic was of little use in this desolate space. The manor seemed to have a will of its own, drawing her into its labyrinthine mysteries, one step at a time.

Pyet stood frozen, her heart pounding in her chest like a wild beast desperate for freedom. The room before her was a desolate wasteland, a forsaken corner of the manor that time itself seemed to have forgotten. The air hung heavy with dust, casting eerie shadows on the dilapidated furniture and faded wallpaper.

Something about this place unsettled her, a presence that clung to every nook and cranny. It was as if the room itself was trapped in a perpetual state of despair, a tragic tale locked away from prying eyes. She couldn't understand why her grandmother's journal had omitted any mention of this place. Had it been intentional or merely a secret too dark to unveil?

Her gaze flitted from one corner to another, searching for a clue, any hint as to why the manor had led her here. But there was nothing of significance to be found, only the ghostly remnants of a forgotten past. Every creaking floorboard and fluttering curtain seemed to conspire against her, making her doubt her decision to explore the manor. Her panic wouldn't wane, like a venomous serpent coiling around her heart, tightening its grip with every passing moment.

How could she have been so foolish, so careless? Pyet's nerve wavered, her courage slipping away like sand through her fingertips.

A flicker of determination sparked within her, a fragile flame refusing to be extinguished. She would not be defeated by her own fears. Slowly, she inched forward, determined to confront the room, to unlock the secrets that it held within its weathered walls.

As she approached a cracked mirror hanging crookedly on the wall, Pyet's reflection stared back at her with wide, fearful eyes. She wondered if she would recognize the person she would become once this dark chapter was unveiled. She wondered if the woman in the mirror would return.

She averted her gaze quickly. Just another mirror she would need to cover with a sheet from the linen closet.

Her eyes continued to scan until Pyet noticed a small, tarnished locket glimmering faintly under the pale sunlight seeping through a cracked window. The locket sat underneath a layer of dirt, strewn across the floor. Pyet cautiously picked it up, feeling a strange connection to its worn surface. Her thumb rubbed across the top, revealing a stunning golden treasure underneath the dirt. When it popped open on its own accord, a gasp escaped her lips.

Inside, a faded photograph revealed a young girl with strikingly familiar features. The paper was rotted with age, but the faded image made Pyet's heart skip a beat as she realized it was her mother smiling mischievously at her from a forgotten era. The photo radiated a sense of joy that was long lost, filling Pyet with a bittersweet nostalgia for a time she never knew. The room suddenly took on a new significance. Pyet knew she was standing in the room where her mother had spent her formative years, a place where childhood memories had been forged. It started to sink in that this was *her* home. This was the bed she slept in, the room she made her home in.

Pyet's fear and trepidation transformed into a profound sadness. The manor had brought her to this room, not as a sinister trap, but as a haunting reminder of her family's past. The neglect that clung to the room was a reflection of the painful experiences her mother had endured. The manor had called her to unravel the enigmata of her family history.

Her desperate need to unearth her mother's past pushed her to explore even the darkest corners, regardless of the lurking shadows that tiptoed menacingly around her. She traced her trembling fingers along the moth-eaten curtains, feeling a chilling presence envelop her. The sunlight filtered through the tattered fabric, casting eerie shapes upon the decaying furniture. It was as if the room itself resented being disturbed, warning Pyet to leave its secrets buried forever.

But Pyet's resolve was unyielding, fueled by the desire to discover her mother's forgotten childhood. She flung open drawers and rattled cabinets, her actions creating an unsettling cacophony within the silence of the room.

One of the old, decrepit looking dolls—that must have belonged to her mother—sat tucked within a cobweb-covered corner, its once vibrant attire faded to gray. Pyet cradled the toy in her hands, her eyes brimming with unshed tears as she imagined her mother's innocent laughter that must have filled the room so long ago. So unlike the mother she had known in her lifetime.

When she saw the journal, ice froze along her veins. This was what the manor was pushing her towards; it had to be. The faded journal had pages yellowed like old parchment, and whispered stories of forgotten dreams and secret fears. Pyet's fingertips trembled as she turned the delicate pages, carefully unraveling the mysteries of her mother's soul. When a small, square Polaroid dropped from its pages, Pyet's brows furrowed as she bent over to pick it up, holding it hesitantly between her fingertips.

It was like she was staring into yet another mirror, and she couldn't help but feel a sense of unease wash over her. It was almost as if her reflection was staring back at her with a haunting gaze; and then, she saw it. The striking resemblance between her and the woman in her mother's journal, the woman who was her grandmother. It wasn't a mirror, but a photograph.

Pyet's short umber hair cascaded down her neck in bouncing curls, just like her grandmother's had in the picture. She traced the curve of her nose, and realized it was the same as well. Even their high cheekbones and dark, intense eyes were identical. The more she stared at the photograph, the more she saw the similarities between herself and the woman in it. She felt as if she was looking into a dark and eerie reflection of herself. She could very easily have been Violet's daughter—she looked far more like her than she did her mother.

Pyet placed the image safely back into the crook of a page, her heart a rapid beat within her chest.

Pyet wanted to devour every word, wanted to piece together the mosaic of her mother's journey as much as she had with her grandmother's story. The house was offering glimpses into clandestine adventures and secret desires, unearthing a vibrant spirit that Pyet never knew existed. In the midst of fear and desperation, she hoped her mother had fought for her dreams, resilient against the cruel hand that life had dealt. And yet, despite all of her hopes, she knew her optimism would run dry. Because she had seen what happened to her mother. She watched as she deteriorated from years of guilt and nightmares. The woman with whom Pyet shared an uncanny resemblance to had broken her mother. She was the reason Juliette escaped Elric to begin with.

Her prize tucked neatly under her arm, Pyet slowly left the room; the weight of her mother's untold story burdened her shoulders, yet an unyielding determination stirred within her. She vowed to weave together their narratives, bridging the gap between generations, until the ghosts of their past caught up to the shadows of their present.

Pyet felt a shiver run down her spine as she stumbled out of the room, the weight of time catching up with her. She looked back longingly, promising to return another day to explore the mystery of her mother more. The house seemed to stir around her, its very walls seeming to groan as if reawakening. Her heart was pounding as she tried to make her way down the dark hallway.

But something was wrong, terribly wrong.

The air was thick with the scent of rot and decay, and she could feel the hairs on the back of her neck stand on end. As she took another step forward, Pyet heard a creaking noise, and then the sound of footsteps. Each time she turned to look, they vanished, echoing against the walls and disappearing into the darkness.

The longer Pyet lingered in the hallway, the more it seemed to come alive. Doors that had previously been locked creaked open, then slammed shut. Voices whispered in her ear, taunting her. Pyet wanted to run, but her legs wouldn't move. Every muscle in her body screamed at her to escape, but she was frozen in place.

Pyet stood in the dimly-lit hallway, her heart racing as she looked around frantically. Every door looked the same, and she couldn't remember which one led to her grandmother's room. Panic washed over her, and she felt her hands shaking uncontrollably.

Suddenly, two women appeared before her, dressed in old-fashioned clothing straight out of a Victorian-era period piece. Their faces were contorted into cruel sneers, and their eyes glinted with a dark, menacing energy.

"You don't belong here," one of them hissed, her voice dripping with malice. "This place isn't meant for you."

Pyet felt a shiver run down her spine. She knew she had to get out of there—and fast. But she didn't know where to go or what to do.

The women continued to circle her like vultures, their sharp nails grazing her skin as they whispered terrifying things in her ear. She tried to back away, but they seemed to follow her every move. Their touches felt so real and tangible, and she worried that they weren't ghosts at all, but real people sent to torment her.

Finally, Pyet let out a scream, tearing herself away from the women's grasp. She turned and ran, not caring which direction she was going in, all she knew was that she had to get away.

As she sprinted down the endless hallway, she felt the walls closing in around her, trapping her in a claustrophobic nightmare. The women's laughter echoed through the empty space, sending chills down Pyet's spine. They didn't follow her, but they didn't have to. They were everywhere, seeping into the bones of her being.

And then, just as suddenly as it had begun, the horror ended. Pyet found herself standing outside her grandmother's room, the door opening before her like a welcoming embrace. Even Kit manifested herself, her yowl a beacon Pyet could tether herself on to. She followed the onyx cat to safety, shutting the door firmly behind them both.

Trembling, Pyet stumbled and collapsed onto the bed, tears streaming down her face. She had never been more grateful to be back in the safety of her grandmother's invisible embrace. Inside this room was a shield, and she never wanted to leave it again.

But, as Pyet looked out the window at the darkened landscape, she knew that the women's haunting words would stay with her forever. She couldn't shake the feeling that they would be waiting for her, just beyond the walls of her grandmother's room, ready to claim her as their own.

She's making me write in this stupid journal again. I really hate doing it, especially now. She doesn't even read them. It feels like I'm collecting memories no one will ever read, or will be interested in finding, just like she did—and grandmother. If it were up to me, I would toss all of these stupid things into the garbage. They just sit and collect dust in the basement anyway. If I were to find one and pitch it, would they even know?

Finish a book, throw it in a box, and so on.

Just a few more days now.

Mother will be furious when I leave her. She doesn't believe that I can do it...run. She said something about how Elric wouldn't let me go. She can't mean the women. They would kick me out themselves if they could. Even without our traumatic and unfortunate predicament, they never grew fond of me. Not in the same way they love mother. Why do they love her?

She is a snake, and she doesn't care about them in the way they think. Mother has been a notoriously fantastic manipulator. She did with Noni, who fawns over every word. She did it with them, even though she is the reason they are here.

How can no one else see it?

How come I can?

There's no way I am the only person in this gods-forsaken place that sees mother for what she truly is. I wonder if that's why she's really insistent I stay. She's fooling herself. Elric can't keep me here. I won't let her take me like she's taken so many others.

I'm going to get out, watch them try to stop me.

DAY 54

1:30 PM

The knock on the front door was loud, echoing across the walls and tile floors. It didn't stop ringing until it smacked against the farthest wall in the room, the wallpaper soaking in the noise and devouring it until there was nothing left.

Pyet was in the foyer, the window in her periphery. She should have seen Winona, but she'd been too distracted to notice. Her family's secrets and the ghosts that soiled the manor plagued her every thought. Pyet didn't feel safe here, but she couldn't leave either; it wasn't like the town was much safer. At least here at the manor there was a hope of discovery. Elric proved to be a steel trap, and she knew that this place had to be a key. Or, at the very least, the corner pieces in a large, disastrously infuriating tabletop puzzle.

Winona's eyes were cupped between her hands, pressed so close to the glass that there was no way Pyet could escape in time. Their eyes locked, just for a moment, but a moment was all it took. Cursing silently to herself, she collapsed to the ground, groaning when both knees slapped against the marble floor. Pyet couldn't help but grimace at the stinging heat trapped beneath her skin. Still, she crawled across the foyer, trying to disappear from sight.

"Pyet, I'm not an idiot, I can see you!"

She stopped, letting the rattle of nerves vibrate through her body. She squeezed her eyes tight, keeping embarrassment at bay until she heard more shuffling outside.

When Pyet glanced towards the window again, Winona was out of sight. She breathed a heavy sigh of relief until the jostling at the manor door resumed. There was no knocking this time, instead the distinct jingle of keys sounded from the other side. Before she could understand what was happening, the lock on the large door unlatched slowly. Pyet watched in horror as the brass handle turned, and flinched as the door punched in, revealing Winona's flushed face.

Too stunned to speak, Pyet didn't move. Her back ached from crawling across all fours but she couldn't move, frozen to the spot once again.

"You're so fucking hard to get ahold of." Winona stared down at her, her lips drawn into a tight frown. The harshness of her tone made Pyet turn her head in embarrassment. She bit her lip, hard enough that she tasted the metallic tang of blood across her tongue. For a moment, Pyet had forgotten that she was avoiding Winnie to begin with—she only felt relief. Somehow, it was easier now that she was standing right in front of her. Not even the scowl that crossed her face could stop Pyet from sitting back and breathing deeply for the first time in weeks.

The manor felt less alone with Winnie in it, and it was as if all of the pent up energy she'd been exposed to in the last few days finally popped like a balloon.

The manor had been waiting for Winona Fairchild to come back to it.

The wind that followed was explosive, flying past Winona in the doorway and ricocheting off the walls, the glass shattering around the two of them. Pyet shoved herself up against the stairway, the sharp angle of a corner digging into her spine as she cowered away from the manor's hauntings.

Winona ignored the ghosts, her hair whipping around her until the air settled around them.

"The manor is upset with you," she continued, looking past Pyet and into one of the many dark hallways behind them. Her frown deepened. "What did you go looking for?"

The accusation made Pyet's back straighten again, her attention focused. Her eyes narrowed and she caught her tongue between her teeth in order to keep from shouting a retort. Instead, Pyet took a second longer than she would normally before she answered.

"It is none of your business what I do in *my* manor." Pyet didn't even think to ask how Winona opened the front door, blaming the house for her allowed intrusion. It was *hers*, and she would stand her ground

Winona's eye twitched, her frown morphing into a small, condescending smirk. "It is when something of *mine* makes it into *your* manor. Which, I believe, you have."

The color drained from Pyet's face.

"This house is more loyal to me than it ever will be to you, child. You think it wouldn't tell me when it houses something stolen from me? You are a guest. I am its keeper."

She sighed and shook her head. "I gave you my key in confidence, Pyet. I promised to give you answers. All you had to do was trust me. Not steal from me."

"As I've said before, I don't have the time to wait for whenever you decide it's the right moment to tell me what I need to know." Pyet pushed herself up and placed her hands on her hips as she stood facing Winona. She felt more in control this way, less a victim to the town and the home that held her captive.

"Pyet," Winona said again, pity lacing her tone, "you have to trust me."

The house was eerily silent, but the overwhelming heaviness was paralyzing, and there was a presence that was deafening. It was like it was waiting for something. The manor knew who it was going to answer to, and between the two of them, Pyet knew it wasn't going to be her.

Winona looked so at ease here; she looked like she was home.

"I don't trust you, Winona."

It was the first time she had been that honest with her, but it had been the truth. She *didn't* trust Winnie. Information didn't come easily in Elric, but Pyet didn't expect to have to spend her life unraveling the secrets of her mother, and of her grandmother.

Perhaps it was naivety.

Winnie's face scrunched together in disapproval, the wrinkles apparent in the creases of her eyes. Something flashed behind her eyes, but it was gone before Pyet could decipher it. The rest of her body was rigid, confident. Winona was nothing but self-assured.

"And why is that?" she huffed, irritated. Pyet rolled her tongue in her mouth, contemplating.

"Because you keep telling me to wait until I'm *ready* to hear whatever secrets you're trying to keep. You're keeping me on a line, but I'm no longer biting. I don't want to keep playing this game, Winnie."

Winona looked as if she was going to say something, but she bit the inside of her cheek instead, leaving Pyet frustrated and disappointed.

"Well." She clicked her tongue, sounding more curt than Pyet would have liked. She didn't know what she expected. Her words were cut short, pointed like daggers, "If that's what you think, then."

It was the coldest she'd seen Winona, and it was not a side of her she enjoyed. The coolness between them made Pyet's wall shoot up high in the air. It didn't matter if the manor wanted her here; Pyet was the only *living* resident in this house, and she wanted Winona gone.

"I think I'd like for you to leave." Even if it would leave her alone again. Even if just these two minutes of seeing her made her feel less crazy.

Pyet had lived her whole life in fear. She never once questioned her mother or complained. Pyet's life was cruel and unyielding, but she had never once made a decision that benefited *her*. Until now.

Winona was taken aback by her boldness. She opened her mouth to say something in return, a mixture of distrust, shock, and fear crossing her features before it disappeared again, leaving the porcelain smooth disinterest it held before. She clicked her heels together once and stormed out without another word, the large door slamming roughly behind her.

Pyet couldn't help but crumble to her knees again once she had the manor to herself. The initial relief that nestled in her chest was gone, replaced by longing and heartbreak. She didn't want to *need* anyone anymore, and she hated that she needed to watch Winona leave. She hated that she wanted to. She hated that she had lost the only person who dared look her way in this darkly enchanted town.

Pyet couldn't live this way any longer. Days had gone by with nothing but drowning in memories that weren't her own and a heaviness that she didn't want to own. She was finding herself stuck, melted glue dripping from her skin and cementing her to the manor, never allowing her to leave.

If time would allow it, Pyet would die in this manor having accomplished nothing. The halls had a way of trapping her, of grasping hold of her wrists and tying her to the property. She had to be careful, or else she would never think of leaving the manor again; Elric would gain another victim.

She needed to get out of the manor.

Pyet didn't come to Elric just to spite her mother, but to find the family that everyone was so desperate to keep from her, including Winona. Getting out of the manor, out of this timeless wormhole, was her best option. If she didn't do it now, she never would.

It was time Pyet paved a way for herself, for once.

She snuck out of the estate, sticking close to the iron fencing as she slunk around corners and dipped into the eeriness of downtown. It wasn't hard to hide in Elric. The grays of her slacks and top matched the grays in the sky. It matched the grays in the outfits around her. People kept their heads down, and she did too, taking the hair from over her ears and pushing it in her face to cover her rosy cheeks. It wasn't like anyone would be looking for her, save for maybe Winona, but it seemed like she was everywhere these days. Or, at least, she was when Pyet was actively avoiding her. It shouldn't be this hard; it had to be karma.

The sun was dipping by the second, but the dark no longer frightened her. In the last few weeks, Pyet had experienced worse things than the absence of light. Soon, Elric's residents would retreat into their homes and close the shutters. As bodies disappeared from the street one by one, she knew they were approaching closer to the impending curfew they took so seriously.

Something had changed, even if she couldn't quite put her

finger on it. Residents still avoided her, crossing the street when she walked their way as if she was a pariah, a leper. This time, though, Pyet didn't notice the familiar glares and whispers she had become accustomed to. Instead they looked…afraid?

One last ring of a bell off in the distance shook the ground beneath her, but Pyet continued, intent on ignoring it. Instead, she pulled her grandmother's journal from her back pocket and tucked it close to her chest for comfort. It weighed heavily on her conscience, but once it was between her fingertips, Pyet felt a certain calm rush over her. She didn't know why it was this journal that she kept in her hands and not her mother's. But it felt like it was the most important, the most dangerous.

This journal was the start of it all, she thought. A tether to reality. As long as she kept it, she wouldn't fall prey to Elric's lies and treachery.

The few remaining townspeople shuffled quickly down the cobbled street. Their eyes kept flicking to Violet's journal, as if they knew exactly what power Pyet held in her possession. She felt strong holding it to her chest. The faded red journal, cracked from overuse, was a weapon she could use, if only she understood how to wield it.

When the stallion's bronzed muzzle faced her, Pyet removed the journal from her chest and undid the leather string that held it together. She opened the book and flipped to a page she had dog eared. The entry in question was full of Winona's annotations, and circled at the top of the page was a sentence her grandmother had written so long ago.

When the bronco looked up, I knew I was standing true north.

Winona seemed to believe that it was important, and though Pyet didn't understand why, she felt like it would have been stupid to ignore it. No wonder Winnie wanted the journal back. It was crucial to some piece of the puzzle.

The stallion never scared me, but it scared them. The women of this house have a terrible history with it. Bloody. Gruesome. Alone. I'm trying to understand them, but to do that, they seem to think that I need to understand Elric. I've lived here my whole life. What in Lantern's name do they think I still need to learn?

There were days Violet seemed no older than a teenager, as desperate for answers as Pyet was. Violet, in Pyet's limited experience, had little to give outside of the fragments of her life and more questions than answers.

And now she was gone.

Matilda's was different after dark. The air was misty, fog coating every atom of oxygen and suffocating everyone and everything in its wake. The silence was eerily similar to her first night in town, and the feeling of uneasiness rattled Pyet. Matilda's also looked darker—not in shade, but in its aura. There was a darker magic that hid here when the sun went down. Her confidence was dwindling as the moments pressed on.

Pyet found a secluded corner to hide in until there wasn't a soul left in the open. She still didn't know where she belonged here; she was not yet a member of their society. Their exclusive celebrations and obvious disregard for her presence made that clear, but it felt so *wrong* being out on the streets this late anyway. Like she was going to disappoint someone with her heedless neglect of the rules.

Matilda wasn't exactly the *outcast* she pretended to be, from what Pyet gathered. People avoided her as they had Pyet, but at least *she* was included in the town's customs and events. Pyet couldn't tell if she actually attended, but she was a staple in the community. Even through the fear, Elric was her home, and they respected her here.

Her shop was only a few doors down, so it was easy to feel along the sidewalk with her feet, guided by the moonlight in the alleyway against the walls. By step thirty-seven she was in front of a gap between storefronts.

Tripping only once as she maneuvered through the narrow passageway, Pyet hung both arms out to touch the sides of the brick. Slowly she dragged each fingertip across the rough surface, hissing through clenched teeth as her index attracted sticky webs. As soon as she was free of the alley Pyet looked around, narrowing her eyes so that she could better make out any signs she might come across.

She hadn't needed to. The door to Matilda's was easy to read, and even if it weren't for the clear bolded letters across the door, the menagerie of hanging plants and crystals scattered across the doormat would have done the trick. Pyet walked towards the door and knocked once, firmly.

Once was all she needed. Matilda's door swung open and an arm snaked across her wrist, latching on and pulling her forcefully across the threshold.

"You're very late," a familiar voice hissed. Pyet jumped backward, stifling a scream. Matilda's free hand rushed to cover her mouth and Pyet clamped her eyes shut. Pain shot through her captured wrist, the old woman's grip unyielding.

"I thought they had you," she chuckled, her raspy voice circling Pyet's ears. "When you didn't come your first night, I thought that house had taken you."

"That house is not a living thing," Pyet reminded her forcefully. She was grateful for Matilda's less-than-pleasant promise of information, but would not let the grouchy old hag intimidate her. She'd had enough of that in her life to want to do it again. And so, she ignored her threats. "Winona told me not to come."

Matilda scoffed, but it sounded more like a laugh as she let go of Pyet's arm and wandered through the back corridor, heading towards a small room she didn't notice the first time she walked into the shop. Pyet followed her cautiously through the darkened storefront.

"I suppose she didn't just stop there?"

"No, she's told me not to come almost every time I've seen her." She decided to leave out the incident from earlier, and how she came into possession of the journal that was pulled tightly against her chest again, "Why is that?"

Matilda glanced at her chest curiously, making Pyet tighten her grip, the whites of her knuckles straining against her skin. There was a spark of recognition and delight behind her eyes, but Matilda didn't say a word. Pyet kept her eyes level, desperately trying to draw her attention away from it. After a few seconds, the moment was over, and Matilda smiled menacingly again. It did not put Pyet at ease, but her hands relaxed a bit against the leather and her muscles breathed in a sigh of relief.

Either Matilda kept this room hidden or it hardly had any use, as handfuls of cleaning materials and several large broomsticks prevented them from waltzing straight in. They both took a bucket in either hand to move them off to the side, Pyet discreetly slipping her grandmother's journal into her back pocket again. As she was moving the last of the mop heads, Matilda turned the doorknob and pushed the door open. Several spiderwebs and a collection of dust unloaded into the air, causing them both to scrunch their nose and snap their mouths closed.

"You're already causing me a lot of trouble," Matilda huffed. Pyet chose to not respond. It was easier not to say anything when the witch was complaining, she feared that saying the *wrong* thing would make Matilda shut her out completely.

If Winona found out Pyet was visiting, she could ruin the tiny fraction of camaraderie she'd built with her—if she hadn't done that already. If she did, Pyet didn't have any intention of driving away this mad woman too.

She hadn't even so much as looked at Matilda's since promising Winona she'd stay away. She was afraid to look at her, afraid to go near her. But as she looked over their crumbling relationship now, Pyet couldn't help but feel empowered at the decision she'd made to come.

She found her way to a dust-covered chair hidden in the corner. Matilda wasn't the helpful type, but she allowed Pyet to move about as she pleased, and smiled from her space behind a cluttered desk as Pyet struggled to move the large upholstered piece of furniture. Pyet grunted, giving up when the chair only moved an inch.

"You're not used to company, are you?" she asked sarcastically, frowning as she touched her butt to the chair. It wasn't comfortable. Matilda's smile only widened. It was as if she fed off of frustration.

"You are in *my* home," she replied smoothly, her tongue tracing the outlines of her lips, tasting the stale air around them. "I need to make sure you stack up."

"This shouldn't be a test," Pyet said with a scowl.

"On the contrary, dear," Matilda tsk-ed. "Everything is a test. You don't think you were pulled to Elric by chance, do you?"

She searched her face, pursing her now wet lips in disappointment.

"Oh, you did," she crooned. Matilda reached a long, curved finger in her direction. Pyet was grateful she was sitting so far away; the distance was necessary in the presence of a witch. Pyet didn't believe the stories Winona had told her, but Matilda definitely leaned into the role. She wasn't surprised the rest of Elric was afraid of her. "Honey, I thought you would be a strong one. If you can't pass this silly test, you have no chance."

"Everyone here speaks in riddles. I thought you, of all people, would be different." Pyet crossed her hands in front of her chest, tightening her grip so hard that the marks on her arms would bruise by morning. Matilda let out an ugly laugh, throwing her head back and banging her outstretched arm onto the table, causing a mushroom of dust to flutter through the air like ashes.

"I take it back. You might have a chance. You're feisty. They won't know what to do with you."

Pyet stared at the old crone, marking each detail in the clouded room. Her hair was long and gray, pulled into several loosely tied braids—more than she'd ever seen one person wear at one time. Her wrinkled skin was freckled with birthmarks. One nail was kept long and sharpened at the tip. Matilda wore the same gray canvas clothes as she did, but hers were decorated with golden ropes that hung from her waist, tied in an intricate knot. Pyet didn't notice them before, but she was the only person in town that had any additions to her garments.

She slouched in her chair, but Pyet guessed she couldn't be any taller than 5'3". Pyet avoided looking directly into her eyes, which took their time as they surveyed Pyet in return. It had been at least five minutes before any one of them said anything.

Pyet would not be the first to break.

"Okay, girl," Matilda gave in at last. She winked wickedly, rapping her fingers along the wood and smiling. "What do you want to know?"

P yet didn't know what time it was. There were no discernible clocks anywhere, and she desperately hated not having any sense of direction. She knew little, but for certain that it was far later than she expected the evening to take her. She was in no rush to be back in the manor among the unknown things that lurked in the dark corners there. Curiosity was going to carve her heart out of her chest, and knowing that Winona could waltz in anytime she pleased didn't sit well in her belly. This place wasn't much better than the manor, though. The longer she sat in Matilda's company, the clearer it became that maybe the stories about her weren't too far off from the truth after all. It was in the odd, unreal movements she made, not quite human. Matilda was ethereal.

"Do you know the story of the Danaids?" Her voice was velvet, sending Pyet into the distraction of a lullaby.

"Can't say it's something I've ever researched," she deadpanned. Matilda chuckled.

"You weren't even well prepared," she chastised again. "Do they no longer teach mythology in schools?"

"I wouldn't know, I didn't go to public school. The only ones my mother taught me were the common Greek ones: Zeus, Hades, Poseidon."

Matilda frowned and her lip curled up into a snarl. Pyet could have sworn that she had seen the old woman huff in a mock laugh, but it was over before she was sure.

"What? It wasn't exactly in the curriculum. You don't know how I grew up, but information did not come easy."

"They only ever talk about the stupid men. When will this world realize that it isn't men that they should fear? It should be women—scorned women—women with a purpose. Women are the real threat. Men are just the vessels they use to execute their will. And yet, they forget."

Pyet narrowed her eyes. She hardly had a good word to say in her mother's favor, but she felt defensive nonetheless. It was Elric that made her the way she was. It was Elric Pyet needed to be upset with.

"Tartarus, that's something you were taught, correct? Surely your curriculum wasn't that far gone yet. Your mother had to have known better than that."

Pyet grumbled a yes in response.

"Good." Matilda took her long nail and placed it in her mouth. Pyet cringed from the chewing sound she heard from where she sat. "Eternal torment, that's what awaits souls that piss off the gods. It's said to be worse than hell, you know." She spat a piece of nail to the side and Pyet felt her body physically recoil.

"You told me you weren't going to speak in riddles."

"You silly girl," Matilda hissed, "these are not riddles. This is history, and knowing it will save your hide. Don't let your pride get you killed."

They both glared at each other, the room filling with tension so high that Pyet felt she might drown if she gave in.

She felt her muscles tense, and Pyet felt the sudden urge to flee from this place.

Winona was right after all.

"This stupid world only cares about its stupid men. They only teach about the crimes their men committed against the gods—but there are women in Tartarus, too."

Pyet didn't believe that Matilda was lying, but her eyebrows cocked in a way that was etched in skepticism.

"There are forty-nine women lurking in the prison Tartarus, Pyet, but not for their crimes against the gods. These women are cold-blooded and ruthless. The Danaids, they are called, were sent to Tartarus for their crimes against men themselves." Her voice held something resembling reverie, respect, and admiration.

"What did they do?" Pyet leaned forward in her chair, causing the furniture to squeak loudly. Matilda smirked, eager to continue. Her words transported her to another world, another lifetime. It felt as if this place was just a waypoint to something bigger. Pyet was never one to show interest toward mythology. Not that it wasn't interesting enough, but her world depended on the realness of life. It needed quantifiable, hard fast rules to follow. Mythology broke all of those rules and rewrote its own.

"There were fifty women in total." The woman sighed as if she herself was sent off into the memory. "Daughters of a man called Danaus. He was a prince of Egypt, and son of Belus, although not his only. I won't trouble you with their stories, as they don't particularly pertain to this one, but it is good to know that Danaus and his twin brother, Aegyptus, were both heirs to their Egyptian throne."

"I'm guessing that went super well," Pyet muttered.

"Clever girl." Matilda smiled, showcasing her chipped, yellowed teeth. "After their father died, he had originally ordered Danaus the king of Libya, and his brother the king of Arabia. Funny how the Greeks thought they could superimpose themselves onto everything, even Egyptian mythos. Both Danaus and Aegyptus were just as any god, greedy, and the two regularly rivaled over boundaries. They wanted *more*."

"I'm shocked." Her voice was low but contemplative. Pyet had never heard of Danaus, Aegyptus, or the Danaids before today, but the story was fascinating. She was drawn into its fairytale, and not even the vibration of her humming was enough to take her outside of the story. Matilda was a natural-born storyteller. Her voice was smooth and dripping with honey—it was near impossible to stop staring at her, transfixed in her own tale. The narrative was being pulled from the fragments of Matilda's mind like finely picked flowers, as if this story was not a story at all, but a part of her life.

"Are you shocked they wanted to take each other's land? I'm sure no amount of land would have been enough." Matilda laughed sarcastically as she shook her head. "Greedy, stupid men."

"I'm starting to believe that your aversion to them is founded in this story," Pyet mused. Matilda nodded reverently. It was meant as a joke, but she was entirely serious in her response.

"Misandry is founded in stories like these. To be frank, they do it to themselves. But Pyet," she tsk-ed, "please let me finish the story. You know I have to open the shop tomorrow, and it's quite late. I can't be here all night."

Pyet refrained from rolling her eyes, but she kept her mouth shut and nodded, dusting off her pant legs with anxious, fidgeting fingers. She wanted to know more, desperately wanting to understand the connection between this ethereal story and the place she was now supposed to call home. It wasn't the information she was promised, but she couldn't find it in herself to walk away from it yet.

And, for someone so interested in not staying late in the evening, she waited for Pyet's return. It had taken a month for Pyet to come back to the witch for her information. Had she truly spent each night waiting for her here? Or had she known that Pyet was desperate today, no longer worried about the consequences of betraying Winona?

She hadn't realized that she was also no longer sitting in her chair, but on her knees against the rough fabric, leaning so far forward that she could have fallen over. Pyet adjusted her position, leaning back into the seat once more. She didn't bother with a retort, as she was sure Matilda wouldn't want her to, anyway.

"Are you back?" Matilda asked patiently. Pyet didn't notice that she stopped in the middle of her story, and her cheeks flushed with embarrassment.

"Yeah, sorry," she squeaked, sitting on her bottom and pushing back as far as she could in her chair.

"This story requires your full and undivided attention. It's critical to your survival here." Pyet was not used to such… motherly chastising. It was far more than her own mother ever gave her credit for. In some ways, Pyet welcomed it.

"I'm back, I promise." She looked around once more and nodded at Matilda to continue. She smiled softly and dove right back into her story. Pyet watched as her eyes seemed to glaze over again, no longer in this world. It really was like Matilda was returning to old memories, and not just a tale people told for the sake of entertainment.

"Danaus fathered fifty daughters, and his brother, fifty sons. Aegyptus encouraged his fifty sons to marry the Danaids. No one knows the reason for certain, but it is told it was to secure easier access to his kingdom and the lands he retained power over. That made the most sense. It was the only thing the two ever fought over."

"Danaus was no idiot, much to his brother's dismay. He understood Aegyptus' plan, as it wasn't well concealed, but he had no intention of letting his brother's sons marry his beautiful girls. They were precious to him at that point, though he'd never once cared to let them know it. Instead, Danaus gave his small kingdom to Aegyptus and fled the country with his daughters, and landed in Greece. Are you familiar with Argos?"

Pyet, unwilling to speak, just shook her head. Matilda scoffed in disappointment once more.

"Argos is the oldest inhabited city in the world. Truly, I do not understand what it is that people teach their children anymore."

"You were the one saying you had somewhere to be," Pyet reminded her coldly. "I don't see how this story has any answers, and quite frankly I'm sick of looking for them. It might be better off if I just leave this gods-forsaken city."

She expected Matilda to contradict her, but was not surprised when she rested her hand against her chin and tugged lightly on a small chin hair.

"I suppose that is not a bad idea," she conceded. "However, it's quite selfish of you."

"Selfish? How so? It seems as if the town would be better off without me in it. No one comes within thirty feet of me, and even less look at me or dare say a word."

"They believe you're cursed,"

"So I've been told. But nothing you're saying is making me believe that staying here, that staying 'cursed' is going to do me much good."

"You are the only one that can maintain that house."

"Winona seemed to be doing a fine enough job of it

before I got here." And she seemed to think that it was still hers to maintain.

"Winona doesn't know how to handle the Danaids." Matilda scowled.

Pyet was getting frustrated with her lack of comprehension, and in her anger, she almost missed the important detail in Matilda's statement.

"So that's what you think?" she laughed. Matilda raised her eyebrows in response. Pyet was listening to an old crone who believed in ghosts—worse than ghosts—daughters of deities. "You believe the Danaids are haunting that house?"

"Your laughter is naive. I seem to recall you coming in wishing for answers. Do not be upset if they are not the ones that you sought."

"You're crazy!" she shouted. Matilda slammed her palms against her desk; it sent a mouse into the corner, scattering for cover.

"Do not disrespect me in my own home," she warned. Pyet could feel rage radiating from her in waves. She shifted back further in her chair. "I will not be yelled at by someone like you. By a cursed child."

Matilda was getting larger, her presence looming over her, and the room felt as if it was getting smaller. This magic was the same as the mirror in her grandmother's room; it was dark and twisted, powerful. For a moment, Pyet was paralyzed with doubt and fright, with the memory of her mirror self clawing at her mouth, her eyes, her skin. She curled in on herself, closing her eyes tightly as if that would save her from whatever power Matilda held.

"I suggest you listen to the rest of the story. *Implore it*, really. I owe you nothing, remember that. It gives me no benefit to fill your mind with nonsense."

When the room stopped shrinking, Pyet opened her eyes again and crossed her arms over her chest, protecting the fragile heart that lay just behind her ribcage. Soon enough, Matilda also settled back down, sitting her brittle body back into her seat. The room started to recede inch by inch.

Pyet could finally breathe. Her breaths came out in large gulps, as if she had been drowning and deprived of air. It felt like it, in this small space. She hated the tricks that were played on her here; it *had* to have been something in the air. There was no way rooms and objects should move on their own, or grow larger and smaller without an explanation. Elric was not like everywhere else; it was something else entirely.

Pyet tried to ignore so much of Elric's mysteries, afraid that knowing them would be the end of everything she'd ever thought true. She didn't want to believe in ghosts, or magic, or the *Danaids*.

She only wanted to find out the truth behind her mother's fears. She wanted nothing but a reason for the life she was forced to live. Where she couldn't leave her home, trapped behind wiry fencing and locks that had no keys. It was a life with a woman so trapped by her own fears that she let it leak into every facet of their lives. Her mother was an empty shell, no room for anything but hurt and violence to fill it.

Gods, she hated that she had been given that letter. She hated that her mother chased her here, to a place she knew she would never get to leave.

Surely death would be easier than this.

Matilda took her silence as compliance and took a large inhale of her own before the sticky honey of her voice filled the air again, unaware of the panic that had started to boil in the pits of Pyet's stomach again.

"Argo was home to Danaus for many years after that, but Aegyptus would not let up that easily. He followed Danaus to his new home, desperate to continue to take the kingdoms he'd conquered. There was something about being better than his brother, a misfounded desire. When his sons presented themselves to Danaus in his new palace in Argos, they demanded the Danaids' hands in marriage."

Pyet hummed lightly to herself, the vibrations of her voice traveling down her arms and warming her from the inside. It helped calm her fast-beating heart.

"Danaus had a connection to Argo that no one understood. Some would say that he would choose Argo over anything else, including his family. He was also growing old, and tired of Aegyptus's games; he had no intentions of conquering or besting him. Danaus refused to let Argo become another battleground, forced to run from his home again. He did eventually, begrudgingly, consent to their proposal, his daughters now soon to be wives to his brother's sons. All to keep Argo as prosperous as it had always been."

Pyet couldn't understand it, Danaus letting his children take the brunt of his weakness—caring more for Argo than he did his kin. Her heart ached for the women whose fates were decided by someone who was so ill-equipped to make choices about their bodies.

"Fucking men," she said in a low, rage-filled voice.

"*Fucking men*," Matilda agreed.

Pyet unraveled herself, stretching her legs out and moving from the chair to a standing position. Her legs were sprinkled with static, and she shook them out one by one. Matilda only watched her, her eyes narrowed—not in suspicion this time—but curiosity. Pyet didn't need her to *tell* the story any longer. She was fully engulfed in it now, the world coming together in the periphery.

Matilda didn't morph with the world around her. They both seemed settled in a vision that conformed to the will of a power higher than hers. It played out before them like a movie.

The sky glittered with stars, deep and beautiful, a faraway place where monsters lurked in corners and people danced around them. The world shapeshifted, and Pyet's vision blurred as the two shadowed figures turned to her before they disappeared, dropping her into a room with less stars. Instead, Pyet looked around, smelling the tingling aroma of sparkling magic. It was hard to be afraid of something so enchanting. It lived in the same family as whatever lived within the walls of the manor, and she knew she had to be wary.

But the world Matilda kidnapped her for was something out of a fairytale.

"Danaus was not weak or stupid, not like his brother thought he was. In the late hours of the night, he planned a betrayal of his own, while quickly preparing the wedding for his daughters in the week that followed. When Aegyptus arrived in Argos, his satisfaction was palpable. The man was overconfident and cocky, and it enraged Danaus."

Pyet could see Danaus in front of her, crouched over his desk, muttering something incoherent in an empty room. He was tall and fit, curly brown hair dangling over his forehead, with long cream colored robes dripping from him onto the ground. Pyet watched him wipe a bead of sweat from his brow. He looked tired, but not just from age; he looked tired of fighting. He looked as Pyet imagined she did.

"It was the night before the wedding..." The witch's old, croaking voice tore her from Danaus. She had forgotten that this wasn't real, even though her vision would tell her otherwise. Her words melted into the air as the world transformed again.

Pyet now followed Danaus as he tiptoed under a blanket of darkness outside, slipping into a small wooden door hidden between street lights into his sleeping quarters and quickly finding a chest that sat at the base of his bed. She moved each leg slowly, feeling stuck to the ground, sinking like quicksand.

There was a gleam in his eyes as he crouched to his knees, unlatching the locks from his chest and looking over his shoulder again. She came face to face with Danaus, her breath catching in her throat. He seemed to look through her, the watery glisten of his irises searching for something—someone—behind him for a second too long before breaking their eye contact. If Pyet hadn't known any better, she would have believed he *saw* her, but of course he couldn't.

It was only a story.

She was unaware of what it was that he was looking for, only noticing the mischievous gleam in his eyes while he searched the trunk, taking various things from it and rustling through until he was armpit-deep into the container. When he removed his arm, Pyet cocked her head and her mouth hung agape. Danaus removed knife after knife, freshly sharpened and glistening. She watched as he threw them to the floor carelessly. She counted fifty in total, one for each daughter. Danaus was no craftsman, with no appreciation for the blades he was wielding. They were scattered around them, blades in every direction. If his brother had entered now, he would have seen Danaus for his cunning tricks.

These knives were just a means to an end.

Before Pyet could say anything, before she could wrap her brain around the implications of this nightmare she was dreaming in, their world blurred again. She turned around to face Matilda, who only sported a Cheshire Cat smile.

"Don't direct your rage at me, girl," she tsked, catching her words before they rolled off her tongue.

"He's going to *kill* them," Pyet said incredulously.

"Nothing you can change about it now. It's already happened." She was so matter of fact, her candidness made Pyet flinch. It reminded her so much of her mother.

"But why? He didn't have to kill them. He could have just left Argos, or at the very least talked to his brother. They were blood!"

"I don't think you understand. Argos was Danaus's home. Anywhere he went, Aegyptus would follow him. He could have had any land he wanted, but he chose Danaus. We have never had much luck with siblings, Pyet. There have been more at odds with one another than there have been those that enjoyed each other. There was no love lost between these two, and from every pair I've seen since." She looked knowingly at Pyet, her eyes brimming with a wild wickedness that glittered in the darkness. She had no siblings of her own, and could only interpret the look as another secret that she was no closer in understanding.

"Pay attention, Pyet," Matilda whispered. She hadn't noticed, but in the middle of their conversation, the world around them blurred again. She had walked right into a war zone. As Pyet removed herself from Matilda's voice, she gasped at the carnage that laid before her feet.

"Kill them, kill them all," Danaus whispered into the air, and the world around them ended.

There was blood everywhere, and Pyet had never seen so much of it. The pools that mimicked a crimson river soaked the ground she stood on, cascading across the stone tiled floor and seeping into the grout. She lifted each foot, her eyes crinkling in disgust as globs of it stuck to her shoe, strings of stickiness latching onto her.

Bodies were draped over furniture, so many that Pyet couldn't tell which ones were alive and which ones were only heaving heavy sobs. Some were hunched, lurching with each gasping breath. Others were torn apart at the seams, limbs severed from their bodies. It was messy work, the skin tears jagged and uneven, rushed. Some hadn't fought back, succumbing to their fate with pained expressions. Torn tapestries littered the ground, some still grasped by tightened hands. It was not just a massacre, but an obliteration.

Danaus smiled as he counted the heads. He bent over to pick up a knife, smiling at the bloodied faces of his daughters, victorious. He wiped it on his soiled robes, looking at the weapon with pride and envy. Women surrounded him, getting up from their knees and huddling close to one another. Wails erupted from their mouths, singing a sweet chorus that caused Pyet to cover her ears from the piercing shrieks.

His Danaids did what they were asked, and the grief of so much death hit her in the pit of her stomach. Pyet felt nauseous, her legs quaking with each step.

The faces of the murderous Danaids before them were nothing but blurred shadows. Either Matilda did not know what they looked like, or had hid those features from her. But they were soiled, hands covered in blood and dirt and grime.

"He asked his daughters to kill their husbands," Pyet said in wonder, wandering around the dream, wading through thick puddles of blood. She kept her distance from the group now retreating from the room. Danaus hustled them out one by one, promising them comfort, relief, safety. He stayed behind as Pyet traversed the crime scene. Danaus seemed to watch her as she walked, solemn as he surveyed his nephews. His eyes held no remorse, nothing but satisfaction at the blood spilled. She could smell salt and sweat in the air, a tangy sourness that stuck to the roof of her mouth.

"And they listened."

Matilda appeared right next to her, gazing upon the scene with well-adjusted eyes. She was unaffected by the gruesome images, unlike Pyet. Her face was like stone, emotionless as she picked up each foot and moved to stand at the back of a girl Pyet hadn't noticed. The girl was leaning over her soon-to-be husband, his chest rising and falling slowly as she cried. At that moment she could have sworn that woman saw her, too. Their eyes locked in a standoff, and the Danaid seemed almost to beg her, to reach out to her.

And then they were gone. They all were.

"There was a lot of death that day," Matilda confirmed, eyes grazing over dozens of bodies before they practically disintegrated at her feet. "But one of the Danaids did not kill her husband that night. Forty-nine men died, and one got away." She looked to where the crouched woman was hovered, trying hard to remember her face but coming up short. The soft rising and falling of his breaths…he didn't die.

"Did he kill her for her betrayal?" she asked softly. Matilda looked grim but shook her head in response.

"The Danaid, though only recently acquainted, felt pity for her husband, and loved him fiercely. When she was brought to court, mythology has it that Aphrodite intervened on her behalf. The goddess refused to see her punished, not when love was involved."

"What happened to her sisters?"

"They were killed. Punished to Tartarus. It was a particularly cruel punishment, as far as Tartarus went." Pyet could hear the wince in Matilda's voice, wavering as she spoke. "They were told their punishment was temporary, and that they would be released if they could carry enough jugs of water to fill a basin."

"A water basin? Surely forty-nine women could fill that in no time," Pyet contradicted. Matilda looked at her with a wounded expression.

"The basin was perforated," she whispered with dread, "The basin would never fill. They were sent to carry water, repeat the same task day after day, knowing it could never be completed."

Pyet didn't know what to say.

"It *is* cruel. And it did no good in the end, anyway. Danaus was slain by the free Danaid's husband. They all died for nothing. It is one of the most tragic things to happen in history, even for the Greeks."

Even still, no one spoke of it.

The room collapsed around them, the bright sunshine of Argo slowly disappearing as if it was truly a dream after all. Blood turned to wood, and when Pyet came to, she recognized the same dirty, brown panels that lined the walls of Matilda's apothecary, and the mess before her on the floor.

Nothing about Elric was what she expected it to be. Pyet looked at Matilda, who sat across from her once more—no longer standing several feet away—and scooted her chair forward.

"I need to know."

"Need to know what?" Her breath was airy, nothing short of a gasp.

"Why do you think the ghosts haunting my manor are the Danaids?"

Matilda may have been a lot of things, but at least she was truthful. Pyet had gotten no further in her pursuit of discovering what it was about Elric that drove her mother away despite Winona's continued promises, until now. There was nothing more she could figure out about the journal, either; she had come no closer to cracking the code, especially with her mother's now added into the mix. It seemed like there wasn't even a code to crack. All Pyet could find was the unhinged extremities of two women, ready to crack.

Then you had Elric, a town unlike any other in the world —as far as Pyet knew—with mysterious people and strange happenings that should have made her run in the other direction. Pyet wasn't religious, in that sense, but she didn't turn away from what was happening here. Elric was something entirely *other*; something *more*. Yet, all she wanted to do was stay; even with everything that surrounded her, she couldn't leave. Elric had dug its claws in, creating gaping wounds invisible to the eye. Pyet could feel it as it sliced her skin, long, deep strokes that carved deeper and deeper until it hit bone.

Gods, those nails were sharp.

There was so much that Pyet didn't know, but not from a lack of desire. Despite the heaviness of her heart and the fogginess of her head, Elric, in all of its gloom-stricken oddity, had awakened an energy in her that Pyet hadn't felt in years. Where time was slow before, it was now moving as if someone pressed fast forward. She felt something stir inside of her, like Elric was where she was supposed to be all along, even if being here was making her sick with fear.

Especially in the presence of a self-proclaimed witch like Matilda.

"You're quick to believe," Matilda noticed, that knowing smirk painted across her lips again. She had moved them both out into the storefront, which was a welcome change of scenery. Pyet needed to get up and move after sitting in that chair for so long. Her legs were stiff, stinging prickles cascading down each limb until her nerves frayed at her ankles.

She still had the images of Argo burned into the back of her brain, blood spilled across the floor and bodies thrown across the scene. She shook her head in a physical attempt to empty her brain of all thoughts, even knowing that they would never leave her. They were a permanent part of her, imprinted on her soul. Pyet felt overcome with a fullness that wanted to weigh her to the floor. She was walking in quicksand, trying to follow Matilda through the apothecary.

"I wouldn't say I was ever a non-believer" she replied, picking up a small unlabeled bottle with a corked top. The bottle was heavy in her hand despite its tiny size. She wanted so badly to know what was in it but didn't ask. Matilda was still looking at her with intrigue, her lips smacking loudly against her teeth. The sound made Pyet squirm; she felt as if she was being dissected. Matilda might as well have her splayed out on her table, picking at her with sharp tools and utensils and pulling the skin back until she was completely bare to her. Pyet didn't know what she was going to find when there was nothing left of her to cut open.

"I believe the things that I can see in front of me," Pyet continued, flinching back from the images that wouldn't relent against the backs of her eyes, "I know what I saw, and with your confirmation, I feel validated. So I guess I *believe*. If that's what that means, anyway."

Matilda shook her head, but smiled thoughtfully, "You rely too much on your head," she chastised. She moved closer to Pyet and took a long string of her hair between a few fingers. Pyet felt a definite tug or two, before side stepping away from the touch. Matilda came with her, with no sense of Pyet's discomfort, nosense of remorse. "You need to open yourself up to all of your senses, not just sight."

"Does it matter now?" Pyet retorted. She didn't just see them, she felt them all around her. She felt the energy inside the manor and as it buzzed underneath the cobbled streets in Elric. "I know that they're there now, and that's really what matters."

"I would not underestimate them." Matilda tsked again, clearly unhappy with her nonchalance.

"I thought they were in Tartarus, I don't understand why you think these women were in my manor, in *Elric*."

"Dimensions, worlds, timelines. Nothing works the way we think they do," Matilda said. It was the first time she said something gently, with care, and precision. Everything Matilda did seemed aggressive, Pyet was surprised that there was even that amount of softness in her. "And nothing works quite the same, either. Everything finds the place, the time, and the world that works best for its purpose. Tartarus is not a place, Pyet. It is much more than that."

"Greece is so far away," she argued, but it didn't sound convincing coming from her mouth, not even to her ears. Matilda cocked her head in Pyet's direction, not even bothering to respond.

"The Greeks knew more than we did. Actually, everyone knows more than we do. But there are some of us that *try* to know more," she said, gesturing to her shop. Pyet wasn't sure which objects she was referring to, but nodded anyway.

"I found this place, and I know it's hard to believe, but Elric was once full of people, children, and laughter. Elric was the place I was running *to*."

It certainly wasn't anymore. Pyet only knew of the gray stones that lined the streets, the buildings that looked real only when they were covered in shadows. She only saw the ends of wispy tailed trees, attached like arms to dead stumps. All of the people that filled its spaces once before were now hiding within their darkened homes, too afraid of what lay outside to leave until they were told. The Elric that Pyet knew was none of those things Matilda spoke of. Somewhere between the passing of time, that world died, and born in its ashes was this place.

"Unfortunately, as you'll come to find out, magic follows magic. I felt as though *something* was going to come here eventually. Maybe not them specifically, but I knew where I went, that magic would follow. The Danaids feed off of magic, and as you can see, Pyet, this shop is certainly full of magic."

"Herbs and liquids?" she asked, causing Matilda to let out a belly full of laughter. Pyet felt—once again—that she was being chastised for her obliviousness, but this time she didn't care. She was finally getting the truth; at least it felt like the truth.

Matilda's eyebrow cocked slyly, but didn't give Pyet the chance to say more before continuing. "Or, maybe it was the

Danaids that had always been here and I was drawn to *them*. I don't believe that things like this are easy to understand or predict. How many women do you remember seeing in that house?" Pyet wasn't in the room long enough to get a full head count, but it certainly wasn't fifty women.

"Probably a half a dozen, a dozen, maybe more."

"And what were they doing?"

"Honest to gods, Matilda—" she shook her head.

"To the Lantern," she interrupted.

"I'm sorry, what?"

"You said gods. The people here do not believe in any gods. They believe in the Lantern, and the Lantern only."

Pyet took a few stops more around the shop, fingering threads of a tapestry.

"Whatever. *To the Lantern*." The words sounded wrong on her lips, even though she'd heard them enough from Winona, the townspeople, and even in the found journals. "I don't believe in any of that anyway."

"Keep that to yourself, lest you want to put yourself in the direct line of fire."

"As I was saying," Pyet continued, tucking that information into the back pocket of her mind, "I didn't stay long enough to see what it was that they were *doing*. They turned to look at me and then I ran. Things fall and the house shakes. Sometimes I see things in mirrors. But if they're ghosts, they can't do anything to me, right? Ghosts are not corporeal."

"They are much more than ghosts, I think. They can do what they please, so long as they're doing their task. It's been so long since I...researched the Greeks and their stories to know the rules."

"Can't we just...call someone to cleanse the place? Do whatever it is that we need, to push them onto a better place?"

Matilda swung her head back and laughed.

Pyet thought that's what people did. She'd read books she pilfered from her mother's old rotted library at home with ghosts hunters and adventurists. She wasn't what anyone would call an *expert*, but she knew the basics.

"The manor is tied to them; it's keeping them there. No amount of herbs or whatever else you think might work will get them out. They have so much more power than we think they do, Pyet. I cannot stress it enough. They are dangerous. They killed their husbands because their father told them to. I believe they are still angry, at men, at Danaus, at us—for still living. The manor has turned into their Tartarus. The world around them morphed to their own hell, and at the center of it, of course, is a man at the helm."

The Lantern, Pyet thought. Elric was a product of the Danaids' magic, of their punishment.

"So then, you're saying I should leave?"

"I'm not saying anything. I'm trying to prepare you. I don't know why they are still here, and I don't even know for sure that it is the Danaids you have haunting your manor to begin with. I feel it in my bones, though. And I do think that you're the only one that can keep them there. Like your grandmother was."

"Violet knew about the Danaids?"

"Violet was the keeper of that house for longer than I know. The people here swear she's been around since their grandparents and their grandparents' grandparents. Hearsay, certainly, but I digress. Violet knew more about that manor than anyone, and she protected it. I can't tell you all of the things that house has done, but know it is enough to make Elric frightened of it."

"So then why not tear it down?"

"And release that evil into the world, girl? Are you mad?" Matilda scoffed, scrunching her nose and stepping close to

Pyet, so close that she felt she was pushing her out the door. She took several steps back, almost backing into a rack of geodes.

The night was starting to loom over Elric, and Matilda was going to throw her out onto the street and expect her to go back to the manor with those stories in her head?

"You have a decision to make, it seems," Matilda said hauntingly. "I hope you make the right one."

"How can I be expected to stay there tonight? Those women might kill me!" She didn't have any incentive to hole up in the manor any longer, not with the knowledge she had now.

"Oh Pyet, why worry?" She smiled crookedly. Her long gray hair whipped around her threateningly. "They are just *stories*, after all. Use your head girl. You'll get it eventually."

Pyet blinked and, at once, Matilda was no longer in front of her, but behind her, the door cracked open just enough for her to slide through. There was a wicked gleam across her features, too much to decipher here in the dark.

"Goodnight, Pyet. Please say hello to your guests for me, *if* you return to the manor." Matilda pushed lightly on her back as she was retreating outdoors, and shut the door behind her completely once she was no longer inside.

Pyet was stuck outside, in the middle of the night.

FROM THE JOURNALS OF

JULIETTE CABELLO

I've been invited to the Danaus Solstice.

I keep hearing the strange voices, whispering from within the walls of this eerie old house. It's enough to send shivers down my spine, and I can't shake the feeling of being watched.

My eyes scan the shadows in the dark, but there's no one to be seen. The voices, though—they keep going. They tell me stories of the house's dark past and it's making me fear the worst. I'm certain I'm not alone here, and my fear won't subside. These women are here. And no one told me what it means, what they mean.

The people around town keep looking at me like I'm crazy. But it isn't me, I didn't do anything. I didn't ask for whatever it is that they're planning, whatever it is that they won't tell me.

I don't know how long I can keep up like this. How can I keep these voices away? What kind of danger am I in, being stuck here? There's only one thing I know for certain: I need to find a way out of here.

The Solstice. That's my ticket. That's how I'll escape.

There were no stars out tonight. It was as if the sky robbed them from view, Elric not deserving enough to enjoy them as a blanket across the horizon. She'd come to expect the darkness and the quiet here, but not as it was tonight. Light could not creep in even if it wanted to; instead it hid in fear.

Pyet's heart pounded against her chest as she crept out of Matilda's, keeping to the shadows and avoiding the piercing glare of the streetlamps. The eerie stillness of the town sent shivers down her spine, and made the hairs on her neck stand up. It was as if the entire place had been abandoned by the living, and now it was overrun by the undead. She didn't want to be spotted, the consequences felt dire. There was nothing that indicated what might happen if someone in town was out past curfew, but Pyet had no intention of finding out. Whatever it was, it scared Elric so completely that no one dared to step foot outside after nightfall.

She weaved through the silent streets, careful not to step or bump into anything that could clatter on the ground. She moved like a phantom, with nothing but the darkness and her instincts to guide her. But as Pyet traversed deeper into the belly of town, she couldn't shake the feeling that someone was watching her. Her skin prickled and her ears rang with an unnerving quiet. She turned around, but the darkness obscured everything, hiding whoever—or whatever—might be there.

The only source of light came from the yellowed flickers of the gas lamps, illuminating small pockets of the streets before flickering out again. Pyet did her best to avoid these beacons, unsure of what creatures might lurk in their illumination. She was entirely too focused on avoiding the lamp posts that decorated the cobblestone, relying on her familiarity to guide her.

Suddenly feeling the need to orient herself, Pyet glanced up. She had expected the grooves of a brick wall to take a sharp right, leading her to the winding road that would steer her to the manor. Instead, her fingers caught on something smooth, drawing her attention away from the fluorescents and onto the scene before her.

She blinked several times, allowing her eyes to adjust to the moonlit Circle. Everything in Elric was different after dark. It caught her in a panic, causing her to suck in a small gasp of air. She let it fill her lungs, only letting go when the pressure in her chest was too much to bear. There was something wrong with the town tonight. It was as if a veil had been lifted, revealing a twisted, terrifying version of the place she thought she knew.

Nothing was in its right place. Pyet couldn't see the store signs swinging near the doorways, or catch the names of the streets from where she stood. It was as if she was in a different town entirely. Before she fell into another spiral, Pyet looked directly towards the center of Elric. Her eyes caught sight of the statue; it was a landmark that she had to see, the piece of this place that gave Pyet an unreasonable amount of security.

What she didn't expect to see was that security lost, gone like the light of the day.

The stallion was a symbol of Elric. Its hind legs reared, and the horse's mouth was open in a neigh that Pyet could have sworn she could hear, despite its hollow metal exterior. But now, though it was the same in its striking pose and overwhelming presence, it was also different, much like the town itself. The statue's features seemed to shift and change before her very eyes, the once stoic expression now twisted into a malicious sneer. It was no trick of the moonlight, it was the shadows in the dark swirling around her. It was another manifestation of the magic that lived here. Its eyes glistened mischievously, its nostrils seeming to flare.

No matter how many times she blinked, the stallion's features would not change. Pyet felt a scream rise in her throat as she realized in horror that it was happening to her...*again*. Elric continued to play tricks on her. The statue wasn't moving—it was alive. And it was only the beginning of the nightmares that lurked in this strange and terrible version of the place her mother escaped from.

Pyet ran.

She ran for her life, following the direction of the muzzle of the stallion that she knew would always lead her home. She sprinted outside of the Town Circle, no longer surrounded by shops and cobblestone, no houses or lamp-lights. The landscape was dominated by gnarled trees and mist that billowed across the ground like ghosts. Pyet's heart was racing as she dashed through the dark streets. She had been careful, wary of potential threats, but now she threw caution to the wind. Her arms flailed and, if she had been able to catch her breath, she would have screamed.

And still it felt like she was being followed. Pyet had

turned around multiple times as she ran, scanning the deserted alleys, but every time she looked, there was no one there. It was as if the night itself was stalking her.

When she finally felt as if she could run no longer, Pyet finally stopped, heaving into the pavement with her hands on her knees. Pyet hunched over, panting as she tried to catch her breath. She had been running for what felt like hours, and her feet felt like they were on fire. When she finally stopped to take in her surroundings, she realized with a start that she was nowhere near her manor.

The street she was on was dark and deserted, and there was a chill in the air that made her shiver. Pyet had always been good with directions, but for the life of her, she couldn't figure out how she had ended up so far off course. She was sure she had been heading towards the manor, but now she was on the opposite side of town.

A sense of unease settled over her as she looked around. She was in a part of Elric she had never been before, and it felt eerie and otherworldly. The shadows seemed to twist and dance, and Pyet could hear faint whispers on the wind. As she lifted her head to orient herself, Pyet felt a pressure in her chest. It was like a weight was pressing down on her, making it hard to breathe. She stumbled and fell to the ground, her vision swimming as she struggled to catch her breath. Through the haze, Pyet could see something moving in the shadows. It was dark and twisted, like a nightmare made real. She tried to scream, but her voice caught in her throat.

As Pyet struggled to regain her composure, she realized with a sickening dread that she had stumbled upon something sinister. Even if she hadn't been invited here, even if she hadn't stepped foot inside the church, she knew without saying that this was where Elric had brought her.

She was always going to end up here.

With her heart racing, Pyet forced herself to crawl towards the church, driven by a primal urge to look, to learn, to fall prey to its charm. Her knees ached and her hands were raw, but she dared not stop for even a second. Every moment she spent out in the open, she felt like she was in danger, but still it was not enough to keep her away. Pyet couldn't tell if it was the story of the Danaids that made her suddenly so alert, brave enough to crawl towards the church that kept her isolated from the rest of town, or if it was Matilda herself.

The crazy witch—though submerging Pyet in a world of questions—promised her honesty for nothing in return, allowing Pyet to fall headfirst into this world. It should have scared her away, but it only made her feel more connected to this place.

She finally started to believe that she belonged, even if it was in this twisted way.

As she closed in on the large building with tall white points, castle-like in its grandeur, Pyet could see the outlines of a fire bouncing like shadows against its marbled walls. It reminded her of her manor, slick and modern, far too beautiful to be in a place like this. Just beyond the treeline, as she got closer, Pyet could make out several distinguishable shapes. They looked too close to human figures, moving in and out between the licking flames. It wasn't until she hid carefully behind a particularly rough patch of brush that she could make out their voices.

The people before her were dressed in deep plum robes, surrounding the fire and whatever it was that lay inside of it. They each looked familiar and not at all, their faces covered by the robes, and the fluidity of their movements. They moved far too fast for Pyet to recognize them, but she was sure she had seen them before.

But it was the fire that held Pyet's attention, its flames dancing in a frenzy that seemed almost alive. She could see something writhing within the flames, something that made her skin crawl. It was hard to tell what was happening, Pyet was caught in a world she didn't believe was real any longer. She had started to question everything that was put before her. It was like the mirror and the manor; there was too much that Elric could do to play tricks on her.

But there *was* something in there. She was certain of that. The robbed figures took turns reaching into the flames, the sound of ripping and tearing overwhelming against their chants. The noise was drowning the hymns, and soon it became the only thing Pyet could hear. It was the only thing she could think about.

Slick smacking of lips and clashing teeth made her squirm in discomfort. She knew what she was watching without knowing. She knew what she was bearing witness to.

Whatever ritual this was, Pyet had no intention of being a part of it.

She shook her head fiercely and snapped herself out of her trance, regaining control of her limbs, though her legs were pained from lack of blood flow. Pyet sat up on the soles of her feet, crouched behind the foliage. She tried to move quickly, but every rustle of leaves on the ground sounded like a death knell in her ears. Pyet felt the weight of fear bearing down on her as she continued to crouch behind the thick bush, her heart beating erratically. She could feel the chill of the night seeping into her bones, causing her to shiver involuntarily.

She knew that if she made any noise, it would be all over for her. Her breathing became shallow and she tried to calm herself down. Pyet took a deep breath and let it out slowly, trying to keep herself as quiet as possible, but fate had other plans for her. As she moved forward, a small twig snapped under her foot, echoing like a gunshot in the stillness of the night.

She looked around frantically, trying to see if anyone had heard her. Pyet could feel her pulse racing, and a cold sweat forming on her brow. As suddenly as it started, the chanting stopped and the robed dancers froze in place. The fire still crackled and hissed, casting grotesque shadows across their faces. Pyet tried to step back, to leave this place of terror, but she found herself rooted to the spot.

With a blood curdling shriek, the group turned as one to face her. Pyet's heart thudded in her chest as she realized with growing horror that their eyes were entirely black, empty of all light and life. It could have been a trick of the light, but without a doubt the blood that pooled beneath them was not. It dripped from their mouths, long tendrils of sticky, red life falling from each jaw.

Pyet heard a distinct sound of chewing, the smacking of lips making her cringe as she backed away from the group before her. She could have sworn a severed finger dropped from one of them, falling to the ground with a small thud. Though the sound was insignificant, it was the only thing she could hear. The world closed in around her, and her world was shrinking before her eyes.

Pyet opened her mouth to scream, the figures now rushing toward her in a hurried scurry.

And then everything went black.

Winnie is the only person I trust to come here. I worry that I'm robbing her of some sort of life she should have. She chose this manor—even after I resisted—and the manor has chosen her in return, at least as much as they are able. I can't make her leave, though. It feels good to have company since Juliette left. She wasn't chosen, but I want to choose her. I almost wish that she was the daughter that the Lantern wanted. But she is no ~~Danaïd~~, not like Juliette.

I hate that I feel so weak. The house is so needy, I don't think I can say no to the help; I'm getting tired of all of it. Does that make me selfish? Maybe. Juliette did the right thing by leaving—no, no she didn't. She ruined us. ~~She destroyed everything.~~

I can't let ~~Winnie~~ think that I'll let her in like she wants. She doesn't need to be caught up in all of this mess. My mess. She will never be Juliette. She can't be.

"Okay Winnie, I'm ready to talk."

She didn't know what made her do it, but Pyet now stood outside of Winnie's magenta home, journal still clutched between strained white fingers. She was done pretending she didn't have it in her possession. She was done pretending that Winnie's lack of information didn't hurt her. It felt like a betrayal, even if Winnie owed her nothing.

She was the outsider, the intruder, the thief; Winona lived here her entire life.

Pyet didn't know how she missed it before, Winona wasn't even trying to hide it. How often did she tell Pyet that her grandmother meant more to her than anything else? How many times did she talk about the manor as if she was the one that owned it? As if she knew its secrets more than anyone?

When she woke up that morning, the remnants of her horrific dream still plaguing her thoughts, Pyet was in a hurry to leave the manor. She had no idea how she had made it home the night before, and the sounds of clashing teeth and slick blood between lips ricocheted in her brain. She couldn't escape it. Her head was no longer the safe space she wanted it to be. It was compromised in some way, and Pyet was convinced her mind kept playing tricks on her.

Matilda's magic. That's what it had to have been. The statue was not alive and moving, and the people she saw last night were not real.

What was real was the bruises on her knees, the dirt under her nails, but not from that. It was anything but that.

Winona appeared out of thin air, her thin lips pressed together firmly. Her eyes hid the kindness she'd kept underneath well. They were strained and tight, only small slits of brown showing. Winnie felt, in that moment, like just another Elric resident. She was not the person who made her feel welcomed, or the friend that had become her own personal guidebook. This was a hardened Winona. A scary Winona.

It was a person Pyet could very well see hiding behind a violet-colored robe.

Her door swung open wide, an invitation for Pyet to step through the threshold.

"I was wondering when you'd come by. Still have my key?"

Pyet nodded as she skirted past her. The house looked very much the same as it did when she was last here, though she didn't make note of that out loud. Belongings were thrown every which way, and Winnie made no effort to clean it up. It felt like this home was both very well lived in, and not lived in at all. Pyet heard the softest click of the door shut behind her.

Once she was trapped, the magic disappeared again. It was a relief, even if the lack of its presence made her wary. Pyet had grown used to the otherness she felt while in Elric—and more importantly, her manor—and here, deep in the depths of

Winona's lair, she felt entirely average. The ground didn't shake, the mirrors didn't move, and the voices didn't whisper in her ear. There were no dreams of rituals. It was just…nothing.

Opening the cover of the journal, Pyet grabbed the key she'd shoved inside and held it out in her hand, an invitation of her own. Winnie's eyes scoured her, landing on the journal with hunger, but she grabbed for only the key held in her palm, shoving it in the waistband of her gray slacks.

"It's rude to take things," she said, matter of fact. Pyet noticed the faintest tilt of a smirk in her direction. She couldn't tell if she was pretending to be angry, or if she actually was. The smirk led her to believe that she had a shot at regaining what she had lost these last few weeks. Her eyes were telling a different story. Maybe Winona was just as confused on how to approach her as Pyet was.

"It's legally mine," Pyet reminded her. She tilted her head to the side and raised one delicate eyebrow. It was a challenge, something she would never have thought twice about before now. Desire for the other journals raged through her. Pyet was so desperate to have her hands on more of her grandmother's words. Her thoughts. Her feelings. Her obsessions.

She had become ravenous for reasons why Elric was doing this to her. What it had done to her mother and grandmother.

"Be that as it may, I remember you distinctly handing them over on your second night here. So really, they're not yours anymore. They're *mine*."

"I felt like I was grossly misinformed about their importance. I was stricken with grief. You know, no person in their right mind would get rid of their relative's belongings right after they passed. And, seeing as it was hidden so effectively, I felt the innate desire to read it."

"Not effectively enough, it seems."

There was a chill in her voice, but it left her as soon as Pyet's eyes reached Winnie. There was a level of hurt she saw behind that hard exterior. The room was still and silent, and after a few seconds, Pyet shrugged to release some of the tension. Winona took that as surrender and finally let a smile rest on her face. Pyet decided she enjoyed that look far more than the other.

"I'm sorry," Pyet said finally. And meant it. Though she was intent on finding answers, Pyet hated this weird aggression that filled the room before them. She hated that she created that, and that she didn't trust Winnie. Hated that she wanted to so badly, but her findings in the journal, and her experiences the last several weeks kept her from it.. "I shouldn't have taken it without your permission."

"You were curious." Winona gestured to the couch. She surrendered, too. "It feels weird to not want to blame you. Your grandmother was a fascinating woman, in a town full of oddities. I'm surprised you didn't push harder to know more. I would have been more shocked if you had seen it and *not* taken it."

"I *did* push," Pyet argued. "You refused to answer me."

"I suppose you're right."

And she left it at that. It was infuriating, not being able to get the answers she sought. Every word felt like a fight, and Pyet was tired of fighting. Everything she'd done and had been through since the bus dropped her off on the side of the road exhausted her.

"Are you angry with me?"

Winona smiled again, tapping her crossed knee with a nail.

"Yes, and no. I'm not angry at you for taking it, but I am angry with you for keeping it from me. I wished you would have come to me. I'm sure you were…confused about some of the things you saw."

Like her notes scribbled across the margins on the page, in between the lines, scratching out her own name. She wasn't wrong, but Pyet held those cards close to her chest for now.

"A little."

"Is there anything you wanted to ask me?"

"About a million things," she answered. "But mostly I was just so engrossed in meeting Violet. I couldn't tear my eyes from the page. Even if some of it didn't make sense to me, meeting her was a gift I wouldn't take back."

Pyet could have sworn that she saw tears in Winnie's eyes. She nodded sympathetically and dabbed at her cheeks with her top. Pyet couldn't tell if they were real or performance. She wanted them to be real so badly it physically pained her.

Why was it so hard to trust the one person who'd only been a friend to her?

"Did you find the answers you were looking for?" Winnie asked. "Violet was always a mystery, but I hope you found it to be resourceful."

Pyet felt her eyebrows draw inward and she frowned.

"No. I didn't." It was too curt. There was a flash of emotion in Winona's eyes that Pyet just missed. She'd been too slow to catch it. Pyet had half a mind to ask her to do it again, just so she could collect every emotion that Winona had in her. She didn't trust anything, or anyone, including herself. Relying on her very human eyes was not enough for a place like this.

"Oh, that's a shame," she said, and Pyet almost believed her. Her lips came together in a pout, eyebrows furrowed together in concern. It was too much to handle, the stillness in the air, the tension that surrounded them. Pyet felt like this conversation mimicked one she had with her mother so long ago, and it killed her to have that here. She *couldn't* go back to that life. She would take the horrors that Elric had to offer over going back to Juliette's home, surrounded by that chain link fence.

"Winona!" Pyet threw her arms in the air in exasperation, and Winnie's eyes followed the journal as it went with her. It was a long moment before she met Pyet's eyes, as if she had forgotten that she was there completely. Her only focus was the faded red journal in Pyet's grip. "This is exhausting. I'm so sick of this game we're playing."

Winona raised a finger in Pyet's direction. It took her a second before she realized it was the journal that she was pointing at, not the girl behind it. Pyet grunted and shoved the journal behind her back, snarling in her direction.

"Of course you did. You came to town, and that was all you had to do. Welcome to the game, Pyet. We're all playing it. And that woman there?" Winona nodded her head in the direction of the journal. "She was the queen. The secrets of that house are a mystery to all of us. Everyone except for your dear old, dead grandmother. I loved her. I wanted to protect that house, but she wouldn't give me any more information than what I am giving you. I can't give you the answers that you seek because I don't have any of the answers myself. *No one does.* And all we wanted to do was find it. I promise, the people who are looking for answers are far worse than me. I wanted to protect that house, I still do."

In that moment, Pyet actually believed her. She *wanted* to. It was in the frustration that leaked from her voice. It was in the way she ran her hands through her hair, slender digits roaming cautiously through golden, glistening, locks. It was in the way she hung her head in exhaustion herself.

"Let's say I believed you," she hedged. Winnie narrowed her eyes again. It was a look of uncertainty, and of suspicion.

"I want to, Winnie, but *Lantern*, you have to meet me halfway."

Pyet made sure to emphasize her exclamation like the old witch told her to. It might have been the only way to get Winnie to trust her. And just as easily as Matilda made it seem, Pyet watched that hard exterior melt away, leaving behind the shell of a broken girl just as confused as she was. It didn't matter that Pyet knew she was hiding things. It didn't matter that she couldn't trust her. She was willing to give this part of herself to save her mother. She was willing to do terribly stupid things for the woman that tried to murder her.

Why was that?

Pyet wanted a home. She wanted a place to accept her, to appreciate her. And she was so sick of Elric challenging her belonging. If Elric wasn't the place she was meant to be, then nowhere was.

Pyet couldn't afford to lose this shitty place, too.

And so, she chose to believe her. Winona's lies and deceit could be overlooked, just as long as Pyet could find her own answers. The rest was manageable.

She hated being so broken.

"Believe what? That I want to protect the house? Of course I do! Pyet, I could have very easily washed your letter away and been done with it. But I didn't. I sent it like Violet wanted me to. She trusted me enough to send that letter after she died. She made me promise. Violet didn't leave the house to me, she left it to *you*. And that sucked, because how could you—a child that she had never met, never once spoken to— help them when I could not? I don't know what it is about you, but you are special, Pyet. You are the person Violet chose to be the keeper of the house."

"I didn't ask for that!" Pyet argued. "You should have just

taken it back, it's not like Violet could have known, she's already gone!"

"It doesn't work like that," Winona snapped. She got up so abruptly, the couch that she'd been sitting on pushed back from the impact and made a terrible screeching sound as it skid across her wooden floors. Pyet jumped, but stayed where she sat, worried that too much movement would make Winnie feral.

She watched as Winona paced across the floors, sliding her feet along, socks catching against the splinters. She shook her head back and forth. It reminded Pyet very much of her mother's episodes. The spiral into delusion was unfriendly, and the most Pyet could do was sit and watch it happen right in front of her.

She was weak-willed.

"I wish I could explain it to you but I *can't*. Not in the way you want. I'm not smart enough," she continued. "It's your blood, Pyet. You are inexplicably tied to that house, because Violet is your grandmother. It is binding, not just legally, but physically. I…can't explain why. I was trying to find a way around that."

"And that's why you wrote in her journals."

"Partially. Sort of. Listen, this is far deeper than you can handle, Pyet. Take this one day at a time. All you need to know is that the house is yours. In body, soul, and spirit. Violet entrusted you. Without you, the house would die. It *will* die if we don't protect it."

"You keep saying shit like that," Pyet spat, growling as she crossed her legs under herself. "What the hell am I supposed to protect it from? I don't see any of the townspeople holding stakes and pitchforks. They do nothing but ignore me."

"It's darker than that, Pyet. Can't you feel it? I know you're not stupid! You feel the magic humming in this town; you picked up on that quickly. You see how they can be dangerous if you're not looking. You've been holed up in the manor these last two weeks, and they've been *planning*. It's dangerous for you here."

She didn't know that Pyet had gone to see Matilda, and she didn't know the nightmare that came after.

"It was dangerous for me at home, too."

"Yes, but this time, you have someone that won't let you leave. Pyet, you're not going to abandon this place. I love this fucking town, and that fucking manor. I will not allow you to leave it to die."

"You keep saying that, but why? I'm so sick of hearing how much you love this damn manor, but you won't say any more than that. Why is it that you love the Danaids so much?" Pyet challenged.

All the color left from Winona's face. For a second, Pyet couldn't understand why. The words just left her mouth, all thoughts of secrecy forgotten.

"What did you call them?" she hissed through gritted teeth. Winona stopped pacing, turning her full attention to Pyet. She could see her fists curled into balls, her breathing coming out in deep pants.

"The Danaids," she said again, stronger. Winona took one step closer to her. "Why do you love them?"

"That fucking witch!" Winona yelled, kicking the floor with so much intensity that Pyet was surprised it didn't hurt. Papers that littered the floor around them scattered, flying through the air and floated around them. Winona grabbed for a pillow resting on her couch and threw it against the wall. Feathers ripped from the inside, adding another layer to the mess before them. Pyet stepped back, practically tripping over empty boxes and half bottles of things that she'd scattered around.

Winona never seemed to be the type to live in a place that looked like this. She looked too refined for that; she looked like she deserved a manor herself, or had spent a lot of time in one. This home was not the place for someone like her. This home seemed temporary.

"You went and saw her, didn't you? After I told you not to?"

There was a deep anger that burst into flame within Pyet. She'd been yelled at, torn up, chewed up, and spit out by far too many people. Winona was one in a long line of people who challenged her, thinking they could get away with it. She stood up, the journal falling to the floor as she walked towards Winnie. She stopped when there were only five footsteps separating them.

"I had no other choice," Pyet snarled. "She was willing to give me answers. She told me *everything*."

"The witch can only give you so much, and all of her magic comes with a price. What did you pay her?"

"She didn't take any money!"

"Not *money*, Pyet. Something much more valuable than that. What did she take?"

"Nothing, I swear!"

Winnie didn't believe her. She started pacing again, shoving Pyet out of the way as she walked, then turning around and doing the same thing again on her way back. Pyet stepped out of her warpath.

"She is tricky. She could have asked you something, a simple question. It might have seemed miniscule, insignificant. That could have been enough for her to weasel something out of you. You don't know what she's capable of."

"And you do?"

"Violet warned me of the witch. Matilda has been here since the town was founded. There's a long, bloody history in this town, and she was the center of it."

"But that wouldn't be possible, that would make her..."

"Hundreds of years old, yes,"

"That's impossible!"

"Not in Elric, it isn't."

"Elric isn't that special!" Pyet threw her arms in the air and turned to walk away from her. She'd almost made it to the door until Winona grabbed onto her shoulder. She pulled Pyet close, spinning them both in a dizzying circle, her face a mask of terror when they faced each other. Her features creased in worry, trying to tell Pyet something she couldn't put into words. She looked far older than she was at that moment. Pyet could have sworn that she saw a tear starting to form at the corner of Winnie's eye.

Pyet's voice caught in her throat. It was quiet, in Winona's home. With the sound of silence bouncing off the walls between them, the tension shifted. She hadn't realized they were as close as they were. It was the nearest Pyet felt to having someone like family close to her. Winona's touch was almost gentle, and she imagined that touch was something her mother could have given her long before all of this. Despite the fear that laced through Winnie, Pyet couldn't help but feel like there was a kinship here she couldn't quite nail.

Although, when no one else in Elric ever paid her any mind, and starving for the attention she grew up never receiving, there was no wonder Pyet wished for it so deeply.

Winnie stepped away, bending down to pick up the journal and held it out towards Pyet. It was a truce, a peace offering.

"Elric is *special*, Pyet. I can't make you believe me. You read her journal, right? You started to *see*? This town won't show you how special it is until you start to believe it."

Pyet started to back away again, still in shock.

"Go, Pyet. I need you to learn."

"I need the journals to do that," she whispered.

"No." Winnie smiled softly. She expected that answer,

Pyet realized. She could read Pyet like an open book. "You can have the journals. I won't keep them from you. But you have to go learn about Elric first. You won't be able to understand your grandmother if you don't learn about how this place came to be."

Pyet ran as fast as her legs would take her away from the house. The only home she had ever felt welcome in here in Elric. Her feet pounded against the ground, her heart racing in her chest. Tears began streaming down her cheeks, a seemingly never-ending river of pain and despair.

No matter how fast she ran, she could not escape her misery. It seemed that wherever she went, someone was there waiting to hate her, to despise her, to make her feel like it was the end. Elric had proven itself to be just the place her mother warned her away from. It was cruel and vindictive, demonstrating a dark magic beyond her wildest dreams. Pyet couldn't understand what was fully happening around her, it felt unreal. But, even with everything she'd seen, and all that she bore witness to, it was a life that made her *feel* something.

Anything was better than the place she left.

She just had to keep running.

Winnie had been trying to tell her something. Something that could change her perception of the world, of this place.

But instead, Pyet ran, blinded by her emotions and unsure of the message she was sending her, though the answer was very clear. Winona had said to learn more about Elric. Pyet knew almost nothing about the place she lived in, so intent on finding the defining moment that changed her mother. Pyet couldn't focus on Elric when she was so desperate to save Juliette.

Feeling entirely overwhelmed, she stopped in the middle of the cobbled road and fell to her knees, wincing from the pain of her fading bruises, her sorrow turning into pure frustration and rage. She screamed in the air, letting free the tears that had been steadily pouring from her eyes.

And then, someone called her name. It was a familiar voice that Pyet still couldn't place. It kept coming, her name echoing through the streets as if it was distant and forlorn. With a tear stained face and her cheeks flushed red, Pyet turned to face it.

Pyet saw a young girl. She was tall, slender and had long hair that never seemed to end. She knew that she had met this girl before, but couldn't recall her name. Did she ever get this haunting girl's name?

"Why are you here?" she grumbled, wiping the tears that were sticking to her cheeks.

The girl looked at her curiously, not paying any mind to the people that slipped past them. Of all people, save for Winona, this mysterious girl was the only one who wasn't afraid to be near her. Who didn't treat her like an outsider to Elric. Not that she felt welcomed around the quiet girl, but she felt *seen*.

"Why are you *still* here?" the girl argued. Her voice was still solemn, but there was a bite of challenge in her reply. It was like she wanted to say something, but couldn't.

"I can't leave. The manor...my grandmother...my mother."

"You keep making excuses," the girl said. "You cannot leave because of your grandmother, and yet your grandmother is dead."

Pyet narrowed her eyes, leaning forward to push herself up from the ground.

"You cannot leave because of your mother." Pyet looked to interject, but the girl continued anyway. "But your mother will not follow you. She would rather die than leave her protected home. She would rather kill *you* than let you come here."

"You know nothing about me!" Pyet growled at her. The people across the street skipped away, too frightened to be near the girl from the manor. The pariah.

"You cannot leave because you don't have a home elsewhere. But you could not leave even if you wanted to. Pyet, you need to leave this place, but you cannot. Much like Violet, this place is your *home*."

She wanted to ignore her, but she couldn't. The girl wasn't wrong. She was in her head, parading her deepest fears in front of her. Pyet couldn't escape her, because she knew too much. Of course Pyet wanted a home. She wanted to belong. She wanted to feel connected to her grandmother, to her mother. She couldn't leave.

Which meant she couldn't give up.

"If you want answers, Pyet, they are right in front of you. You are so close to figuring it all out. Just. Look. Up."

With that, the girl gave Pyet a kind smile, nodded goodbye, and then disappeared. She was there, and then she was gone, like a gust of wind now shaking through the trees that surrounded her. Pyet had no idea who the girl was or what her words meant, but she had offered Pyet a new glimmer of hope and comfort in her time of need. She was hard and rough, but she was the only honest person Pyet encountered in Elric.

Pyet stood, shaking off the dirt from her gray slacks and wiped her eyes again. When she opened her eyes and blinked a few times, she did look up, just as she was told.

And all of her questions *were* answered.

Sitting in front of her was a library; Pyet didn't even know that Elric *had* a library. Now that she was staring right at it, there was a happy, hopeful lump in her chest. This was what Winnie was telling her. The library had to have *archives*. It was fate that brought her here, that took each foot and placed it in front of the other. It was fate that made her run from Winona, run to *here*. Maybe Winnie didn't know exactly where she was going, but this was what she meant, certainly.

They weren't the journals that she was wanting, but it might be a start. Who knew the secrets that Elric's archives might have?

Pyet crossed the street and walked up to the doors of the old library. Like the other shops in Elric it had a rusty-looking sign, swinging lightly in the breeze. It squeaked threateningly as it swung back and forth, dusty from months of neglect. There was no one inside that she could see, townspeople or workers alike.

Pyet first knocked, even knowing that shops were open across town. She wasn't expecting an answer, and she didn't get one. After a few seconds, she pushed through the door anyway.

Pyet stepped inside the library, feeling the familiar creaks of an ancient and abandoned building. Everywhere she looked, dusty shelves seemed to groan from age, much the same as it looked from the outside. All was still and quiet in the library; there was no sign of another living soul. Not one person in Elric was there. Not reading within the stacks of books or behind the information desk.

She hadn't realized since leaving Winona's house, but the

magic was back again. It coursed through her bones, over-whelming her racing heart. It was even here, despite the emptiness of this place. The magic was different, though. It was darker, older, staler. Pyet felt like the library had contained that magic, isolated it and kept it for as many years as it stood standing.

It didn't matter. The magic was beginning to feel like home. It was becoming a comfort, even if she had no idea how to use it. Even if the people here didn't accept her. Even if Elric still scared her.

Even if she was starting to see the beauty in it.

Reading Violet's journal lifted the veil off of Elric. It was no longer deep blues and grays, but something just a little bit brighter. It was becoming a place that Pyet wanted to stay in, despite the rest of it.

Pyet hesitantly walked through the bays of books, occa-sionally glancing over her shoulder for any signs of danger. There would be none, of course, not while there was no one in this small space; she could hear nothing but creaking wood as she walked. Nevertheless Pyet couldn't help but keep snapping her head back and forth. She wiped at her red face, rubbing it raw.

After a few minutes of aimlessly exploring, she eventually stumbled across an old dusty book on a wooden desk in the corner of the room. It was the only book she could find that looked like it had been touched at all. She dusted it off and opened the cover, cracking the spine until it laid flat against the desk.

With her heart beating nervously, Pyet breathed in deeply before turning the first few pages. The book was worn and aged, the writingin a foreign language she did not under-stand, and, at first, she wasn't sure if it would be of any use. It seemed like it was written in the same language her grandmother often spoke in her journal. It looked like *ancient Greek*. And of course, she couldn't read it.

Pyet shut the book with a frustrated slam.

"...Is someone there?" a small voice squeaked from behind a covered wall.

The voice startled Pyet, causing her heart to beat rapidly and her feet to crumble before her. She lost her balance, using the desk she'd been standing near to hoist up her weight.

"Hello?" the voice said again.

"Y-y-yes?" Pyet stammered. She couldn't catch her breath, instead letting out short and shallow pants to settle herself.

"No one ever comes here, anymore." The voice manifested itself as a small, plump man rounded the corner. He looked so similarly to the store clerk she'd met on her first day here that Pyet had to do a double take. He was friendlier-looking, though he glanced at her quizzically, as if she had gone and gotten herself lost.

"Why is that?" she asked. He didn't introduce himself, but he did close in on her, touching his hand down on the desk she was at. Pyet narrowed her eyes in his direction and shuffled back a few feet.

The old man noticed her apprehension, and he let out a guffaw. It sounded more like he was choking on his own words. After a few seconds he stepped away and turned his attention to an unshelved cart of books a few feet away.

"Call it what you want," he hummed, grabbing a book and sliding it into an empty spot on the shelf. He didn't even seem to notice the dust that littered the air as he disturbed its resting place. "But they stopped coming here a long time ago. They don't need these books anymore, not according to the Lantern. I'm here simply as a placeholder. People don't, and aren't expected to, come here."

"Doesn't Elric have another shop that sells books not far from here?"

The man nodded, grabbing for another book from his cart.

"That's my brother," he said, matter of fact. Pyet nodded, accepting his explanation for his familiarity. She would have taken any answer if it meant she could have some sort of stability again. She shuffled her feet and the man turned his back completely on her, focusing his attention to the cart.

"Do you…want me to leave?" she asked. He turned his head over his shoulder and shrugged.

"Stay if you want, I guess."

Pyet slid the book away that she'd been looking at initially and continued to browse at each shelf. There seemed to be nothing that would aid her, and the hope she'd been feeling just outside was disappearing by the second.

The librarian let her alone for a few moments, keeping himself busy and running around to several bays that needed attention. Pyet noticed that he kept glancing her way, but everytime their eyes met, he would look away in embarrassment and continue to keep himself busy.

Pyet wanted to say something, but nothing would come out. Each time she tried to start the conversation, something stopped her. It was hard to trust people in a place like Elric.

"Can I help you find…anything?" His voice was small and quiet, and if she hadn't been acutely aware of his presence, then she might not have even heard it. Pyet turned to face him, relief showering her features. She could feel the red creeping up her cheeks. Now that she had the spotlight, it was proving difficult to form words that made sense, that made her feel like she wasn't spiraling.

"Yes, actually!" She took several hurried steps towards him, stopping only when she realized that he was matching her steps, but backwards. Pyet couldn't be surprised that he was just like the rest of them; afraid of her, wary of her. It was exhausting, and isolating.

Especially with her relationship with Winona so…uncertain, she was feeling incredibly alone.

"I'm sorry," Pyet whispered, embarrassed, "But I was hoping there was a book here or something that could help me find out more about Elric. About how it was created?"

The man looked at her like she had grown two heads.

"You want…to know what now?"

"Elric. I want to know more about Elric."

Pyet was so tired of feeling like she was the crazy one, and couldn't help but frown as the man shook his head incredulously.

"I don't think you're going to find anything here, Pyet."

There it was again, the feeling that everyone in this goddamn town knew exactly who she was, when she knew absolutely nothing about them. Pyet's teeth ground uncomfortably.

"Why not? This is a library, right? Why don't you have any history books?" The man raised his hands defensively, as if he didn't expect her to come at him so aggressively. The tone in her voice surprised her too.

"Woah there, sugar. Don't get all tied up. I'm surprised you don't know is all. You live up there in that house just outside of town, right? *The* house?"

She nodded curtly. "Right, the house everyone is afraid of. It's why they avoid me, too. Worried I'm carrying something contagious or whatever." Pyet rolled her eyes and scowled. She must have looked ridiculous, her arms crossed over her chest so tightly that she could barely breathe. The old man dropped his hands and burst out into amused laughter.

"Your grandmother was a piece of work, you know that? The people here were afraid of her."

"But *why?*" she asked. "I don't know much about her. The

most I've learned is through goddamn letters!" His eyebrows raised, and the man leaned forward with interest.

"You've read your grandmother's journals?"

This town was so small; these people knew everything about each other. They knew everything about *her*. Pyet stood her ground, ignoring him. She tapped her foot impatiently, which allowed the man another minute of nervous laughter. He shook his head again.

"Fine. Have it your way. *Because*, darling, she owns that house. She protects that house. That house is Elric's best kept secret. And Violet doesn't let anyone forget it."

"Until she died."

There was a moment of silence, where both the old man and Pyet had nothing left to say. He looked at her and she could have sworn she saw tears in his eyes. Who the fuck was Violet Cabello to all of these people?

"Yes," he said finally, dropping his head to his chest. "Until she…died."

"And now, because *I* own this fucking house, I'm the town's pariah."

"It's not your fault."

"I know it's not my fault!" Pyet seethed. She hated that he felt sorry for her. He had the same look in his eyes that Winona had every time she looked at her. It made her feel like she was weak. She was never this small until she arrived in Elric; Pyet didn't know who she was anymore. Elric was making her someone else entirely, someone she couldn't recognize.

"You're the one that asked," the man said defiantly. He turned his body back to his cart of unshelved books.

"I'm sorry," Pyet muttered. "I just want to know why. I want to know why she was so important to this town. I want to know how Elric became this place. I want to know why my mother was so afraid that she left."

He stopped touching the books on the shelves, but he wouldn't turn to face her. The man instead walked away, turning the corner into the stacks of more dusty, old texts. Pyet could hear the cluttered bangs and sounds of shuffling. That must have been it; he was done with her, with their discussion.

Pyet was exactly where she started.

It was only a few minutes or so, but soon Pyet looked up as the man came back around the corner. She wasn't expecting him, assuming he had just left like everyone else did. He came close to her, hesitantly, at first, before swallowing hard and reaching towards her. She watched as his Adam's apple bobbed. She held so much power, with all of these people afraid of her. It was too bad that she had no idea how to use it to her advantage.

Pyet shrunk back from his reach before realizing that he was trying to hand her something—a lot of things, actually. The man shook his hand again, desperate for her to take it. When Pyet didn't, he grunted in frustration and dropped them on the desk in front of her.

She bent over and inspected the papers, touching them gently, like they would disintegrate if she handled them too much. They were incredibly old, torn and frayed, browned from years of weathering. Pyet fingered through them before looking up at the old man. He was back at work, refusing to look up at her again. It was as if he'd given her a gold mine, like he had done something incredibly illegal, and was trying to act as if he hadn't.

Pyet huffed.

The first page had large bolded red letters.

MISSING PERSON.

The picture underneath the letters was someone she

didn't recognize; Pyet didn't know why on Earth she thought she would. Like this would be her big revelation. That this librarian had, in fact, given her a gold mine.

The girl from the page looked back up at her, eyes wide and youthful. She had blonde hair that ran long past the edges of the frame, and her cheeks held a healthy glow of someone that didn't belong in Elric. The further she read, Pyet noticed that she wasn't from here at all. The missing woman in question was from a place just outside of Elric, a place she remembered passing on the bus as she drove in.

"Why did you give me these?" she asked. There was no response from the old librarian, much as she suspected. Pyet frowned and went to the next page. It was another missing person page, though the lettering was different than the last. It was slimmer, not as bolded. But the sentiment was the same. Another person missing, another town she remembered vaguely a few miles from here. In fact, each subsequent page was similar. A lot of faces, old and young, stared back at her. All missing.

It didn't make any sense.

Pyet closed a fist and continued flipping. At some point, the missing persons pages stopped and other various articles replaced them. She read each one from beginning to end, never once stopping before jumping to the next. This was important, she decided. She couldn't decide how or why, but the librarian sent worrying looks at her periodically, and Pyet continued to devour each and every page.

In the end, when she was so full that she couldn't take any more new information, Pyet rested her head on the desk. She closed her eyes and breathed in deeply, not knowing how long she was sitting in that position. When it had seemed that hours had passed, she felt the lightest of feather touches on her shoulder. Pyet's head shot up, and she swung her head back and forth until her eyes landed on the librarian, who smiled sheepishly.

"I'm sorry," he said softly. "I can't have you falling asleep here."

"I wasn't—" she started, before shaking her head. "Never mind."

"Did you learn anything?"

She wasn't sure how to answer that. On one hand, Pyet *did* learn something. There were enough missing person flyers to fill an entire town. On the other hand, she felt like she didn't learn a goddamn thing. What did this have to do with Elric? Why did this plump little librarian hand her a pile of nonsense?

"I learned…" She hesitated, not knowing what answer he was looking for. He did look at her expectantly, wanting something. She wished at this moment that she could read his mind. She wanted so badly to do something right for a change. It seemed that since she stepped foot in this town, nothing she did was the right move. There were no good decisions, no *right* way to feel. She felt wrong.

Pyet wondered if she should have just died instead. It would have been easier that way, letting her mother glide the delicate blade across her throat. It would have been quicker, less painful.

"Pyet?"

"Yes?" she whispered, not loud enough to be as affirming as she wanted to be.

"Welcome back." The librarian looked sad as he shook her out of her daydream. He still had that expectant look about him, like he was still waiting for her to say something. What did he ask her again?

"I learned nothing," she said at last. The man had the audacity to look disappointed. Just another person to add to the list.

"Pyet, you need to *think*. I know Juliette taught you better than that. If she was anything like the girl I remembered, she had a sharp mind about her. Always curious, too curious. She knew where to look."

For some reason, the mention of her mother's name made her irrationally angry. Pyet curled her fingers into fists again, ready to shove the librarian that had given her nothing but piles of useless paper.

"You knew my mother?" she growled, turning to him sharply. His look of defiance came back, and he stood rooted to the ground, unmoving.

"I was hoping she would teach her own daughter some wit," he snapped. What right did he have to be angry? He hadn't even answered any of her questions, not directly.

"They worried that you were smarter than this, Pyet. They had too much faith in you! You're proving them wrong, and they'll still be the ones that benefit. Don't you see that?"

"I don't know what it is I should be looking for," she pleaded.

"You have all the answers in front of you!" he yelled at her. He must have realized how loud he had gotten, looking sharply from one side to another, as if there were someone nearby that could hear him. The librarian sighed before lowering his voice. He still towered over her aggressively, but she was no longer afraid of him.

"I can't do all the work for you, Pyet," he said finally. "At some point, you're going to have to stop asking me. The Danaids. Matilda. Winona." Pyet noticed the distinct disdain that laced his voice when he mentioned her friend's name. "You're going to have to go back into your manor and fight your own demons. You're going to have to do the work needed to find your place here. Stop denying it. Elric won't accept you until you learn to accept it in return."

She was dumbfounded. Pyet didn't know how he knew so

much about her, but she felt her heart breaking. She hated that he was right.

Her mother taught her better than this. *She* was better than this. Pyet was not weak.

She grabbed the papers from the desk and stood up from her chair.

"You don't know the first thing about me," she hissed. The chair she was sitting at screeched against the floor, but it only added to her sense of urgency. She turned to walk away from him.

"I'll leave you with one last piece of advice, Pyet. And then you're on your own." She didn't turn back to face him, but she stopped nonetheless. Her shoulders tightened, her breathing coming in heavy pants as if she had just finished another long run. All she had been doing was running. When he was sure she wasn't leaving, the librarian talked in a low, hurried voice.

"I don't have archives here. There *is no definitive history of Elric that's available to the public.* Coming here to learn, to research, is not welcomed by the Lantern. I've given you everything I could, and your grandmother gave you the rest. You've read it before, Pyet. You know how this town came to be. You know about the Witch and her ghosts. You know why they are afraid of your manor, and the danger those women threaten our safety with. You *know*, Pyet. You have to open your mind to the possibilities. Be smart."

She was done listening to him. Pyet wouldn't allow this man to insult her intelligence any further. She had gotten everything she needed here.

Pyet left the man in the library, and his ominous threats behind.

She was tired of running.

It felt like that was all she kept doing. She ran from her mother's home. She ran from her grandmother's house. She ran from Matilda and Winona. And now, she was running from the librarian she didn't even catch the name of. Pyet was proving his words to be true, proving to be the dumb little girl everyone thought her to be, and not the person she was raised to be.

In her home, her mother was harsh. She was protective, but she knew it was her own twisted way of hardening Pyet. Her mother prepared her for Elric, even if she hadn't known it.

In her youth, it felt like these were things everyone learned. It wasn't weird that her mother had them practice safety drills each week. It wasn't odd that she had to crawl in a small space Juliette built under the stairs whenever someone rang the bell to her home. It was normal.

It was why Pyet was so afraid of Elric to begin with.

She could pretend to be brave all she wanted, she could let the guise of saving her mother be the crutch for the decisions she was making, but in truth? She was frightened. Pyet didn't want this place to be everything her mother told her it would be. She didn't want it to be a place she couldn't find a home in, because then where would she go?

Her travels brought her back to the stallion at the center of town. It was always this fucking stallion. It was the only place she could really feel centered, and that wasn't because it happened to be the middle of Elric. It righted her, made her feel like she could make sense of the world. Even after seeing the statue come to life before her very eyes, she felt safe here.

Pyet lifted her hand and touched the rusted metal, loving the coolness as it shocked her fingertips. She looked up at its muzzle, relieved when it was only slick and smooth metal, the familiar features of a horse frozen mid-neigh, facing the direction of her manor once more.

She had to figure out how Elric came to be. She had to figure out how the Danaids got here, and how this magic worked. She needed to understand the Lantern and her grandmother, and why the people couldn't dare speak her name

And she already knew?

It seemed unlikely, given that she was here contemplating the old man's words. How could she already know something she was still trying to figure out? Pyet bit the bottom of her lip and caught herself in a small squeak. When she brought her fingers to her lips again, there was a small bit of blood that left traces on the pads. She sucked the saltiness into her mouth, swallowing.

The pain sharpened things. Just as it had when she first finished reading her grandmother's journal, her hurt made the world around her more...present. The deep grays in the sky lightened to a beautiful indigo, the buildings were no longer living in shadows. Even the brushes that littered the

Town Circle were less dead looking. Everything cleared up.

Pyet sought out a bench, the same one she sat on the first day she arrived in Elric. She still had the papers she'd taken from the librarian in one hand, and pulled the leather journal from the waistband of her gray slacks. Everything she needed was right in her hands. She just had to think harder. No more questions, Pyet needed to figure it out for herself.

What did she already know about Elric?

She knew the people were afraid of her manor. That was a consistent narrative she'd played a part in since she first arrived. It was the first bit of information that was given. It wasn't a secret, and Matilda told her why. The Danaids.

The women that killed their husbands. It was more than just a story. Pyet didn't believe in mythology, but maybe she should. It was clear that Matilda was leading her to believe that it was more than just a tale you told to scare your children. It was real, and it was haunting her manor on the hill.

Even Violet was distrustful of those murderous women in her letters. Pyet was convinced that she was the last person coming to terms with the fact that her house was home to at least a few dozen ghosts. All of the voices, the visions, all things she tried to ignore. It was them, it had always been them, and they weren't even trying to hide it. Pyet ran a hand along the grooves of the leather, playing with the string that held it together.

Matilda told her story, acting as if it wasn't fiction at all, but she couldn't go back there and ask her for more. The witch wouldn't entertain her even if she wanted to. Pyet was sure no one would give her any more than she'd already taken from them. Everyone was doing the work for her, and Pyet finally understood that she had to do the rest on her own. Just for herself. She wouldn't be able to continue on if she didn't try.

People were starting to slow as the day moved further along. The sun was settling in the middle of the sky, once again covered by looming clouds that threatened to burst with rain, but never did. Elric's residents moved under the awnings of various shopfronts to avoid getting wet, or went inside completely, never to come back out. The figures had become only obstacles. Pyet stopped looking at their faces, not that the townspeople ever cared to look her way anyway. They were blurred faces of people she felt she would never fully get to know. What they looked like was irrelevant.

Besides, Pyet liked being here in the Town Circle when there was no one else around. It was far more peaceful when she didn't have to worry about people's death glares or frightened, erratic movements. The tension in her shoulders lessened, and for the first time in days, she felt like she could relax and focus.

Finally, as if she was waiting for the climax to hit, she opened up the journal. It looked much the same as it had the last time she touched it. Violet's name was printed in the front, her familiar looping signature full of warmth on the first page. There was no immediate lightbulb, no magical memory that arrived with vigor in her mind. It was still a mystery, even here.

Pyet only thought of the photo she found in her mother's old bedroom. Touching her face with delicate fingers, it was easy to imagine the same rounded features, the same cola brown eyes that ignited with…survival. Pyet had never imagined she'd look so similar to Violet. It made sense why Winona always stared a bit too long, or why her mother couldn't approach her unless she was in a drunken stupor. Dragging her index finger across her cheekbones, she almost wanted to look into a mirror, just to confirm it.

But the mirrors here in Elric were dangerous. Since her last encounter, she hadn't looked in one since. Even the promise of seeing her grandmother in her reflection wasn't enough to persuade Pyet.

She tried not to be frustrated. She was so close to the truth, but it alluded her with the speed of a feral cat. Pyet dropped her hands from her face, shaking her head once to continue flipping through the journal she held in a tight grip. She flipped through each page slowly, paying special attention to the margins, eyes darting across each word and every marking to avoid missing something.

She'd been so preoccupied with her grandmother's erratic behavior that sometimes she skimmed Winona's notes completely. They were as unhinged as the entries themselves, with words circled in blue ink, or small notes of just exclamation marks dotting sentences. She underlined a lot of it, with arrows connecting several paragraphs that Pyet couldn't connect on her own.

So what was she missing? What was Winona seeing that Pyet could not?

Her favorite page was one close to the end. It was labeled as number 65, and it was one of the last in this journal. Winona's presence was the heaviest here, and it felt the most important, though that could have been because Violet's tone had changed drastically. In her previous entries, her voice was low and hurried, like she was frightened and unsure of herself. This one was an anomaly.

There was a moment that happened between this one and the last, a moment that wasn't documented for her to see. But the words that lay bare before her were charged with a knowledge that wasn't present in the other entries. It was the version of Violet that Pyet felt her mother got. Confident, Demanding, Rigid. It was the closest Pyet felt to the person Violet was before she died. The person her mother and Elric residents feared.

She skimmed it a few times, almost positive that she

could recite it word for word at this point. The entry wasn't in any riddles, at least not all of it. But there was something hidden in between the lines. Winona thought so too. Pyet could see it in the various question marks and introspective thoughts she wrote in the margins. Something *big* loomed. It was as if Pyet was not looking at a journal entry, but a time portal. Everything was blurry, but it was there, waiting to be found.

If Pyet could understand what it was that made Violet so sure of herself, and sure of the truth she believed to have witnessed, then this would all be easier. Pyet could connect the missing person pages and the journal, and how all of it related to her. She could figure out the secret that this damn town was trying to keep from her.

FROM THE JOURNALS OF

VIOLET CABELLO

Now that I understand, I'm no longer afraid. It all makes sense now. Why was I so scared of the destiny that was laid out before me? I am not allowed to say much more than that, but I am no longer afraid.

The Lantern tells me that I've been chosen. I can't tell if they're upset with me, but if they were, they haven't shown it. I was always meant to play this role, and now that I know the life they've groomed me to lead, I am excited.

My daughter will have a family that will cherish her. That will groom her, too. She will remain an intricate part of Elric's history, and she doesn't even know it yet.

But she will.

It's in her blood.

The Lantern has been gracious with their knowledge. This town was built on secrets, but also on love. It was Aphrodite, after all, who said that love, though painful, was our foundation. I think he meant to say that Aphrodite blessed this town. She was the reason we were still here, after she punished those that were unworthy of it.

Those fucking women.

Juliette will not be like them. She will find a nice man in this town, she will marry him, and have his children. They will be perfect clones ripe for picking, I am sure of it. Wouldn't that be the dream?

I wish I could share more with you, but alas, that is a story for another day (and another journal). For now I hope you are blessed with the knowledge that my girl has changed my world. She, one day, will love Elric as I have come to. She will love the people, and she will love its history, and she will protect the house. She will protect Elric, no matter the cost.

That way, we can preserve the basin, and continue to make sure that these women never escape it. Our journals are our stories. They are our myths. They are the way the Cabello women pass down our history. I can't wait for her to be a part of it, and her daughter thereafter.

Lantern be with you, Lantern guide you. Like a moth to a flame.

There was something there that she hadn't caught before, something Pyet simply glanced over. Her grandmother mentioned the name Aphrodite in her last entry. Aphrodite, the goddess of love, the same one Matilda spoke about before.

Pyet flipped through several pages, seeing the name pulled and mentioned in multiple entries. Of course, she had never been interested in mythology, and she wished desperately that she was. Looking at her grandmother's journal was like looking at an ancient piece of text that hadn't yet been translated.

In Matilda's story, Aphrodite *saved* Aegyptus. She had given him clarity and retribution, damning Danaus' daughters who slaughtered their husbands and sent them to Tartarus. She had taken just one mercy, that of the one who refused to kill. So what had happened to her, the one that got away? She must have escaped; Pyet could not fathom a world in which she would be able to stomach watching over a dozen of her sisters be sentenced to death, no matter their wrongdoing. It made no sense for her to stay, unless she wanted them to suffer. Unless she truly believed that they were evil.

Pyet continued to let her thoughts wander, closing her eyes as she tried desperately to pull strings of memory to the surface. Things she could have missed, other moments she might have looked over, until she could grasp onto something. And it did come, eventually.

Aphrodite's punishment included a basin.

Matilda believed, at least in what she had told Pyet, that the Danaids were in her home. The town was frightened of it, yes, but they always had someone to protect it.

Pyet squeezed her eyes together and scrunched her nose, leaning her head forward into the journal and kicking out her feet in frustration. She was so close.

You are right there. A voice whispered in her ear sharply. It caused Pyet to jolt, but not fully open her eyes. It was probing, insistent, but it was not frightening. It was a voice that was familiar, that was excited. It caused a rush of electricity to flow through her bones. *You know there is magic here, Pyet. Do not rule out that which you do not understand. Look closer at those things. You will find that the answers are right in front of you.*

"You all keep telling me that!" she hissed, cracking her knuckles across the leather from the pressure. "Stop stringing me along and just *tell* me!"

The voice in her head laughed, and that was when she placed it. It was the same sort of laugh she remembered coming from the apothecary. From the mouth of the person who had told her the story to begin with. Matilda.

It is no fun just giving away information. You have to earn it. Your mother had no patience. She couldn't handle it. There was a bite in her words. *She left. And good fucking riddance.*

"GO AWAY!" Pyet shrieked. Her head snapped back and she opened her eyes. People on the street stopped and looked at her. They didn't avoid her face now, as they had since the moment she arrived. Every single person in Elric was staring at her and now they wouldn't look away. This time, their faces showed no resemblance of hatred. It was curiosity, eagerness. It was as if everyone was waiting for this moment, ready for it.

Like this could change everything.

Matilda's laugh filled her head again, loud and obnoxious.

Girl. You can't get rid of me. This town is mine. *This history is* mine. *Those girls are my* sisters. *That house was my* home. *You will figure this out because you MUST. I will not let them die because you are too stupid to understand.*

And then she disappeared. Just as quickly as she appeared, she vanished, and yet, Pyet could still feel her. Matilda was everywhere; she was in front of her, she was behind the eyes of every Elric resident looking at her. She was right behind the stallion. Pyet got up to round the fountain, eager to catch a glimpse of her, to prove to herself that she wasn't crazy, and there she was, just as she imagined.

Matilda was not the same old crone Pyet remembered. She was young, with wide eyes and long blonde hair. Even in this state, Matilda seemed familiar. She looked so much like…

And then she was gone, completely this time. Before Pyet could place her, Matilda disintegrated right before her eyes. Pyet walked along the fountain until she was sure she couldn't see the witch in her periphery, and then returned to her bench, cursing silently to herself.

She grabbed for the journal roughly without stopping, and started to pace.

Matilda did give her more information than she promised. She gave away her sisters, the Danaids. If she hadn't been feeling the electricity running through her veins, and the overwhelming sense of *otherness* from Elric, Pyet wouldn't have believed her. But she did. She believed that Matilda was the one Aphrodite saved. She believed that the women that were haunting her house were the Danaids from her story.

The manor did not want her here, that was for certain. Pyet was no closer to winning its favor as she was when she first arrived. Even trapped in their endless version of Hell, they still found the time to torment her, to force her out of this town.

Matilda did not want to see them suffer; she said so herself. But she was also intent on keeping Pyet here, giving her just enough to want to keep knowing.

Matilda was manipulating her, making her want to stay.

And it was working.

The two narratives did not line up, and it only compounded the confusion that circled her mind. Pyet felt herself clench her fingers together, her nails finding soft skin. The pressure caused bruising and she winced from the pain of it, but she didn't relent. She wanted to feel it, she wanted it to ground her. Pyet was afraid that if she let herself slip too much, she would end up just like her mother; too afraid to find the truth. Too afraid to stay. Maybe it was this that was her mother's undoing. Elric was too much for her, and so she left, just like Matilda said.

Pyet refused to let that be her. For her mother's sake. For hers.

She didn't know where she was heading until she noticed the familiar homes along her side street. Pyet's heels clicked against the cobbled stone, her head down as she walked. This route felt commonplace now, intimate. Like always, the people of this place crossed the street when they saw her. Though this time they seemed to avoid her because she wanted them to, and not because they had to anymore.

She tried not to think about it.

When Pyet was back at her manor it felt like it had been three years since she last slept in it, though it had only been several hours. She had no desire to go in, no desire to approach the Danaids, but Pyet knew that she must. She wouldn't know the truth until she confronted the people behind that door.

The iron fencing was far more intimidating than it should have been. It stood six feet tall, and Pyet guessed that it had been standing for longer than she'd been alive. This entire property, she finally noticed, was horribly old. The front was beautiful and large and marbled. It was grand, but it still showed its age. The color was dulled, the gardens not kept up with. Pyet had really let this place go to the dogs. She wasn't the type of protector that it wanted, or needed.

They let her abandon them.

They *wanted* it, she thought.

It was with that consideration that she trespassed her own property. Pyet stepped through the iron gate and a feeling of wrongness overwhelmed her; she sensed that she was unwelcome here now. So much had changed in such a short amount of time.

Though it wasn't deep in the evening like it had been the night she arrived, Pyet was timid again in the house she had become so accustomed to these last few months. The house that she had made hers. Though, it hadn't really been hers, had it? Pyet had nothing when she came to Elric. No photos, no furnishings, nothing. Everything in this house was *theirs*.

The key slid into the lock easily, and Pyet pushed through the door and entered the foyer. As she passed through the threshold, something large and heavy flew past her, colliding with the wall. The base of what used to be a lamp smashed onto the floor, its glass bulb shattering into a thousand tiny pieces. Its crisp white shade lay crumpled on the floor next to her.

It was *them* letting her know that they were here.

They were communicating to her in the only way they knew how. Shards of glass were cracking underneath her feet as she stared at the scene before her. Her fingers curled into her fists, her body quaking from the aggressive energy that was palpable from where she stood.

Pyet didn't ask for this. She didn't ask for any of it.

"Show yourselves!" she screamed. Her voice echoed off the walls, up the stairs and down the long forgotten hallways. The hallways her grandmother once walked. The hallways her mother escaped from so long ago.

There was silence as her echoing ceased. If Elric forced itself into a bubble in the world, the manor was even more isolated. The air was sucked out of each room like a vacuum.

And then they spoke.

"*You cannot force us outside of our own home,*" they warned. All of their voices were in unison. They were all one person, but they were many. Pyet felt the goosebumps along her arms raise, and the hair rose along the back of her neck. They were here. And she was welcoming them with feisty, angered arms.

"This is *my* home," Pyet told them. She spoke loudly and clearly, and even if she didn't believe it, she hoped her voice made her sound as confident as she wanted it to.

"You are such a stupid, silly girl." A voice separated itself from the pack. She was shrill and high pitched, and her flustered breathing made it seem like even just the smallest sentence was enough effort to tire her. She sounded exhausted, already; and yet, exhausted or not, she was still full of threat. "This world is not meant for you. And this is not your manor."

"You don't even think it's true. Look at you!" Another

voice sounded from her left, making Pyet jump. It sounded so close to her, yet so far away. She felt prickles along her backside. "You're so weak. So pathetic. A little *girl*. You're not your grandmother, or your mother. This is no longer your home. This is *our* home. We will be prisoners no longer. We will be…"

The wind rushed around her, the curtains flying off their racks, the walls rattling. Pyet could hear shattering glass in the distance. The house came to life before her, and she was too weak to turn it off. There was magic all around her, but no magic *inside* of her. Pyet couldn't fight the power of this home, she couldn't fight the Danaids and win.

"You are *not* that powerful!" she screamed at them, trying to hold back the tears at the corners of her eyes that were threatening to break free. Since the first day she saw them, Pyet had convinced herself that they were illusions. They couldn't be anything harmful, just a home with too many memories. The stories her grandmother wrote were much of the same, just memories and the ramblings of a young person afraid of the dark. But memories couldn't harm her, not really.

And yet, these women were screaming at her. Throwing things at her. They very much *could* harm her. And she had been living here, too oblivious to their true motives to do something about it. She should have pushed it with Winnie, she should have stayed until Matilda—damn that witch— taught her what the mythology meant. There were so many things Pyet wished she had done before this moment, where her hands were wrapped around her head and she was crouching close to the floor to avoid the objects flying around her.

"*Girl*," they whispered, and Pyet almost sobbed. The voice was the house now. It was coming from in between the walls.

It was coming from the heart of it. *"We are more powerful than you could imagine."*

"We loved her," an isolated woman said, seemingly weeping from the corner of the room. "Your grandmother. She protected us from all of them."

The chill in the air settled around her, and Pyet looked up once the sudden gusts of wind had all but disappeared. The house was in mourning, wincing from the layers of hurt that were being peeled before her. They were wounded, left alone after the death of Violet Cabello. Of course they loved her.

"I'm sorry," she murmured, breathing in deeply. She needed to keep them lost in their history as she constructed a plan. Her mother had always taught her to have a plan, and several weeks in Elric seemed to be enough to make Pyet forget all she'd been taught.

A dangerous, fleeting idea flashed across her mind. *What if her mother was right, all this time?*

No. That couldn't be. Things in Elric were uncertain, but she had founded an unlikely friendship in Winona. She found herself within the discovery of this beautiful mystery of her grandmother. This was where she felt like she belonged, for the first time in her life, despite everything happening within it. How was it that she could find too many reasons to leave, and yet not one of them was strong enough to make her jump on the bus home? Pyet *knew* her grandmother, even with just one journey within her diary, and her mother had drawn a knife to her throat.

It was so much easier to side with a dead woman. Pyet didn't need to go home; she just needed to find the strength she had built after a lifetime of trauma to break through this fog.

"We don't need you to be sorry," they all hissed together in unison. *"We need you to get out of our way."*

"I just want to live here! I want to learn!" Pyet was practically begging them now. "Please let me understand my grandmother. Why my mother left!"

"Your mother was the only smart person in this town. We made her leave. It was the only way to save her."

"Save her from what?" Their words were feeding her, giving her a reason to keep her eyes open. Pyet crawled along the floor, starving for information, wanting so badly to inhale each and every word they would give her.

She almost forgot that she was trying to find a way to escape them.

"Save her from this town, Pyet. What else?"

There were so many moving pieces that Pyet couldn't keep them all together. She didn't know who wanted her to go, or who wanted her to stay. There were so many haunting memories in Elric, so many moments of hurt and betrayal. Pyet had never felt so...invigorated. This was what being human felt like, something her mother so desperately wanted to keep her from. She wanted to feel everything, even if it hurt.

"You know nothing but the walls that keep you here," she argued. "You don't know what it's actually like out there."

"You, who have lived here for less than a year, cannot tell us what we know, girl. We created this town. Elric is here because we died. How has it taken you this long to understand?"

"I don't understand what you mean."

"I thought we taught Juliette better than this," one snapped at another. Pyet could visibly feel the shrug in the air. The disappointment.

"Juliette was fractured. She was broken. It is not her fault her daughter knows nothing."

"Then we must teach her."

It didn't matter that they put words in my ears every day. I knew the truth. I knew what was coming, and I would continue to serve those people that had given me everything, that continue to shower me with what I've been searching for. Elric was my home, and they will not tarnish it.

Those women are putting bees in my brain. And I won't let them do this to Juliette, too.

I like that our names rhyme. It's such a little thing, but it makes me smile. I've been needing more of those types of things lately, things that make me happy. While I am forced to live here, I need to search for any little thing that I can.

Danaus Solstice is approaching.

I am preparing, but I was told I cannot

participate as I'd like to. I think that is for good reason. My role in this has shifted. But someday, my daughter will participate.

I think that thought gives me enough happy to last a few days.

When Pyet opened her eyes again, she was no longer in the manor, but in a field. There were flowers everywhere, the sun was sitting high in the midday sky, and yet, there was a feeling of melancholy that surrounded them. She was not alone. There were dozens of women around her, wrapped in garments akin to what she had been used to within Elric. It felt oddly comforting, to be fully enveloped by so many people. There was safety in numbers, and she was nothing but a needle in the haystack. Falling to the shadows felt good for a change.

Pyet tried to catch her barings, starting with placing herself. She couldn't tell where she was at, though common sense told her that she was in Elric. She had to be. There was no other place the women in the manor would take her. Not if they were trying to teach her something, not if they were trying to get her to understand. This had to be Elric, though it looked nothing like the town she was in now. This was an earlier time, a much simpler time.

She felt an overwhelming sense of calm rush through her. It was here, circled by people she didn't know, that Pyet felt fully in control of herself. With her wits about her, she felt steadily grounded. Pyet was comforted knowing that she was still herself, even if her mind was trapped in this illusion.

The women around her didn't look alike, but they all seemed very close. Some held hands, some kissed the others' cheeks. All of them were talking in hushed whispers to one another. The sense of sisterhood they seemed to share made her heart twitch with jealousy. To have a family like that was something she craved, and the feeling sat in her belly like a heavy stone.

The only woman who stood out was standing to the side smoking a cigarette, away from her grouping. Pyet could tell that she wasn't exactly a part of the gathering, but she wasn't an outsider either. The woman just seemed…other. She had no hushed conversations, and no interest in inclusion. Instead, she just flicked the bud of her cigarette and frowned into the distance.

That was, until she stared right at Pyet.

Pyet's heart jumped, and she felt the goosebumps rise on every inch of skin. This woman was dangerous. She was an enemy. Pyet took a step backward, eyes flitting side to side before she crouched close to the ground to avoid her gaze. Hidden behind two women who giggled at her conspiratorially, she tried to make herself smaller.

The woman's eyes did not follow her movements.

Instead, they continued gazing upon the gaggle of others before her—a feast to be worshiped. She had the pick of the crop, and Pyet could tell from the hungry look in her eyes that she was searching for someone to take a bite out of.

But, at least she hadn't been staring at *her*. The woman's eyes stayed trained on her prey, like a predator stalking behind tall grasses, and then she was on the move. She weaved between the others, though they were not mad. Some grasped her shoulder gently as she walked by. Others looked at her with bashful gazes and longing sighs. She was something of an idol, a leader.

A god.

The woman respectfully disentangled herself from the grouping, making her way towards the front of the large crowd. They were all eager for whatever it was she had to say to them, and as they stared at this chosen woman with disdain and jealousy in their eyes, Pyet finally understood.

They worshiped her. They wanted her. They wanted to *be* her.

"My loves, this is the place. It is ours, and I am happy to say that we've done it. We've escaped the terrors that awaited us in the neighboring hell holes, away from those gruesome *men*, and we have created something new. Something good. Something extraordinary, even. Today, you are brave. You left your homes, your husbands, your children, to follow me. I am so humbled to have your trust and devotion."

What things could a woman like that say to get them to follow her so blindly? What was she giving them that made them abandon their homes?

As Pyet looked away, trying to find her way back home, a familiar face caught in her periphery. She had seen that face before. She was sure of it. It was swimming in her memory, just waiting to be caught by a line. She grasped for it, squinting her eyes and tugging, reeling it in with every ounce she had left in her.

When it hit her, it was like she was being run over by a truck. Of course she's seen her before. So recently, in fact. Pyet had seen her within the missing person's pages she'd retrieved from the library.

The longer Pyet looked around, faces were becoming clearer and more recognizable. She'd seen several people around her within those pages. If she kept looking, Pyet was certain that she could have placed every single missing person's image to their respective page. All of these people were from different places, families, lifestyles.

So why were they here?

"You've chosen this path, to leave the world as you knew it behind, and to the future that is ours. A future where you never have to suffer at the hands of men again. I, Amorette Cabello, will make sure you are safe. That is my promise to you. "

Several heads nodded in unison. Pyet moved her head along with them, begging to not look out of place.

"I promise you freedom. I promise you eternal life. If you believe in me, if you believe in Matilda and what we can do together, you will have no fears. You will have no worries."

Pyet could have sworn she saw tears in the eyes around her. Her gaze was transfixed on Amorette, taking in each feature she could. It was her great-grandmother, it had to have been. It was a person that started it all.

Pyet felt like she was going to faint.

"Oh, dear moths…there's work to be done."

"Yes, Lantern," they all chanted in unison.

When Pyet awoke, she was back in her own bed. The comforter was tucked into her sides, the feeling of disorientation making her head tilt to the side. Her head lolled as she blinked. She couldn't tell if she was still in a dream, or if anything she remembered happened at all.

The Danaids played a trick on her, that's what this was. They were planting things in her brain, trying to confuse her, trying to make her feel like there was something else she should believe.

As if they weren't the dangerous ones. As if they wouldn't kill her on the spot.

But why for? She didn't want to believe any of it. She had seen things in Elric, but Pyet couldn't help but cling to the hope that all of it didn't exist. It wasn't as bad as her mother wanted it to be. If it was, then all of this would have been for nothing.

They keep telling me to leave, but I can't.

The Danus Solstice is tonight, and everyone is watching. No one told me who would be here or why, but there are eyes everywhere. Whoever they are, they're watching me. And, Mother would kill me if she saw me even near the door. But still the ghosts, the women, they won't stop their haunting. It's getting ridiculous. Everywhere I look something is broken, someone is moaning, or the walls are quaking.

I thought this would be it, but I think I got ahead of myself. Elric is impossible to escape.

I wasn't invited to the Solstice last year, but I'm not sure I want to be a part of this one, even though I desperately wanted to be included last year. It's much more frightening than I pictured.

They keep looking at me like something special is going to happen. They're looking at me like they're scared, but also like they're expecting something. They're whispering when they think I'm not looking, and those around town are jealous when they glance at me. As if I had something to do with this, as if I chose this.

No one prepared me for the Solstice.

Mother tells me I have a choice to make tonight. It feels important, and she's making it seem like the fate of the entire world rests on that choice. It didn't feel like this last year, or the year before. Mother was the one making the choice that time. But whatever it is, it'll keep us here, she said. It will help keep Elric strong, and young, and thriving.

It's how these people I've known my whole life have stayed the same. No matter how much time has passed, the witch lets them stay if we make this choice every year. She keeps us alive.

I'm terrified for when they tell me what this choice actually is. Whatever sacrifice we're having to make to stay here isn't worth it. It can't be. My mother hasn't been the same since she was chosen, and I don't want that to happen to me, too.

I'm nervous to drink from the fountain. I'm nervous for this dinner. I don't know what's going to happen, and I'm afraid that if I find out, it'll be the straw that makes me break.

It'll mean I have to leave for good, and not just talk about it anymore.

And who will make the choice then, when I leave?

Will I be the reason for Elric's demise, or will they find someone else to use?

DAY 60

11:30 AM

Pyet could still feel the tendrils of the nightmare wrapping around her mind like a sinister serpent. The vivid images of the dream still played in her head, taunting her with their twisted reality. But deep down, Pyet knew that what she had seen was no mere figment of her imagination. As she stumbled out of bed and made her way to the window, she could feel the magic of Elric pulsing all around her. The town was alive with a sinister energy, one that sent shivers down her spine. And as the sun's rays spilled into her home, she couldn't shake the feeling that something was waiting for her just beyond the threshold.

The air was thick with a musty scent, one that seemed to seep into her very soul. Pyet tried to ignore the creeping unease that gnawed at her. The world seemed to twist and writhe around her, as if it was alive with some kind of malevolent force. She tried to convince herself that it was just her imagination, that her mind was simply playing tricks on her, just like the women in the house, just like the nightmare they trapped her in. But she knew better.

The sun was setting, casting an eerie orange glow over

the town, cascading into her window and down the stairs. Pyet's heart hammered in her chest as she crept out into the deserted foyer, the only sound the eerie hum of magic all around her. Her bare feet tapped against the tile, her mind a blank slate.

And then it all came at her, barreling into her with a force that practically pushed her back into the railing. Pyet stumbled, reaching out her hand to catch herself. As she fell through the darkness, the pieces finally clicked into place. The missing posters she uncovered in the library were not a mere collection of antique articles, but people she had already *met*.

The pain was unbearable, her wrist shooting sparks of hurt throughout her arm, but Pyet forced herself to focus on the puzzle unfurling before her. She tried hard to remember each face, memorizing the contours of their cheeks and the gauntness of their eyes. Squeezing her eyes shut, she knew she had it. She tugged harshly on the string of memory, letting it lead her through the labyrinth she'd created within her mind. And now, as she approached its frayed ends, she knew that she had seen each of those faces deep within the memory her ghosts had placed her in.

Elric was founded on those people, stolen from homes not far from here; corralled, coerced...persuaded?

Though, they didn't seem like they were forced at all. In fact, the townspeople seemed too willing to follow in the footsteps of the woman at the helm. A Cabello; her family, her ancestry.

Realization happened slowly, but the longer she stayed in the silent foyer, she knew the Danaids were giving her time to think. And it *was* coming, Pyet could feel each gear in her head turn, and welcomed each epiphany that manifested within her until it felt like she was entirely new.

Pyet was no longer befuddled, her eyes no longer glazed

over with the hazy glow of a crystal ball. For the first time since stepping into Elric, she felt completely clearheaded.

The manor came to life before her, the remnants of broken glass still littering the ground, sunshine flowing through its pieces and creating faded rainbows against the wallpaper.

Pyet slid barefoot between each slab of glass, careful not to step on their sharp edges. She stood in the very center, the chandelier that adorned the ceiling swinging dangerously from side to side. She didn't realize it before, but the chandelier looked just like her family crest. Pyet wondered if that was what inspired it; the same teardrop shaped crystals hung from delicate chains as it did from their triangular tapestry. They moved back and forth with an invisible wind, threatening to fall on top of her.

As if the manor was warning her, once again.

And then, three loud knocks sounded on her front door.

Pyet's head snapped to attention. She hated that this was how they always found her, and it was always Winona. In fact, she was the only person to ever walk up the marbled staircase leading to the manor besides her; no one in Elric besides the two people who saw it as home. The scene that played out before her was just like the others, like she was stuck in a loop.

The silhouette was the same, her elongated body casting shadows far larger. Winona's shadow was tall and imposing, and Pyet could have sworn she saw several clawed nails curl inward before she tapped on the door again.

Pyet slowly walked towards the door. It felt like quicksand, her feet sinking further and further down into the tile, elongating the seconds between her and the door. When she reached for the knob, it turned on its own, and Pyet had to jump backwards to avoid the heavy door as it swung back on its own accord.

She felt like she was experiencing several bouts of déjà vu. Winona's arms were now crossed, a scowl etched across her face. Her eyebrows arched so high they could crawl off her face, and her eyes were laced with an emotion Pyet couldn't decipher. Worry, maybe?

"Pyet." she said curtly. Winona's gaze penetrated the deepest parts of her soul. She was looking for something, Pyet realized. Winona was practically looking through her, trying to seep into her mind. After their last conversation, she shouldn't be surprised. She wondered what it was Winona would find there, and if she would like the answers she received.

"We don't have much time."

She blew past Pyet, walking through the house as if she lived there herself. Winnie looked so comfortable, maneuvering through the hallways as the manor catered to her every move. Pyet watched as the walls expanded and retracted, breathing in deeply as Winona made her way to the kitchen. It morphed around her, shifting as she moved.

Pyet followed her silently, staying several steps behind as if to not be caught off guard. When she reached the threshold of the kitchen, her feet would not move a single inch further. She hadn't come by since she'd seen the women cooking in it that first week. It seemed so long ago now, but the image was burned into her retinas, and she couldn't quite shake the visual. Without warning, memories of her hauntings invaded her body again. The cruel images in every mirror—now covered with sheets from the linen closets—and the angry touches that wouldn't end.

"They won't hurt you here." Winona sounded confident, but it still was not enough to allow Pyet's feet to move on their own accord. She felt a slight pressure on her backbone, and shivers shot up her spine. Another push and Pyet was forced into the kitchen, her head snapping back to see her assaulter, but finding only the empty halls behind her.

"You came with a purpose," Pyet finally let out, wrapping her arms around herself. She pressed her back against the farthest wall, keeping as far away as she was able to be. "I learned what I could, but your secrets run deep. Every time I feel like I'm getting close, it slips from my grasp again."

Winona stared at her, eyes no larger than slits.

"I am not here to beg you to do more research, Pyet. Your time is up."

She didn't know what that meant, but by the way concern flashed across Winona's features, Pyet felt her heart rate quicken. It pounded so loudly in her chest that she couldn't hear anything else.

"I'm not quite sure what you mean."

The worry was gone now, replaced by hard, creased lines and furrowed brows. It was as if Winona couldn't decide what she thought of Pyet. Some days, it felt like she pitied her, and others it felt like she was no better than the townspeople, thinking Pyet a pariah. She was always speaking in riddles, and Pyet couldn't quite decipher what she meant. As she tried to wrap her head around her confidant's cryptic message, Winona's frustration reached a boiling point.

Without warning, she slammed her fists onto the countertop, making Pyet jump. The impact reverberated through the room, causing the windows to rattle. Winona's eyes burned with anger as she glared at Pyet.

"You really are dafter than I thought you were," she hissed, her voice barely above a whisper. "You had all the time in the world, but your mother never taught you as well as she should have. Juliette...the *traitor*."

Pyet could feel her heart pounding in her chest. As if sensing her confusion, Winona let out a dark laugh. "Oh, you poor, poor girl. Don't you see? It's already too late. They're coming. And when they get here, they won't spare anyone. Not even you."

Pyet's mind was reeling. Who was coming? What did Winona mean by "they"? But before she could ask, a deafening roar shook the ground beneath their feet. The lights flickered, and the room was plunged into darkness.

Pyet's eyes managed to adjust to the dim light, and she could see Winona's silhouette against the window. She was staring out into Elric, her hands shaking.

"Winona, what's happening?" Pyet asked, her voice barely audible.

"They're here," Winona whispered. "They're finally here."

Pyet's back was pressed back into the cabinets. She could hear movement from the front of the house, but she didn't want to go. They would come eventually, just like Winona said. The sounds grew louder, things were tossed to the ground, and Pyet could hear the thunderous footsteps as they echoed through the hallways. It was mere moments before she saw them, large hooded figures with shadows over their faces crashing through the kitchen in a pack.

She watched the figures saunter into her home, uninvited and unwelcome, feeling powerless as they rifled through her cabinets and climbed her staircase, making themselves at home as if they had every right to be there. They were so calm, so methodical. It was as if they already knew what they were looking for and where to find it.

As they disappeared upstairs, Pyet's instincts told her to run, to escape before it was too late. But something inside her refused to give up her home so easily. She felt like a warrior defending her territory against an invading army.

She turned to face Winona, who had been watching her reaction curiously.

"You can't do anything, Pyet. They will not leave."

"Why are they here?" Her breaths were coming out in short pants, her heart beating to the pace of each hurried whisper.

"The *Danaus Solstice*." Winona said it with reverence. There was a beauty to the phrase when it left her lips; it sounded ethereal. She said it with so much confidence that Pyet knew she should have done more. She should have tried harder to understand. Surely someone who was this entranced by it meant there was something special coming.

And yet, she couldn't stifle the fear that laced her veins.

"Every year, we come together in this house," Winona continued, walking around the kitchen island and stepping between hooded figures as they searched the cabinets. "Every year we invite someone into our world. And we make them eat."

It wasn't the answer that she was expecting, but Pyet clung on to every word.

"We had to have smaller celebrations of course, every now and then. That was a more recent development. We'd been starved of *the right one*, for several years. The Solstice didn't work once a year like it had been. It required…more. But, Pyet, I have a feeling that you're going to change that for us. I think, *we* think, that you're the solution. You're going to help Elric become whole again."

"We've been waiting for you for a long time," Winona continued. "I wondered if you would be like your mother, but it turns out you're more like us, after all. Not as flighty as she was. I think Violet would have liked that in you. I think she would be a bit sad that she wasn't here to watch you be memorialized."

The figures now surrounded them, closing in from all ends. They reached out to her, like a family. Pyet knew she had to run, but she couldn't help herself.

It felt good to feel needed.

The hooded figures sat around a long table, their faces hidden in shadows. Pyet could feel their cold, penetrating gaze on her skin, sending shivers down her spine. Her heart raced as she frantically tried to remember how she had ended up in this strange room that seemed to have appeared from the depths of her nightmares. With every passing second, she felt an urgent sense of dread engulfing her as if something sinister lurked just beyond the shadows. The walls were ancient and decaying, covered in thick cobwebs and dust. It was as if this room had been locked away for centuries, only to be opened for this terrifying dinner party.

The silence was oppressive, only interrupted by the occasional sound of shifting robes or a scraping of a fork against an empty plate. Pyet found herself unable to speak, to break the tension. Her legs felt like lead, and her arms were heavy as she tried to push herself out of the chair, but the combination of fear and inertia kept her firmly seated, as if the chair had rooted itself to the floor. She felt like a fly caught in a spider's web, unable to move as the hooded figures surrounded her, with herself and Winnie at either end.

"Would you like some wine?" Winnie's smile was large, her lips stretching until Pyet could see the whites of her teeth from across the long dinner table. Pyet kept her mouth clamped shut, her eyes flicking from Winona's face to the empty plate sat in front of her.

Winona nodded her head towards the hallway that led to the kitchen, where another robed figure emerged with a singular stemmed glass on a silver tray. The red liquid that sloshed inside of it spilled over the edge as they walked, dropping speckled red stains across the carpet. When the glass was placed in front of her, Pyet couldn't help but stare as its deliverer retreated.

It was deep and dark like the color of fresh blood and swirled with a dangerous elegance, inviting the unsuspecting victim closer. As the liquid settled, the scent of ripe berries and aged oak crept into the air, a hint of its origins and potential dangers. Pyet breathed in deeply, capturing it in full as the audience around her sat in stoic silence, waiting with bated breath.

As she lifted her gaze, the mysterious individuals had removed their hoods. Her heart dropped into the pit of her empty stomach. The faces that now stared at her were ones she'd seen before; the faces of the men and women the ghosts presented to her in their memory. Pyet scanned each face, identifying the crooks and features that made each one so unique, and she was sure of it.

These people, who had followed her great grandmother into the furls of Elric's creation, were sitting right in front of her. They invaded her home, they walked the same streets she had for months. But how did they withstand time's cruel aging for so long? They were carbon copies of what she'd remembered, not aging though time had passed.

Winnie paid no attention to her unmasked confusion. Her smile was curling in on itself, the maleficent delight that sparkled in her eyes defining the moment so poignantly that it burned into the back of Pyet's brain. She knew, all along.

The realization was not new. Pyet's instincts had certainly picked up on the otherness of this place since she arrived. The strings that tied her moments together in Elric were becoming intricately knotted, and she pulled hard on them so as to watch them fall before her. It felt good to be right, and it felt right to be frightened. But Pyet was so proud to have finally unraveled her family's secrets that she almost didn't care about the rest of it anymore.

She proved herself worthy, even if the task was assigned by herself and to her herself alone. No one would praise her, and no one would acknowledge this small success but her. It was worth it, she thought, despite its consequences. Whatever those may be.

The glass trembled, as if eager to unleash its sinister secrets onto her, but she couldn't look away from it again. She pulled her gaze away from the missing townspeople, focusing solely on the offered wine. Its appearance alone was enough to make one shudder, imagining the twisted paths that led to its creation and the demons it may have awakened. The red wine in the stemmed glass was not to be trusted, a harbinger of doom waiting for its next victim.

And yet, her delicate fingers wrapped around the glass, and she lifted the wine to her lips.

This was her reward for solving Violet's mystery, the rich coating of grape and berries as it traveled down her throat.

December

DAY 61

3:33 AM

She dreamt of moths.

There were hundreds of them, thousands of them. Just her, the moths, and the darkness. Pyet wasn't sure why, but she wasn't afraid, either. There was something about moths that calmed her. Maybe it was because they were traveling in a pack. Swarms of them surrounded her, crafting large shadows that moved in unison in the umber glow. Moths of all shapes and sizes fluttered, their powdery wings casting an eerie glow in the darkness. Pyet studied the moths, taking in every detail of their iridescent wings and delicate antennae.

Pyet was nowhere, in a place like limbo where there was no beginning and no ending. She felt as if she might have been at the center of the universe, but there was no telling if that was true.

All she knew were the moths.

They reminded her of Elric, flocking together. Moths, like the townspeople she had come to know, were creatures drawn inexorably toward the light. They couldn't help themselves, even though they knew it would be their undoing. And just like the moths, Pyet had always been drawn to the light of the townspeople, their closeness and big, fancy houses calling to her even though she knew there was something dangerous lurking beneath the surface. That was not to say she was the only one. The townspeople, too, followed their light. The mysterious Lantern, who she had only seen from a distance, was the god they worshiped. He was their undoing, too.

But the moths were more than just beings attracted to light. Pyet's mother once said that they were also symbols of death, and the longer Pyet fell into deep limbo, the more certain she was.

She was going to die.

Her eyes closed, but not for long. She realized that there was something in her mouth. Something fluttering, alive. Pyet's eyes shot wide as she opened her mouth and dozens of moths flew out, their wings beating furiously as they took to the air. Pyet watched in horror as they circled her head, their papery wings brushing against her face.

What was happening to her? She stumbled, still coughing and choking as more moths escaped from her lips. They were everywhere, swirling around her like a cloud of living darkness. Her feet tripped over something in the dark; Pyet fell hard onto the floor, knocking the wind out of her lungs. Still, the moths didn't stop. They flew in and out of her mouth, filling the air with their soft fluttering.

As she lay there, gasping for air, tears streamed down her face.

She was no longer in control of her own life. The moths were now her masters, and she was nothing more than a puppet on their strings. With a cry of despair, Pyet closed her eyes again, pressing them hard together. Maybe if she tried hard enough to wake herself up, it would all be over.

But deep down, she knew that the nightmare was only just beginning.

She awoke on top of the very same table she drank at. Pyet couldn't move, her hands tied to the legs, tightened so much that any type of movement caused her pain. She whimpered, the constant wobble of the table as the world moved beneath her turning Pyet green with sickness. She turned her head sideways, leaning her cheek against the polished wood. It was cool to the touch, a small relief as she was carried.

She *was* being carried.

The thought should have frightened her, but she was, in fact, grateful. It was like a dream, her brain hazy with little recollection. There was peace in not knowing where she was, and what was awaiting her. It should have worried her, but the fogginess that clouded her mind wouldn't let her. It wouldn't allow Pyet any free moment to stress and worry. It made her comfortable. It made her feel…nothing.

Ignorance was bliss.

She was far from her home now, and as Pyet turned her head back to face the sky, she noticed nothing but deep, navy blue clouds. It was as if the hyperbolic gloom of Elric had lifted like a veil. The town was rejoicing in her freedom. Because Pyet *did* feel free. Maybe not in the literal sense—she tried once again to move her wrists against the restraints with no success—but in her mind, she was liberated.

She had no reason to fear, not in this semi-drunken, delusional state. She didn't have to worry that her mother would perish without her. There was no more desire to find buried secrets. She had no fear that she would never find a place that she belonged. Pyet was, for the first time, able to let herself breathe.

And Elric did this for her.

Whatever had been in that wine was strong. It knocked her out cold, so much so that Pyet couldn't remember any of her dreams. It was another welcomed relief. Everything in Elric was brighter now. Everything was more colorful. There were no longer any shadows that lurked in alleyways, no dark covers of eerie night looming over them all. Elric was celebrating.

Pyet took a second to get her bearings. She kicked her legs out and realized that those, too, were strapped down tight. With her limbs as useless as they were, she had to rely on her eyes to see. She blinked them once or twice to clear the blurriness that formed at the creases of her eyelids and focused on what she could find within her periphery. Beyond the blueness of the night sky, there was nothing to allude to daylight breaking anytime soon. This told her that she hadn't been asleep for too long.

She must have only been out for a few minutes at most. Maybe less. It was dinner she'd been served, after all. Time in Elric was beginning to make absolutely no sense to her. She didn't know how they could have gotten her here in such a short amount of time, but they had. And here she was.

To her right, she could see the Elric buildings pass her by. She could tell as they took each step that they were moving slowly, but the hare never did beat the tortoise at the race. She didn't mind the slowness. It allowed Pyet to take in the beauty of the homes she lived near. She had taken it for granted as long as she'd been here.

They were large and grand, but they started to feel like home. Even her manor, in all of its oddity and haunting.

The ones she passed were ones she had walked beside for months. She recognized the landmarks—the graying pillar on the house down the street from the manor that had a deep crack running down its base, the window at her neighbor's overflowing with greenery that she could never replicate with her black thumb.

Everything was familiar.

To her left, Pyet could see nothing past a large man that held the table she was lying on. She didn't recognize the face, their features covered in a dark gray hood. The garment looked like it flowed behind him, though she couldn't see past his waist. They all looked like that, she noticed. There were at least six of them surrounding her. They each ignored her, but Pyet wasn't keen on speaking to any of them. She felt as if she shouldn't say a word, feared that it would be a mistake. She was tied to a table, after all. Anything Pyet could have done in that moment felt like it would have been a mistake.

She didn't want to disappoint them. Violet's letters talked about how wonderful Elric and its people were. She was starting to see it herself, the more the colors bloomed before her eyes. How could someone not love a place as close as this one? Pyet was desperate to cling to that. Violet was the only person that had made her feel like she could create a home here. Elric made her feel something again. Not every emotion was a good one, but it was better than feeling nothing at all.

As they moved her, she tried to focus on the noises

around her. It was easier to do that than to spiral through her thoughts. That was what Pyet was craving; any way to *forget*. Even though these people had tied her up and drugged her, she only wanted to fall deeper into their clutches. Pyet longed to avoid having to think; for once, she wanted just to *experience*.

The even, rhythmic steps of the figures beside her were too hard to ignore. They were the only noises, in fact, that Pyet could focus on. Even if there was something else echoing in the distance, she wasn't sure she would be able to think about much else. Her fogginess was beginning to fade, and what remained was an overwhelming sense of unease. Her wrists and ankles were pained from rope burn, and each step beneath her wobbled the table so that she rocked from side. Liberated or not, she was not free. She was trapped here, underneath these restraints.

The people that carried her hummed something she couldn't recognize. It was almost too low for her to hear at all, but it was there. Small, unusual noises that sung to a melody, welcoming her home. They were chanting something in another language, something that sounded achingly familiar. That was when it hit her. Their singing struck a chord inside of her, and Pyet's heart twisted so tightly in her chest that she wanted to grasp at it. It was the sounds that personified the language Violet sometimes expressed in her journals. It had to be. They were singing in Greek.

The sounds that followed secured the realization in Pyet's mind; she was utterly captivated by it. She could see it written out before her, as if Pyet had the journal right there in her grasp. This was the language of Elric, the language of her grandmother, and it was beautiful to listen to.

While she was entranced by their chanting, she didn't think to pay attention to the other happenings around her. But, at once, the men that held the table she was strapped to stopped, and Pyet felt the jolt as they lowered her to the ground. She could hear the wooden legs of the table creak as it hit the pavement. All but one took a large step away, as if she was contagious. Pyet strained to look at them, but her head couldn't move far enough and she couldn't see.

The one that stayed behind tore a blade from his robe, and her heart skipped when she saw the reflection from the knife as it sat in his grasp, reminding her so much of her mother's movements as he cradled it. He brought his hand to one of her wrists, sawing at the rope until one cuff was free. She brought her arm to her chest immediately, keeping it close and out of harm, grateful for the tingles that sped through her veins at the lax of pressure.

He did the same to the other arm.

When their chanting finally stopped, Pyet blinked. With both of her wrists now free, she could move again. She was hesitant to sit up, worried that she wouldn't be welcomed by the sight that was inevitably awaiting her. Her daydreams felt much more safe to be in, and she longed to stay in that space for as long as she was able.

But something was calling her, and she felt her body move without her mind's permission. Pyet moved her hands to press against the wood beside her and pushed herself up into a sitting position. Her head buzzed with blood rush, and she shook it before daring to open her eyes.

At first glance, she saw nothing past the people in robes that carried her here. They were all sorts of sizes, and Pyet thought she recognized a few of them. It was hard to say. Their hoods were pulled over their heads and were covered by shadows, but she thought that they were familiar.

As the horizons cleared, more and more familiar faces crossed her line of sight. People from shops she'd frequented, some that never once spoke to her but looked from a distance. It was almost as if the entire town was here, waiting for her.

What were they waiting for?

"Pyet." The voice from the hooded figure before her echoed in the distance. It bounced off the ground, surrounding her with sound. It was omnipresent. Pyet hadn't recognized the Town Circle before now, but as she glanced around, it was obvious. They were situated at the base of the old, rusted stallion, the water spouting from its mouth for the first time. She didn't think it was possible. The fountain hadn't been running since she set foot here. Now the stallion was hooves deep in a shallow puddle of water. The fountain was only half full, never going past the eroded water line at midway, and she could have sworn that the horse blinked. Around them, the brush and grass were more alive then they'd ever been. It was as if the life of the stallion was seeping into the pores of the Town Circle. It was giving it the life they'd been craving so badly. The greenery lapped at the opportunity, blooming to a point where she might have said it was overgrown.

It wasn't possible for it to be this way in such a short period of time.

What was this magic here?

"Are you with us?" the voice said again, but it was far away. She wanted to answer them, but it was proving to be impossible. Pyet couldn't focus on anything other than the beauty of the Town Circle, the stallion behind her, and the people sitting before her. They were an audience, and Pyet couldn't figure out why she was the main attraction.

"You shouldn't have put so much in her wine. She needs to see. She needs to understand. She can't when she's basically useless." They waved their hands in front of her, and Pyet struggled to follow the movement with her eyes.

"I did what I was told," someone hissed from the crowd.

Pyet looked, trying to focus on the blurry faces that were sitting before her. When they started to clear, she could have sworn she knew the person who was talking.

And she did.

It was Winnie. Winona drugged her drink.

She couldn't say she was surprised. It was Winona who had begged her to drink the wine. To relax, to prepare.

Winnie was preparing Pyet for this…whatever it was.

For the *Danaus Solstice*.

No one had told her explicitly, but Pyet knew that this was it. This was the elusive event that Violet so often referred to in her writings. She was never explicit about what it was, or what it entailed, but Pyet knew that she was right. She could feel it deep in her core, rattling her from the inside. It wasn't the dinner after all, but *this*.

And, though she wanted so badly to experience what her grandmother had so long ago, for the first time since waking, she felt fear. There was nothing normal about being chained to a table, nothing normal about being put up for slaughter in front of an audience.

They all quieted around her, and Pyet looked frantically from left to right.

"Hey, hey, hey," Winnie said softly, getting up from her seat in the front. The hooded figures held out a hand to stop her, and Winona growled in frustration. "It's going to be alright. Don't panic."

I don't know how to stop, Pyet wanted to scream. She couldn't open her mouth, the after effects of the drugs she was on prevented her from being able to do anything else but stare.

"She won't stop thrashing!" one of them complained, reaching to pin her hands back down to her sides. Pyet hadn't noticed, but she had been swinging her arms around recklessly and kicking her feet against the last of the restraints. She looked until she caught Winnie's sightline. At the familiar warm gaze, she calmed immediately. It reminded her so much of her mother, and for the first time, Pyet felt like she was looking at an image of her grandmother, too.

"This one was *mine*," Winnie said forcefully. She tried to take another step forward, but the hooded guards stopped her again.

"Not yet," they said in unison. It came forcefully, aggressively. Even Winona was offended. Her lips pursed into an aggravated pout and her eyebrows narrowed as she rested her arms against her hips. This was the person Pyet remembered from her first night here, nothing but business. This was the person that meant what they said. Winnie had an air of authority that she couldn't turn off. She wholly, fully, belonged here in Elric.

"No, you listen to me." She frowned. "This one was mine from the moment she stepped foot in this town. You don't get to touch a single hair on her damn head. You hear me?"

Pyet felt her face flush. She hated feeling like she was just a toy, a plaything for others to enjoy. Winnie's claim was both endearing and frustrating all at once.

"Enough!" A loud voice sounded from behind her. Winnie turned around, her face paling. She immediately sat back down, rolling over on her belly in the midst of the sight before her. Pyet craned her neck to see what it was that made her surrender so easily without another word. There were few people who could make Winona Fairchild shrink like that.

Pyet sat up straight, the hairs on the back of her neck rising, the phantom touches of electricity shaking her bones. It was the Lantern.

The elusive figurehead that everyone loved, that everyone feared. It was the person that had made the most impact on her since she arrived, and yet she hadn't so much had more than one conversation with them. The Lantern was a sight to behold. He was large in stature, standing over six feet tall with broad shoulders and a face that held no sympathy.

His hood was up, but not for long. Pyet watched as he carefully paced forward, like he was a predator stalking his prey. He slowly lowered the hood from his head, revealing sharp features. He had an over-amplified brow that hung over his striking green eyes. His cheeks were pointed and rich with color. There was a long white scar that traveled down the left side of his cheek, and didn't stop until it was well past his collarbone. He wore the same gray garments as everyone else in Elric, but his were still different. The Lantern had embroidered gold swirls that adorned it, that made him stand out amongst the crowd.

He was the one.

When Pyet reached his eyes, the Lantern smiled. His grin was confident, sympathetic. That look changed when he tilted his head in Winona's direction. It shifted in a second, from the overconfident smile to one of severe disdain. Pyet watched as Winnie shrunk into herself. She cowered as he approached her, dipping her head when he was just a foot in front of her.

"Winona," he said, voice as low and as powerful as he looked. She didn't look at him, continuing to keep her chin to her chest. The Lantern took out a meaty finger from his robes and placed it underneath her chin, tilting it up to face him.

The air was quiet, and all eyes were on the interaction in front of them. Every Elric resident sucked in their breath, as if one word would tear down the reality they've created here.

"When I speak, you will listen, *girl.*"

She blinked once, and Pyet could have sworn she saw a

flash of defiance in her eyes, but it left as quickly as it arrived.

"I'm sorry, Lantern," Winnie whispered. It was almost sad to see her so defeated.

"She is Elric's property. Not yours. We do what is best for the town, not for the individual, you of all people know that."

"I understand."

"This goes for all of you," his voice rang out into the crowd as he turned to face them all. The Lantern removed his finger from under Winnie's chin, dropping the weight of her head until it hit the center of her chest again. She didn't even try to resist.

"We have you gathered on this glorious day, to serve as a reminder to us all. A life for a life. It has been our way of survival for several generations."

The crowd stayed eerily silent, captivated by every word.

"I know you are worried. I know you are unsure. I know you are frightened. This year's Solstice has been long awaited. But it has also been our most…uncertain. When Juliette left us so long ago, we were left in an unfamiliar predicament. With no one to take the helm, we were left without a mother. Without someone to look over us. Left to take more of our own because of one Cabello's intense greed."

Winona's eyes started to gloss over, as if she was about to cry. Pyet felt like she wasn't here at all. She was no longer the prime attraction, but a spectator in the theater. She was not bothered by the restraints around her ankles, or the pain in her rear from sitting on such a hard surface for so long.

She was just as captivated by the Lantern as they all were.

"When Violet left us, I saw the change it made in all of you. For the first time in many years, you thought we were over. You thought that we had failed you. And while I understood your concerns, I felt hurt. I was not your mother, I knew that. But I wished that you had some faith in your town. In the people that kept you thriving."

"The witch made us this way!" someone in the audience screamed. His voice was piercing, and it echoed around them.

"She is the reason we are aging!"

"And you *protect* her!"

The Lantern just laughed. It was booming and ominous, and it seemed to fill the entire Circle with its condescending tone. He acted so cavalier, as if their threats and protests had no effect on him. As if he didn't care at all. He mustn't. The Lantern was too important to let the ramblings of these insignificant people sway him.

"Matilda is not your enemy," he said with finality. Their hushed whispers stopped almost immediately. Whatever bravery they had felt a moment before was lost, almost as if it had never existed in the first place.

Except for one.

"She killed Violet!"

In the frighteningly still, quiet air, you could have heard a pin drop. Even Pyet felt it. And soon, the quiet turned into a small, flickering flame in her belly. It was something that was being corralled, groomed into a fury that filled her up from the inside. She could feel it so much that Pyet thought she might be consumed by it. If she was going to die here, it would be by her own rage.

That woman killed her grandmother. She was the reason Pyet was here, strapped to a table. Matilda, *that witch*, who had given her all the answers, was the reason why Violet was dead? Pyet hadn't looked in the right places. She didn't get the right answers. It was hard to believe that anything that happened to her in Elric was real. Had they all known? Had they all kept this from her?

Was this the reason why they all avoided her? Pyet,

unknowingly, was the one they all pitied. She was the grand-daughter of the woman the witch killed. She was nothing special, nothing more than that, not like they all pretended she was.

"Matilda killed my grandmother?"

It was the first words that she had spoken since dinner. Pyet looked over towards Winona, whose lips were pressed into a straight line, no emotion left to escape. She didn't even dare to glance at Pyet. Her eyes were strictly placed on the Lantern, awaiting his command. And the Lantern, though he looked as if he would rather look any other place, finally rested his gaze upon Pyet, sitting strapped at the center before the statue. Limp and useless. His brows were narrowed and his eyes flickered from her face to her torso, seemingly uninterested. Disgusted, almost.

"Pyet," he drawled, taking a step towards her. Pyet flinched from his attention, trying to crawl back as far as she was able to but coming up short. She felt a deep-seated panic set in her chest, smothering the rage and fury that made home there just moments before. The restraints burned against her soft skin and she kicked a foot out, panting as the ropes dug deeper and deeper into her skin.

"It was so nice to finally meet you," the Lantern contin-ued, until he was so close he could reach out and touch her. Pyet wiped the stray strands of her hair from her face, pushing them behind her ears to avoid his touch. He frowned.

"I'm sorry you had to find out like this," he continued, placing both hands on either side of her dining room table. He tugged on it until she moved several feet, the screeching of the wood on stone making her cover her ears with both of her hands to stifle the noise. The crowd remained silent, awaiting their leader's next move. Awaiting *her* next move. "It was unfortunate that your grandmother was last seen with

Matilda. But, alas, no one really knows the full story, do they? They make assumptions…it's a shame, really."

"Lantern, I—" Winona's voice vibrated through the crowd. His head turned with a quick snap, and Pyet noticed her lip quiver under his intense gaze. She held firm, though, to her credit. Pyet wanted to beg her to back down, but her mouth wouldn't work anymore. The words wouldn't come out.

"*Silence!*" he screamed. Pyet shrunk back and Winnie jumped, but the rest of the audience stayed where they sat. Too afraid to move a muscle.

"I—I was told it would be me. That I was the one that was going to do it. It's my right, my blood."

"You don't know anything, girl," he hissed at her. Pyet seemed to be the only one surprised that Winona had spoken out of turn. There was an unusual hierarchy that Pyet was unaware of. They all looked at Winnie, not as an equal, but as someone who they needed to answer to. Even the Lantern, whose presence was nothing short of a nightmare that towered feet over her, was taken back by her abrasiveness. He clenched his hand into large fists that rested on either side of him.

"I know that you are standing at a throne that is not yours. It needs to be *me*."

"It was *never* going to be you."

The voice did not come from the Lantern, or from Winona. It came from no one in the crowd. The voice was isolated, small, and quiet, but it had as much power in it— more power—than the man that stood in the gold embellished robes before her.

And it came from behind her.

Pyet's head turned in unison with those sitting around her, and faced the fountain. Water was still running from its mouth, the basin still only half full. Pyet almost squeaked when the head started to turn. Soon, the entire body of the statue rotated until its muzzle was facing them, and a panel opened from its base. It was not alive like she once thought it was, but it might as well have been.

It was not so much a door, but a compartment only visible to those that already knew of its existence. The panel sunk into the statue's base before sliding to the left, revealing a large space full of darkness.

The voice had come from within it.

A figure emerged, ducking to crawl through the space with ease, and stepping feet first into the fountain of water. It wore nothing but the dark gray slacks that Pyet had grown accustomed to, save for the same gold embellishments that adorned the Lantern's. When the figure stepped into the clearing, it shook the water from its garments and removed its hood.

The face that was staring at her was one Pyet never thought she would see in her lifetime.

It was a face she recognized instantly, the one she had found deep within her mother's bedroom. It was the face of the person Winona trusted with her life. It was the face that brought her here to begin with.

Violet Cabello stared at her with malice lacing her features.

She looked far older than the picture she'd seen in Juliette's room, but it was unmistakably the same woman. She had more lines wrinkling her face, and her scowl was more pronounced. She had an air of authority to her, and with each step she took, the people of Elric held their breath. Before Violet took her last step out of the fountain, she lowered her hands to cup at the water filling the basin. Violet lifted her hands to her lips and took a large, desperate gulp. As if she would never get the chance to drink again.

At once she was lively. The wrinkles in her face cleared, and her eyes didn't crinkle in such a dramatic way.

She looked as if she was stepping out of the fountain of youth.

The world around them stayed quiet for a long time. Elric was shocked. The entire world around them stopped moving, because there was a ghost in their presence. This woman wasn't alive. She couldn't be.

The witch had killed her.

Right?

"Mom?"

Winnie's voice was barely over a whisper. If she didn't seem just as surprised as Pyet felt, Pyet would have lept off her table to run. She was so sick of the secrets and betrayals. She couldn't believe her eyes. Her hands went up to wipe at them, even knowing that when they were gone she would see the beautiful woman in front of her.

Pyet's heart pounded so hard in her chest, she felt as though it might explode. She could scarcely comprehend the truth of the figure before her. Her grandmother, who she had believed to be long gone; now stood before her, imperious and fearsome, like a queen from an ancient world risen again from the grave. The flickering firelight danced upon her features, casting an ethereal glow about her. Pyet's thoughts jumbled together like a thousand strands of tangled yarn, but one thing rang true deep inside Pyet's soul: this moment was something sacred.

Her grandmother was standing right there, and she wasn't dead.

An evil cackle erupted around them, and Pyet knew without seeing that it was the laugh of the witch. Matilda was nowhere to be found, but her laugh encased them. The people of Elric looked around, trying to pinpoint the source of the sound, but she was nothing but a memory. Matilda disappeared just as strangely as she had come.

Violet ignored her at first, and Pyet as well, stepping around her and her table to address the crowd in front of them.

Their faces held the truth. Shock. Awe. Relief.

Winona let out a heaving sob and lurched forward. The still hooded figures stepped to block her from approaching Violet, three at a time. They didn't try too hard, instead letting her fall into them. She didn't like that, shoving at their chests until they let her through. Winona didn't want or need their pity. Pyet watched as Winnie crumbled at Violet's feet, her words drowned out by the heaving gasps and wails.

"Mom, you're alive!" she wept.

It was like the entire world stopped after that. There were moments in Elric where Pyet could feel the electricity vibrating underneath her. She could feel it just as if it was a tangible magic, forcing her to experience the wonder of this odd, unearthly place. It vibrated now too, and Pyet could feel a direct tingle in her wrists, running through her veins until it touched every single nerve in her body.

It must have been a mistake. Winona had known Violet for so long that it was obvious that she could have easily grown accustomed to calling her mom. Pyet was not privy to that relationship, not in the way that it mattered.

She tried hard to ignore the string of jealousy that flowed through her. It was short-lived, seeing the look of rage that crossed Violet's features as Winnie sobbed at her feet. She looked disgusted, not warm. She looked nothing like how a mother should look. She looked very much like Pyet's mother, like her *real* daughter.

"Get off of me!" Violet snapped, kicking Winnie off of her foot. Winona was trapped by her own despair, glued to the floor beneath them. "You look absolutely pathetic. I raised you better than this."

Winona sniffled, but her cries did stop eventually. She looked up at her onlooking crowd, embarrassed, and shoved her knees to her chest. Pyet couldn't help but forget her own predicament. There was so much happening around her, and none of it made sense. She mimicked Winnie's movements, trying to kick her knees up as far as the restraints would allow, which wasn't far.

Violet turned her attention back to Pyet again, a small, evil smile placed upon her lips.

"Pyet, my dear. It has been so long."

Pyet opened her mouth to speak, but nothing would come out. It was as if she was paralyzed yet again.

"Moth caught your tongue?" She smirked. Pyet closed her mouth instantly, the dream of moths infiltrating her insides plaguing her as her nightmares had.

"Say something, my love. You know you want to."

"Y-y-you're…"

"Alive? Of course. It seems to be that way. Riveting. Any other observations?"

The crowd started to laugh uncomfortably, and Violet flashed an award-winning smile all around them. She walked up to the Lantern and he bowed before her, his head so low that it touched the ground. She raked long fingernails against his scalp, grasping the hood in her hand and tugging so hard it could have choked him.

"You and I will talk later," she growled, with no intention of keeping her voice low. "You took to your role almost too easily. You even had me fooled."

"Violet, how are you alive?!" Pyet managed to gasp. It took more effort than she wanted, the aftereffects of the drugs still interfering with her speech. Violet tilted her head to one side and made slow, casual steps toward her, dragging the Lantern by his hood until she tossed him casually to the side. As the Lantern had before, she placed two hands on either side of the dining room table, staring directly into Pyet's eyes.

"How am I alive? Don't tell me you still don't understand?"

She pressed her lips together tightly, scrambling to keep her feet pulled back as far as she could. Violet reached out and caressed her bare foot gently. It was as if she was just as shocked that Pyet was sitting in front of her. In her youth, Pyet was a spitting image of her grandmother. As they stared at one another, that only became more clear. It was like Pyet was looking into a mirror. Violet seemed to think so too, and after a moment of silence, she was forced to look away. As if it was too much for her, too.

"Of course, your mother was a piece of work."

"Don't you dare talk about my mother!"

"I will talk about *my daughter* however I would like!" she roared. Pyet could see Winona start crying again in the outskirts of her vision, but her focus remained entirely on her glaring grandmother before her. "She was useless! Primed as the Lantern, and groomed to perfection. She was going to be everything this town needed. But she was weak."

Violet tore her grip away from the table and turned around, pacing the Town Circle, hands now clamped together in front of her. She took a moment to look at each face, eyes glazing over in love and appreciation. That look was far more motherly than the one she directed towards Winona.

"Pyet, Elric was founded on a myth. I know that sounds nonsensical, but that's the easiest way to put it, anyway. Aren't all myths founded in real life?"

Violet continued to walk and weave between her residents, not really waiting for Pyet to answer. They were enchanted by every word, their eyes closed and their bodies still as she slid past each one. She touched their cheeks and ran fingers through their hair. She treated them all like they were her family.

Pyet longed to feel the same.

"When Matilda approached my great-grandmother, so many years ago, she told us a story. A story about a man who took advantage of us."

At the mention of them, Pyet could see the faces of the men around her curl into themselves. There weren't many of them. She could count on one hand the number of men that adorned the city at once. How was it that she didn't notice it until now?

"Men are a plight among us. How dare they kill our sisters? How dare they believe they were worth more than the dirt and grime that collected on our shoes?" There were hums of agreement that sounded around her. Smiles and laughs and a deep-seeded awoken agreement that grew from the crowd. Pyet couldn't help herself, she found her head nodding along with her grandmother. It was unlike her to be so violent; that was her mother's skill.

And yet, after knowing the story, after living in the dream Matilda showed her, she couldn't help but agree. Women died because of men's greed. Hadn't she seen that, living in the manor?

"Matilda's sisters were damned by the horrid gods. A fate worse than death, a fate they could never escape." Violet pointed then to the fountain behind her. Pyet turned around to face the large, rusted stallion she'd been so enchanted by since stepping foot within Elric. The fountain had never once held water in it, not until today. And even now, it never filled past its eroded markers.

The Danaid, though only recently acquainted, felt pity for her husband, and loved him fiercely. When she was brought to court, mythology has it that Aphrodite intervened on her behalf. The goddess refused to see her punished, not when love was involved.

Matilda manifested atop the stallion, riding it as if it were a live animal. She swung her legs over one side, and stared at the fountain below her sadly. Reminiscing. The Danaids were *her* sisters.

"The fountain, Pyet. It does so much more than house the torment of those lost souls. This fountain gives us life. It gives us youth. It is something to be thankful for."

"And so, when Matilda came to our ancestors, broken and looking for a way to keep them alive, we made a deal." Violet's twitching mouth was the only thing that took Pyet out of her trance. It was something even she didn't seem too happy with. But it was Elric, and this town punished those that did not uphold its promises.

"You seem to not like this deal," Pyet dared to whisper. It was barely audible over the spill of water in the half full basin behind her. Violet's head snapped, her eyes narrowed, and she took several long strides until her face was only about a foot away from hers.

"You don't know what I like, *cursed one.*"

Pyet physically recoiled from the words, as if it was slapped across her face. She didn't like hearing that curse from her mouth. It felt like a betrayal, like the woman whose journals she'd devoured was no longer here; this was not the same Violet.

This Violet was hardened by years of Elric.

"Once a generation, two women were born. In *our* blood line, dearie, if you weren't following. One to take the throne, to become the Lantern. The light to guide these moths back home, to choose the sacrifice. The second, to watch, to provide the next generation."

At once the members of their audience tilted their heads back, their eyes glazing over white as their mouths gaped open. A loud, moaning chant erupted from them in unison. They were all under the same sort of trance, and Pyet had no idea what the trigger was. The only exception was Winona, whose typically warm gaze was cooled over, looking at her with a dangerously hungry glare. Pyet looked back and forth, avoiding both Winona and Violet's eyes, instead starting to pick at what was left of the restraints. They were bound tightly around her ankles, digging into the skin. The two women gazed at her thoughtfully, not deigning to stop her. They knew as well as she did that there was no way to escape.

"Your mother was chosen. My first born. My dearest, darling Juliette." Winnie hissed from somewhere behind her, but Violet ignored her. "But she proved to be the wrong fit. She was too weak to choose the sacrifice. She chose to listen to the ghosts in the manor. My trophies…"

She wondered what happened to the souls of the ones her family had chosen, generation after generation. One soul for one Danaid.

"Your mother left. And I was left with my infertile half wit of a second born, who's been nothing but a disappointment since. Do you know what it's like, having two daughters who failed you?"

"But I have proven my worth!" Winona begged. Pyet looked her way, frowning as her friend…no, aunt, finally rose from her knees. "I brought her here, I did what you asked of me!"

"Yes," Violet hummed, contemplatively, "I suppose you did. You did exactly what you were told to do, Winona, though I'm disappointed you believed in my death so easily. That you believed Matilda would ever cross me is a burden I hope you always carry."

"I chose for us, Mother. I chose Pyet."

Violet did smile then, clicking her tongue against her

teeth and nodding in appreciation. "It was not the obvious choice, but it *was* dramatic. Juliette was always known for her dramatics, so it was a delight to watch it become the route you would take in the end, Winona."

"Juliette took this from us. It was only fair that I took something from her in return. Please, Mother, let me be the one to do it. I promise I can. This was my place, not at your side like a second born puppy."

Violet's smile fully blossomed, her teeth coming into tiny sharp points, pinching where they met skin.

"Very well, daughter."

That was all the permission that Winona needed; she shot up and eagerly took her place by Pyet's side. There was no way out of her restraints, and Pyet was paralyzed with fear as her family stood before her, panting from desperation, ready to devour her.

The men that held her table closed in on them, chanting in that foreign language again. They gathered something from behind her, and as one gently pressed against her back, Pyet's breaths quickened as he lowered a headdress onto her.

It was the same type of headdress she'd seen that night she left Matilda's. Except it wasn't a mystery figure that was wearing it, but *her*. The floral arrangement was intricate, the smell of fresh flowers encasing her.

This headdress was always meant to be hers.

Once it rested upon her head, Pyet felt different. Her eyes were now covered, her ears halfway so. From beneath the flowers, all of her senses dimmed. And she felt...calm. The world around her was empty, and there was nothing but Winona and Violet before her. She wondered how much of that was the magic laced in between the stems and petals causing her blindness, or how much of it was just her desire to connect with the two people in her life her mother kept her from.

Pyet couldn't help but resent her mother, at least a little bit. No matter what her predicament was, no matter what table in what town she was trapped in, Pyet was happy she was here.

Juliette might have escaped, but Pyet didn't want to. Pyet was home.

"I promised." Winona's voice was loud and clear. Gone was the meek figure that bowed before her mother. This Winona, her aunt, was speaking like she was a god.

"I promised, Elric, after Juliette betrayed us, that I would care for you. I promised that I would make the hard decisions, that I would put the town before myself. And have I done that?"

"Yes!" the crowd chanted in unison.

"I bring forth Pyet Cabello, first born to my sister. Though unconventional, she is the beginning of a new wave in Elric. We will no longer suffer our daughters. We will make our own rules, and we will survive."

The humming amongst the crowd was getting louder now, until she couldn't hear Winona at all anymore.

It was time.

With everyone surrounding her, Pyet felt like she'd been wrapped in a blanket of calm, despite the better half of her head screaming at her to run. She couldn't leave, not with these people around her, accepting her, bringing her in. Making her a part of their life, *finally.*

Pyet hadn't felt this way since she first moved to Elric, though the overwhelming need to vomit was so strong that her stomach gurgled.

The night was dark, and all of Elric sat still, waiting on this night of the Solstice, because that's what this was—the time had come to make their great sacrifice, and for the first time, Pyet felt like she was a part of something greater. The Danaids. Elric. The Witch.

Winona approached her. She could tell it was her by the graceful, lithe movements she made, and leaned forward to whisper in her ear. Even with the headdress, Pyet could hear her fully and clearly.

"You look content, Pyet. For the first time in your life."

Pyet only hummed in tune with those around them. Winona's voice came again from her other side, and small flicks of flame surprised her feet. She kicked them back but the heat of it was a welcomed friend.

"I *chose you*. Pyet, my niece. For the first time, someone is choosing *you*. How does it feel to finally be home?"

The fires of her pyre had been lit, and the air was full of smoke and ash. Pyet's nose scrunched at the stench of charring wood, and her mouth prickled at the taste of burnt flesh. She couldn't even find it in her to feel pain anymore.

Pyet needed to run. But she couldn't. She felt so at peace, here.

I am home. Thank you.

She thought she said the words out loud, but no one replied. Her family was all around her, and though Pyet could feel the flickering flames at her face now, she could only focus on the presence of Elric circulating her.

The townspeople gathered in a circle around the pyre, with their leader, Violet, at the center. She smiled from under her cloak, the real Lantern, chuckling to herself as the people of the town kept chanting their ancient prayers, singing songs of reverence. At some point, they had pulled at her limbs, pinching her skin until it tore from her body. She could hear the gnashing sound of teeth grinding as they inhaled every piece of her.

As the flames of the pyre licked the night sky, the eerie silence of the ritual settled over the gathered group of people. They sat in a circle, staring at each other with cold, empty eyes. Their hunger was palpable, radiating off of them like a foul stench.

With no words spoken, they began to slice into the flesh of what was left. Blood sprayed across the clearing as the fire still burned. The sounds of chewing and slurping mingled with the sickening smell of burning flesh. It was a ritualistic dance of carnage and consumption.

Pyet, now almost gone, could no longer think. She was no longer an important chess piece, or someone worth remembering. She was just someone who was dealt the wrong hand of cards, who had the best intentions. She was someone who couldn't, no matter how hard she tried, change fate.

And when it was over, when nothing was left but scraps and bones, the people of Elric walked away with red-stained teeth and dulled, glossy eyes. It was the cycle of their lives, the twisted path that led them down into madness. A path that they embraced with a horrifying, gleeful fervor.

From a distance the witch now stood, back facing her apothecary. She had no need of being near the festivities any longer. A shadow of a ghost whisked past her from the direction of the fountain, making Matilda's long hair swirl around her and her skin prickle from goosebumps. She smiled.

"Sister, it is so nice to see you."

The ghost looked back at her, reaching her hand out to touch her. As the fire by the stallion roared to life and the floral headdress rained burnt flowers around them, Matilda closed her eyes.

When she felt the ghost's fingers thread through hers, she opened them again.

Standing before her was a beautiful woman, dressed just as she had the night of her wedding. Though her garments were covered in familiar streaks of blood, she looked nothing like the person Matilda had remembered. The softness was gone, hard lines carved into her face from years of work and desperation. She was not the first, or the last person Matilda planned on saving. But she was here now, thanks to Winona, Violet, and ultimately, Pyet.

Lantern be with you. Lantern guide you. Like a moth to a flame.

Magic was a fickle creature. And though it was something no one would truly understand, Elric was still harnessing it in a way others might deem impossible. Matilda clung to Elric tightly, and would continue until each life of her sisters had been saved. One life would not be enough, even if it was Violet's granddaughter. She would have to continue to take them, each Cabello, one by one until every woman burnt by the gods was welcomed back home. A small price to pay. Even if she had to lie to them, even if far more lives would be lost in their endeavors than was necessary, it would be worth it. The Danaids were worth it.

Elric was not the only place that housed the pits of Tartarus, or the darkest. It was not the furthest from human-ity, or the worst.

It simply pulled people in, and never let them go.

It was their undoing.

EPILOGUE

11:45 PM

They just finished sweeping the Town Circle, though after the fire had gone out, it hadn't taken any longer than an hour or so. This Danaus Solstice was far less messy than their previous ones. Usually, Elric had a harder time keeping their victims still enough for the fire to catch. It was a welcomed surprise that Pyet had been so willing, so *easy*. She was caught up in belonging, in finding a place where she could keep her feet grounded. It worked in their favor.

Winona didn't think that Elric would ever become that place for her, but she'd been surprised before.

She almost missed the girl who'd found her way into her life. She wasn't a bad kid, if she wasn't her sister's daughter. Winnie smiled as she picked up a dried, dead flower from the ground. It nearly crumbled as she held it, as anything nice always did. She was used to that.

Her hand curled into a fist, destroying the last remaining memories of the girl she'd lured to Elric, and her heels clicked against the pavement as she traversed the Circle.

Clean up first. That's what her mother had always said.

Mother.

Just remembering that her mother was here, alive, sent shivers tingling down her spine. Winona had lived for years without the person that raised her, without the person that kept Elric living, for longer than she thought she was able.

Violet was a cruel, terrifying woman, with harsh features that never softened and a heart that was wrapped with iron. She never did give her daughters—Winona, anyway—the life they deserved. Winnie felt, on some level, a pang of sympathy for Pyet. She had escaped the home of her sister, who Winnie knew was in a dire state of duress when she escaped. It was no surprise that she had done to her daughter what their mother had done to them.

Sympathy or no, there was work that needed to be done. Winona had to do her part, feelings aside, and bring her here. Extort her, turn her.

Sacrifice her.

It had worked out in the end the way it needed to, but there were questions that still needed to be answered.

"Mother," Winona snapped as she approached Violet, who turned around elegantly. She hadn't known how she thought her mother could ever die. The cold, callous person that stood before her was invincible, immortal.

"Winona." She mimicked the sharpness in her tone with her tongue. Violet raised her hand to touch Winona's hair, frowning at it as if she had done something wrong. Kit curled up around them both, doing figure eights in between their legs. Winona had to resist the urge to crouch and scratch her head. She couldn't show any more weakness to her mother, but she loved her family's cat as much as anyone could. Kit was the only light that lived inside the manor.

"It's nice to see you alive." She squared her shoulders to her mother instead, frowning.

"Oh, but isn't it? I'm so glad that was over with. I hated

the stuffiness of the tunnels. They are no place for a Lantern, you know."

"It would have been nice to have been a part of these intricate games you play, Mother." Winona couldn't mask the hurt that laced her voice. It was not unusual for Violet to play sick, twisted fun with her, but to go this far?

"And where would the fun in that be, darling? You know I couldn't let you know. It was the only way."

"But you had some...pathetic nobody take your place? Do you really think so little of me?"

"Every Cabello in Elric has to prove themselves to get here. You are no exception. And besides," Violet said, tossing her robe out behind her dramatically, "Uriel might be pathetic, but from what I remembered, you didn't once contest his appointment after my death."

"Because you wrote a will!" Winona tried to contain her frustration, which had started to manifest in large waves of her hands. Instead, they stayed curled at their sides. "The same one that instructed me where to find Pyet to begin with."

She couldn't help but notice the curl in her upper lip at the mention of her granddaughter. Juliette's escape had hit her mother hard, and Violet knowing that she had a granddaughter that could have kept her legacy was not an easy pill for her to swallow.

In fact, it filled her with rage.

"That girl," Violet hissed through thin lips. "My blood. It was a disgrace to have her here."

"But the right choice."

"Yes," she conceded. "It was what Elric needed. Using our daughters was not sustainable. Not when my other daughter was...dry."

Winona winced at the words.

"We are lucky Matilda renegotiated her terms. And with

the fountain sustained for the next year, we have time to prepare for our next Solstice."

Anticipation prickled at her fingertips. Winona had proven herself worthy, she had shown what her sister could not, *that she could pick*. She could kill. She could become the person her mother needed her to be.

"We are preparing for next year already?" She hadn't expected it to come so soon. It was typical to have a few months of peace and solitude, even though Pyet had caught them not just a few weeks before in the midst of another ritual. The plumes of smoke from the pyre would stick to the sky, casting shadowy grays across their small, dome-like town for the rest of the year. Only daring to let go come next Solstice.

Elric was used to living in darkness.

"Yes, my dear. You did well, but you have a long way to go. And, with you at my side, we will show the world the power this town could truly hold. With the fountain of youth, we will be infinite."

Violet opened a palm towards her daughter in invitation. Winona's smile was small, triumphant, as she took it. Their fingers laced together, and for the first time Winnie's heart was mended. She was no longer the spare, the forgotten. She was *important*. For a second, she wondered if this was the source of the smile that was pasted on Pyet's lips when the fire took her. It felt so good to be loved. There was no wrongdoing that could take this feeling away from her.

Immortality. That was what the witch promised them. One life every year, and they would stay young. They will keep their faces, and Elric's town will grow. The Cabello family can be infinite.

"It's time to bring forth another one, daughter. You were lucky Pyet was invested so quickly. I doubt you'll have the same stroke of luck with the next. It will take *time*."

Winona nodded, that smile growing into something cruel and otherworldly. She looked out towards the apothecary, into the eyes of the witch she had hated so deeply these last few months. Matilda's expression matched her own, her teeth elongating and her body morphing until she looked like a small nightmare.

"Then there's no time to waste."

PLAYLIST

- **cult leader** - KiNG MALA
- **Like a Stone** - Audioslave
- **everything i wanted** - Billie Eilish
- **the fruits** - Paris Paloma
- **The Sound of Silence** - Disturbed
- **Become the Beast** - Karliene
- **mad woman** - Taylor Swift
- **Burn the Witch** - Shawn James
- **Panic Attack** - Liza Anne
- **Save Me** - Shinedown
- **Ritual** - Ghost
- **Madness** - Ruelle

ACKNOWLEDGMENTS

I'll start with my standard dues.

Eternal thank you's to my ride or die editor, Alexis Aumagamanaia (@threemuses_editorial). Words will never be enough to express my appreciation. You will always be the first one I thank, each and every book.

To my fine-toothed comb, Bear Lee (@bearleebooks). Your attention to detail and incredible eye for style really made my book the best version of itself. I am keeping you forever. Thank you for sharing your talent with me.

Thank you to my cover designer, Quirky Circe Book Design (@quirky.circe), and my map maker and interior art designers, Alyssa Konkel (@alypaca.doodles) and Jacob Konkel. I believe that using art *in* my art is important, and I love finding the best of the best to do it. Showcasing other creatives is the coolest part of the job.

This part of my acknowledgments will always look different for every book, simply because of the circumstances of existing. The names that follow are just what *Elric* needed—and what *I* needed—in this period of my life.

Several people saw me through the depths of my woes and the heights of my highs in *Elric,* and those people are some that I will always keep close to the heart. Katelyn,

Tiffani, and Whitney, you continue to remind me of why what I have to say is important, and I thank you for it wholeheartedly. This book would not have seen the light of day without our group chat and our friendship. You have become so important to me, and I value every day I get to be around you all. I love you infinitely.

To Sheldon, Audrey, Katy, Tony, Vic, Kristen, Jenn, and every other B&N friend that has touched my life; thank you for your never-ending support of me, my career, and my writing.

To Dani (@daniwantsalibrary), Aly (@thelittlelibrarian), and Tatyana (@theliteraturellama2.0); our friendship is what drives me to continue doing the creative thing, so thank you. Seriously, you inspire me daily.

To Delta, my soulmate; I'll just text you what I'm feeling so that I don't monopolize this time with how much I love you. So I'll keep it short this time, thank you.

To all of the authors and creators that I've met during my career; I am so humbled that I get to be around such amazing and talented people.

To my Creatures of Chaos; you make me feel welcomed and important. Thank you for accepting me with open arms, and for helping me find my footing in this genre and community—and bonus love to Jessie (@punkybookbabe). You loving my books gives me a reason to write. I would literally only continue writing just to have you in my DMs. It means so much to me.

To Ari Aster, whose films inspired the contents of this book; your creative direction was the reason I fell in love with horror, and I hope I did your work proud with this one.

To my husband and animal babies; for keeping me loved, fed, and watered.

And of course to you, reader.

I hope this spooks you.

ABOUT THE AUTHOR

Cassandra Celia (she/they) is a Maryland bookseller, turned author. She writes gothic, horror, and paranormal fiction, such as her debut, STARS AND OTHER MONSTERS, and her latest release, THE ELRIC UNDOING. Cassandra obsesses over stories with love, death, ambiguous endings, and everything in between. In her books, she takes inspiration from dark, haunting art and media, and she absolutely loves writing about angry, scorned women.

Stay up to date by visiting her website, www.cassandracelia.carrd.co.

9 798985 865974